second
first
impressions

Also by Sally Thorne

99 Percent Mine
The Hating Game

sally thorne

second first impressions

PIATKUS

PIATKUS

First published in the US in 2021 by William Morrow,
An imprint of HarperCollins Publishers
First published in Great Britain in 2021 by Piatkus
This paperback edition published in 2022 by Piatkus

1 3 5 7 9 10 8 6 4 2

A CIP catalogue record for this book
is available from the British Library.

ISBN 978-0-349-42893-2

Printed and bound in Great Britain by Clays Ltd, Elcograf S.p.A.

Papers used by Piatkus are from well-managed forests
and other responsible sources.

Piatkus
An imprint of
Little, Brown Book Group
Carmelite House
50 Victoria Embankment
London EC4Y 0DZ

An Hachette UK Company
www.hachette.co.uk

www.littlebrown.co.uk

For Taylor Haggerty

CHAPTER ONE

One of the "benefits" of working in the front office of Providence Retirement Villa is I receive feedback on every aspect of my lifestyle and appearance, whether I want it or not. (I do not.) Here are the three questions the residents always have for me:

- How old are you? (Twenty-five)
- Do you have a boyfriend? (No)
- Why not? (Miscellaneous reasons, none of which will satisfy them)

"There's more to life than having a boyfriend," I once told Mrs. Whittaker as we walked up the rain-slicked front path to her town house, her arm hooked into mine. "I'm right where I want to be, helping you all."

"That's true, Ruthie, honey. You're a good worker," she replied to me. "But boyfriends are a very nice part of life. I once had three at the same time." She shuffled inside, her walking stick clicking on the tiles. Just as I was thinking I'd misunderstood, she said over her shoulder, "They knew each other, so it wasn't awkward. Boy oh boy, I was exhausted. You're prettier than I was, why don't you try doing that?"

I was left on the doorstep, fighting the urge to ask some follow-up questions, primarily:

• How?

It's likely Mrs. Whittaker could still get more action than me, and she's eighty-seven. I think about that conversation a lot.

While my boss, Sylvia, is on her cruise, I get her desk with the good view. I'm emailing maintenance, and I'm also grappling with my daily three P.M. wave of melancholy. I save a yogurt for this exact moment. Sitting at my usual desk is Melanie Sasaki, the temp. She doesn't understand the concept of pacing oneself, so she eats her lunch at 10:30 A.M. I can hear her stomach growling as I peel open my snack.

In a desperate outburst in the silence, she says, "Ruthie, I was thinking about you."

I wish she wouldn't. "Let me just finish this email to maintenance, then we can talk."

I know I sound like a prissy jerk, but to survive these next two months as acting office manager, I've been trying to enforce a quiet-time policy. When Sylvia is here, I never speak to her if she's typing. Or clicking. Or unless she speaks to me first.

Hey. I haven't been this relaxed in years.

Melanie would probably talk while under a general anesthetic. "Let's make you a dating profile."

I break my own silence rule. "How do you know I don't have one?" She's teasing me, I know it. The residents of Providence are, generally speaking, brutally honest with me. But it's always well intentioned.

She says, "You don't even have an Instagram account, so you're not exactly the type to put yourself out there. Am I wrong?"

She's not. "Let me just finish this, Mel." Quiet Time Shields Up.

I reword my request to maintenance from a *where the hell are you guys* to a more diplomatic *as per my last email.* There's only so much DIY I can learn from YouTube.

When that's sent, I find a Word document titled "RUTHIE_ PROFILE" in my personal folder. According to the file history, it hasn't been accessed since I wrote it in a weird lonely moment last year, when online dating felt like a good idea for about thirty seconds. Maybe it's not that bad? A workable base draft for a dating profile that will find me my Mr. Right? If Melanie wasn't staring at me, I'd read it through my fingers.

Can I Take You Home to My Churchy Parents?

I'm a very old soul (24 going on 124). I've only seen one penis firsthand (briefly) and was not impressed enough to seek out another (probably should, though). Seeking patient, safe cuddle-bug soul mate to tell me when my cardigan is buttoned crooked. I live and work in a retirement villa. At this rate I'll retire here, too.

Okay, so the only update to this I'd make is I'm now twenty-five going on a hundred and twenty-five.

Like she's my impatient supervisor, Melanie asks: "Are you done now?"

After deleting that incriminating evidence, I counter with, "How's that new resident profile you're setting up for me in the system?"

Melanie purses her lips like, *Spoilsport*. "I don't know why you wouldn't want to utilize my true talent. The one I can't put on my résumé." She pauses for dramatic effect. "Getting peeps all loved up. If you only knew who you had here sitting across from you, you'd be jumping on this chance."

When someone is that confident in themselves, it does make the offer tempting. "Well, you do have a lot of things on your résumé."

Melanie stretches her arms above her head. "You know I'm livin' dat temp life. I'm dating all the jobs, until I find my perfect match. And I'm dating all the boys, too. Answer this quick without thinking: Are you ready to be in love?"

"Yes." I don't have enough strength to hold that word in, and it's humiliating how much force my answer had.

Every night as part of my security rounds, I walk to the western edge of Providence to check that the roller door securing the dumpsters is padlocked. I know that no one wants to steal garbage. I lean on the chain-link fence and stare at the town lights below. The knowledge that my cuddle-bug soul mate might be just there under that particular streetlight star, but I'm too chicken to go find him, makes my heart feel like a toothache. If I don't attend to it soon, it may have to be pulled out altogether.

Every night when I check the padlock, I look at the lights and apologize to him again.

Melanie is looking at me with such naked empathy in her expression that I scramble to try to cover up how much that word *yes* means. "I mean, everyone hopes they find—"

"Shush, shush, shush," she repeats until my face-saving caveats fade away. "Don't worry. I'll help you."

In the three weeks that she's been here, Mel's had at least four first dates, all at a tapas bar she calls "the Thunderdome." Before each one, she puts in an excessively long black pony-tail extension and makes me check it from all angles. She also writes down the details of each date, "in case I'm murdered." She trusts me to be her police witness? I'm conflicted about how honored I am.

I recheck the calendar. She really has only been here three weeks. Maybe I should take the opportunity to consult with this seasoned professional. She's like an electrician for my love life. "Well, what's your dating profile say?"

Her phone is always in her hand. She can open the app without having to glance down. "Mine says: 'High-maintenance twenty-two-year-old half-Japanese princess who makes no apologies. Take me on adventures. No weirdos, little dicks, broke dudes, or fugs.'"

I can't categorically say any of those would be a deal breaker for me. "What if your soul mate is one of those things? A . . . broke weirdo, or . . ." I study the banana and the ChapStick on my desk. The world is full of a lot of variables. My neck is getting sweaty under my ponytail.

Melanie shakes her head. "He won't be. You believe in soul mates? I wouldn't have picked that." She studies me with an *Aaww* expression. "You secret l'il romantic you."

"You don't need to help me, I'll work it out myself." I try to backpedal but it's too late—she's taken the case pro bono.

Melanie turns to a fresh page in her sparkly notebook. "Name: Do you prefer Ruth or Ruthie Midona?"

"Ruthie's fine." Less rhymes with it. The teachers used me as their airplane black box if they left the room and came back to chaos, hence my school nickname *Truthful Ruth*. I was the church girl with thrift store shoes; my classmates had ponies and Jet Skis.

Melanie is also distracted. "Oh, got a message. I'd give that a four out of ten. See? A dick." She holds up the screen to me; it is indeed a dick. I need a banana or ChapStick for scale. She smirks as she prepares a response. "I always reply with a photo of a zebra's dick. Gives them some perspective." She shows me that too.

What human dick would get a ten out of ten? It dawns on me that this is the first page of a lawsuit. Dicks in the workplace: Sylvia would be furious. "We should do some work. I really don't have time to date." I file some paperwork under *B* for *Boring*.

"You've definitely got the time, let's be real. How have you worked here for sixteen years?"

"How old do you think I am?" I see her eyes lower to my clothes. "Mel, I've worked here for six years. Not sixteen."

"My contract goes until Christmas and that's an eternity, no offense." There's complete desolation in her tone.

The only reply I can give to that is, "I've got a spare yogurt if you want it."

"God, yes, please." We find the strength to carry on.

"I'm twenty-five," I say, feeling weirdly embarrassed by the fact.

"Twenty-five" she says in a marveling tone as she writes it down. "Only three years older than me, how's that possible? But you have great skin," she amends, realizing how that sounded. "You're just so grown-up, running this place. That's all I mean."

I'll follow her suggested profile format. "Low-maintenance twenty-five-year-old peasant who makes a lot of apologies."

She snorts in amusement and taps her pen. Her dark eyes assessing me critically, she asks, "How do you know that you're low maintenance?"

"Look at me."

"It's not just about looks." Melanie is charitable. I'm okay-looking but I'm not fancy. "Do you like the guy to be all over you? Texting you all the time, taking you out places, giving you presents? Do you want him obsessed with you, or someone who gives you space?" She thinks of something. "Oh, whoops. If you're not into guys, that's cool too."

"I'm really not sure." I watch her blink several times and clarify, "I like guys. But I don't know if I want him all over me."

(Liar. I'd love that.)

(I think.)

"What was your last boyfriend like?"

"He was . . ." I can't think of anything except *very religious*. I make a praying shape with my hands and hope that's enough. "A long time ago."

She narrows one eye. "How long ago, exactly?"

I cannot answer that without opening myself up for a total crucifixion. "Quite a while ago."

If this were a teen movie, they'd intercut a couple of scenes here: Me in a prom dress slow-dancing with a Devout Young Man, literally named Adam. Cut to us in a single bed, partially naked. Adam is facing away from me, his shoulders shaking with sobs. If you think that memory can't get any worse, what if I told you that:

- My dad is a reverend?
- Adam went to my dad for counseling the next morning?
- Counseling re: the sin he committed with me?
- Yeah.

My counseling was outsourced to Mom and she told me that Dad was "deeply disappointed" by my "choices." Apparently, he was so disappointed that we haven't had a proper talk since, and I've never made a bad choice again.

"Looking to jump back into the dating scene." Melanie

writes that down. "I've written all my friends' dating profiles, and for my older sister Genevieve. My bridesmaid's dress is this pistachio color. That's the thanks I get."

An engaged sister? Melanie has some heavy-duty credentials. But this feels like the start of another teen movie and I have no intention of starring in it. "Please don't actually post anything without my permission."

"I won't," she replies, so puzzled by my suspicion that I'm ashamed. "We'll create a schedule of homework activities starting out very easy, until you're down at the Thunderdome getting your neck kissed by some sexy guy. We won't just pick the first one who comes along. By the time I leave here, you'll have someone."

I gape at her. "That is literally impossible."

"Not when you follow the Melanie Sasaki Method." She writes that down and underlines it many times. "The Sasaki Method. How catchy. That sounds just like a self-help book. That sounds like a Netflix series." She's sold the rights within ten seconds of having the idea.

She's not the only one jumping way ahead; I'm still caught up on the sexy-guy-neck-kissing concept. By the time she's worked her magic and left, I'll be watching the Christmas special of my favorite TV show, *Heaven Sent*, on my couch with someone who wants to kiss me. Is it actually impossible?

"So you in? The Sasaki Method?" Melanie grins widely. "It'll be a lot of fun."

I'm a sleep-on-it person. "Can I think about it?"

"I want a reply by Friday, close of business." Today is Monday.

She turns to her computer and begins typing. Just as I think a miracle has occurred—she's doing some work—my computer chimes with a meeting request for Friday five P.M. Subject? The Sasaki Method, of course. I click accept, and just like that, the conversation is not over, just rescheduled.

CHAPTER TWO

After our yogurts, Melanie begins setting up the new resident profile in the system, but now that she's working, I kind of wish we were still chatting. It's a beautiful afternoon. Through the open office door, I can see the neat path leading to the residents' accommodations. There's perfect hedges, emerald grass, and a tiny sliver of blue sky. "I like Sylvia's view from this chair."

Melanie replies, still typing, "Are you angling to get her job?"

I nod. "If nothing disastrous happens, she says she can retire with confidence." I think she means, she'll retire before things get serious.

Prescott Development Corporation (PDC) acquired Providence eighteen months ago. They have a reputation for giving their acquisitions a glamorous, repurposing makeover. Would Providence become a wellness center? A boutique hotel? A set for a reality TV show? Time passed and nothing happened. There was no visit, no call, no bulldozers, but eventually a decree was issued on PDC letterhead: All tenancy agreements have been altered to have the same end date of December 31 next year.

"That's fine," Mrs. Whittaker (she of the legendary three boyfriends) told me when I dropped off the paperwork explaining the tenancy amendment. "I'll be dead by then, honey. Got a pen?" The attitude of residents has either been cheerful don't-careness or gossipy conspiracy theories. The calls from their families were stressed-out questions we still can't answer. By next Christmas we could be packing up this office.

We keep trying to impress PDC with the perfect investment they've made, by sending through regular financial reports and cute newspaper clippings about our contributions to the community. But our corporate daddy's too busy to notice our A+ report cards and flawless ballet recitals. We are the forgotten achievers. And I'm really okay with that.

Melanie's head turns. "Oh, I hear a scooter. Tag, you're it."

"Part of your duties is assisting the residents. Probably your top duty."

"They're all so old with see-through skin. I can't handle it." Melanie gets up and goes into the bathroom, phone in hand. I walk outside to create a drive-through service.

A sharp voice shouts, "You'd think for the price we pay, they'd do something about the turtles." Steaming down the hill toward me are the Parloni sisters. The older sister taking the lead is Renata. She's just turned ninety-one. I put a birthday card in her mailbox and it was returned to me, torn into pieces. It's okay—I knew she'd do that.

"Be more careful, they're endangered" is what Agatha

(Aggie) replies. She is younger at eighty-nine years old and she is correct: They're endangered tortoises and they're everywhere. Providence has the highest concentration of golden bonnet tortoises of anywhere on the planet. They swerve their scooters around the slow-motion lumps dotting the path and my heart is in my throat.

Renata bellows back, "I'm the one who's endangered around here. I want to turn them into hair combs." When they reach me, they brake to a stop. Britney Spears blares from a portable radio in Aggie's front basket.

Renata was once a fashion editor. The devil wears brands you've never even heard of. YouTube has footage of a fashion show in 1991 when she called Karl Lagerfeld "Weekend at Bernie's" to his face. He called her something far worse in French, but she considers it a triumph. *He had no creative reply.*

HOT OR NOT magazine is long gone, but Renata is not exactly retired. I can pick out brand logos all over her.

Her sister, Aggie Parloni, is my style goal. Gray suit, white blouse, and black loafers. She has fine white hair cropped close to her head and is smart, neat, and reasonable. I get along with her great. Aggie is a quiet person, but she's noisy because of her radio. The local station has a competition: Win $10,000 if they repeat the same song in a day. Aggie doesn't need the money, or any of the random prizes she's always trying to win. It's the what-if feeling between entering and the prize draw that she is addicted to.

I ask her loudly, "Any luck?"

Aggie turns down the volume a touch and holds out some

envelopes to me. They're prestamped and ready for the afternoon's mail run. They'll be twenty-five-word-or-less entries. Collect-ten-coupons. Name This Yacht for a Chance to Win. "I did have a small windfall," she says carefully, like she knows she's about to be teased.

"She won a Frisbee," Renata cackles. "Let's ask the neighbors to toss it around, shall we? Break a few hips."

The mental image almost pixelates my vision. "Is there anything else I can do for you?" The fact that their assistant isn't in tow is a very bad sign.

Renata smiles, and it's pure evil. "We need a new one."

I know exactly what she means. "What happened to Phillip?"

She ignores me and lowers her sunglasses, cooler than I'll ever be, and looks through to Melanie's vacant chair. "Where's your pretty Asian minion? Or is that not PC? Inspired by her, I ordered a lovely black wig."

"You absolutely cannot call her that." I hold eye contact until I see she understands. "But in regard to the wig, Melanie will be very flattered. She's busy checking her social media in the bathroom."

Renata's cackle always hits my bloodstream like a drug. It's the Providence equivalent of making the popular girl at school laugh. "The youth of today. On the toilet, right where they belong. I wish I'd had 'the Instagram.'"

"Is it too late for you to try it?" Aggie's a quiet instigator. Thanks a bunch. Before the day's out, I'm going to be taking street-style shots of Renata leaning against a brick wall.

Renata narrows her eyes like I'm a magazine cover and I'm Not Hot. "You're looking very old today, young woman. Where's the visor I bought you for Christmas? You are asking for LIVER SPOTS," she booms, loud enough to scare birds. "Look at my spotty OLD HANDS. This song was playing this morning," Renata says to Aggie abruptly when the radio changes tracks. "Quick, call them."

Aggie consults her notebook. "It was 'Billie Jean' at 9:09 A.M. This is 'Thriller.' Tell her what you did to Phillip."

Renata is triumphant. "I gave him the joke pair of panties and told him to iron them. Who knew such a simple request would be the last straw?"

"He just picked up his keys and walked out," Aggie says wearily. "Two and a half days. He lasted longer than most."

For entertainment, some people go on safari. Renata Parloni prefers hunting a very specific type of game. She's reloading her weapon when she says, "We haven't had a Goth boy in a while. I want one that's constantly thinking about his mortality."

I steel myself. "We had an agreement. We're putting up a sensible advertisement. I'll go get it." Imagine being able to tell Sylvia that I fixed the Parloni situation once and for all.

Renata says when I'm back with my file: "Read the old ad. I want to hear what's wrong with it."

"'Position Vacant. Two ancient old women residing at Providence Retirement Villa seek male assistant for casual exploitation and good-natured humiliation.'"

Renata interrupts. "What's wrong with that bit?" Both sisters are jiggling slightly on their scooters now. No one could stay still to "Thriller." I'm shifting foot to foot, trying to hold the dance in.

I explain, "It's illegal to discriminate based on gender. This says only males can apply."

"I have no desire to boss around a female. Read the rest," Renata bosses me. Aggie gives me a deeply empathetic look.

I continue, "'Duties include boutique shopping, fast-food fetching, and sincerely rendered flattery. Good looks a bonus—but we aren't picky.'" I appeal to Aggie. "I'm not sure that's legal either. You can see that isn't going to get anyone who will be any use to you. All you've gotten so far are—"

Renata interrupts again. "Skinny boys with skateboards and dark circles under their eyes. Useless kids who don't know how to peel an orange or drive a stick shift."

I pull out my draft advertisement. "'Wanted: Experienced aged-care nurse to provide assistance to two active elderly women residing at Providence Retirement Villa. Domestic duties, outings, and errands. Driver's license plus police check required.'" I try not to cringe under Renata's poisonous stare. "We had a deal."

Aggie is on my side. "Ren, I think we need to go with this new ad. It would be nice to have someone who could actually complete tasks. Laundry. Making the bed. I am too old to live in this kind of mess because of your strange hobby."

Renata fires up. "We agreed that when we were rich and old—"

"That was fifty-five years ago," Aggie cuts in. "You've gotten

16

your revenge on the male species. Yes, having young people around the place is enjoyable. But I have no clean clothes. I have no clean coffee mug. Let me live comfortably. My hands are no good anymore." She has peripheral neuropathy, causing numbness in her fingers.

Renata's expression softens. "One last boy and I'll retire. I'd better put in a good effort to really break him in. Find him for us, Ruthie." She adjusts her visor. "I need a strong drink. But I have no boy to make it for me. Drat."

"Maybe we'll win the lottery with this last boy," Aggie says to me with not much optimism. "Got to be in it to win it, I suppose."

"I'll go and sort out that ad for you and take your mail. Have a lovely afternoon." I must have a shred of optimism left in me. I nearly make it back to the door before Renata stops me.

"We need you to put gas in the car. We need snacks. And get us some dinner—Thai, but nothing spicy. No noodles or rice. No soups or coconut. Absolutely no cilantro or mint."

My pulse bumps at the thought of leaving the grounds this evening, but I can't exactly leave them up the hill to starve. "I was busy tonight, but . . . okay."

Renata snorts. "You? Busy on a Monday night? Puh-lease. Look, keep this good service up and I'll write you into my will." (A common tactic. Her sister and I interject with admonishments and she moves on.) "Get us some fresh flowers—some sort of elegant mix. But no lilies. You know I don't like feeling like I'm at my own funeral."

I know exactly what sort of flowers will get me yelled at. I turn my face to the sky and send up a request: *I can't take much more. Please send us the One.*

Renata revs her scooter and accelerates off. "Then come up and register me for the Instagram. Then fix our DVD player." Her voice is fading into the distance. "Then stay and watch a DVD with us. And then you can wash all of Aggie's . . ." (inaudible).

My only plan for tonight was walking 127 steps from the office to my cottage, to have a hot bath and then watch *Heaven Sent*. But it sounds like I'm going out instead. Gas is one of the only things that can't be delivered, unfortunately for me.

"Thank you, Ruthie," Aggie says to me. She has been struggling to liberate her purse from her smart handbag that I secretly covet. She peels out two hundred-dollar bills from an inch-thick stack. "Is this enough? I wish we could have you as our assistant, but Sylvia would never let us. Girls like you are gold dust."

If Sylvia gave me to the Parlonis, I'd age ten years in a week, and that would make me 135. "I'll find someone reliable. You need someone who can run your house for you. Life will be much easier." *For you and me.* "I hope when Sylvia comes back—"

"Don't worry. I'll tell her you managed the place just fine." Aggie peels out a third note from her purse. "I apologize for Ren. Here is a thank-you present." She hands me the most perfect hundred-dollar bill I have ever seen, her eyes on her departing sister.

18

"Oh thank you, but you don't need to." I try to hand the money back, but her purse is in her bag. In the distance, we can hear Renata still shouting. I say, "Aggie, this is too much."

"It's not against the rules, you can take it. Go buy yourself something indulgent." She looks at my plain outfit with kindness rather than critique. All the pieces are clean and in good condition, but they're all thrifted. "Be twenty-five years old. How nice it must be, to be so young. That's the only prize I can never win again." She scoots off.

I put the windfall into my pocket and go back inside. Melanie is back at her desk. A white earbud dangles from her ear and she's wearing no shoes. I put the job file into her in-tray and Aggie's envelopes in the mail tub.

"We're going to put their job ad up for a few days, then we'll change it to my new version. Could I leave that with you?" The local recruitment agency we got Melanie from won't deal with the Parlonis any longer. We throw out the net and trawl the internet for fresh boys. I think of my dating aspirations and wince; will I be doing the same?

"Sure thing," Melanie says. "I'm stuck with this new resident setup. What do I enter here, for tenancy end date?"

"All contracts end December thirty-first next year."

She looks up at me quizzically. "What happens after then? Their tenancy gets extended?" She thinks of something. "Is this because they're all . . . you know? Old?"

"No, it's our new corporate policy. We actually don't know what happens after that date." I reach back behind me and find

Sylvia's file labeled "PDC DEVELOPMENT." "If you run out of work, you can read through this for some background. I might go for a walk and check in on a few residents."

Melanie flips open the file, decides it's boring, and says, "Think about the Sasaki Method. Think about giving a smile to the next cute guy you see."

I do think about these things for a long time as I walk up the hill, moving tortoises off the path with my hand in a latex glove. I give each one a flirty fake smile. I know that when I circuit back around, they'll be on the path again.

No one can say I don't try my best.

CHAPTER THREE

Time to saddle up and hit the trails on this gleaming borrowed steed. For the journey, I'll be needing:

- My cool cardigan (it has foxes and mushrooms)
- A freshly retightened bun with no escaping wisps of hair
- Brushed teeth and some pink lip gloss
- Some courage, which I know is weird

Hold on to your hat, partner, we're about to ride out into the valley and . . . who am I kidding? I'll sit here and simmer in my own nerves. I once googled how much the Parlonis' car cost, and my brain instantly forgot the amount like I'd experienced a trauma. I hate leaving here. What if something happens? Someone falls, a hydrant explodes? A tortoise sprains its ankle? I make myself start the (very valuable) engine, because the sooner I leave, the quicker I can get back for tonight's episode of my favorite show.

I haven't told a real-life soul this, but I'm one of the founding creators of the longest-running *Heaven Sent* online forum, Heaven Sent You Here. *Heaven Sent* is about Pastor Pierce Percival; his wife, Taffy; their studious teen daughter, Francine; plus twin eight-year-old girls (Jacinta and Bethany), who are always up to mischief.

The forum hosts an annual global rewatch of the entire show. Tonight we're up to Season Two, episode eight. That's the one where the homesick twins think they've seen the face of Jesus singed onto a marshmallow at Bible camp. When I get back from my errands for the Parlonis, I need to rewatch this episode to refresh myself on it and start a discussion thread.

With this goal in mind, I begin the trip. Holy moly. I'm in the outside world. I'm filling the car with liquid gold at the less-busy gas station when I realize I am staring at the back of a young man. He has very long black hair that puts Melanie's hair extensions to shame. Resplendent, gleaming hair is wasted on men. I bet he doesn't even condition or get the ends trimmed. He sits there sideways on his motorbike, ankles crossed, that unearned glory lifting on a breeze in an inky swirl.

He's oblivious to my presence. Fine by me.

This particular specimen is in his twenties. His skin sits tight on his body, inked all over with tattoos. I see a scorpion, a knife and fork, a diamond ring. It's like his body is the page he's been doodling on while on hold to the electricity company. An upward trail of butterflies, a switchblade, a donut. The artistry is lovely. This is a guy who took a lot of care getting trivial, unrelated things printed all over himself.

Nothing's been colored in, and I want to unzip my pencil case and get to work. I'd start on that big unfurled rose on the back of his arm. Actually, I think I'd use a pink lipstick. The slanted tip would be just the right size for the petals, each the size of a woman's kiss.

He turns his head, feeling my eyes like an animal would, but he doesn't look back at me. I stare at the concrete until he re-settles. I put my hand on my neck; I can feel my heartbeat. This is an interesting development: My body knows it's twenty-five.

Melanie told me to take a chance and smile at a guy. I look down at myself. Mom told me once that I have nice calves and my reflection in the car's window is perfectly fine, maybe even pretty when I soften my face.

Imagine being a guy. How would it feel to sit on a neat butt that doesn't spread out like a hen when you sit? If I was turned into a man for a day, I'd spend the first hour carrying around hay bales, making myself sweat. Then I'd muster the courage to unzip my pants to make a decision on whether seeing a penis is a worthwhile priority moving forward. As the minutes tick on, the Rolls-Royce guzzles and he continues to sit motionless. I can't see a second helmet. He does have a very full backpack. I worry for that zipper.

I lock the car. Then I check each individual door. I say under my breath: "I locked the car doors." I mostly believe myself as I walk inside to pay.

As I'm deliberating over what soft-looking chocolate bars I'll get for Renata, my ears tune in to the gas station clerk's hushed telephone conversation. "He's going to steal it."

I rush to the window to check the car, but Tattoo Guy's sitting where I left him. I lay my purchases on the counter.

The clerk says into the phone, "It's been more than ten minutes. He's filled his bike, can't pay for it, and he's deciding what to do." He begins scanning my items and mouths my total at me. "Yeah. As soon as he touches the ignition, I'm calling the cops."

I look through the dusty windows. It's evident from the set of this guy's shoulders and the stark deliberation on his face that he is sitting inside a terrible moment. I was oblivious as I admired his butt. Then I suspected him of theft. Is it true that he has no money? I was in a similar situation once. I was only a few weeks out of home and my card kept getting declined. My neck was hot from bottling up the tears. A motherly type paid for me and disappeared into the night. All she'd said was, *Pay it forward.*

Time to settle my karmic debt. "I'll pay for him. How much?" I dig out my special hundred-dollar bill.

The clerk hangs up the phone. "Twenty dollars. Aren't you nice?" The way he says it doesn't make me feel that nice.

I'm almost back to the car door when the clerk says over the loudspeaker: "Pump number two, please thank your Good Samaritan. Your gas has been paid for and you can leave."

We are the only customers. So much for me just melting away into the night. I give it a try anyway. Tattoo Guy says behind me, "Ma'am, thank you so much."

"No problem." I fumble with the car keys and drop things. "Don't mention it."

"You've just saved my ass—I mean, my butt. I'm having the worst day ever." He's closer behind me when he adds, "I left my wallet somewhere, but I always find it. The world's full of Good Samaritans, just like you. If you give me your details, I'll pay you back as soon as I can."

"Not necessary," I say, but now he's right behind me. I smell the cotton on his body when a breeze blows through it. When I look down at my loafers, there's big inked hands picking up my dropped groceries.

No way am I going to say *Pay it forward*. Men probably think that's girlie nonsense. But I'll try to have an exciting story to tell Melanie. I turn on the balls of my feet.

"Here you go," he says when all the chocolate is gathered up. When he straightens to full height, he's obviously surprised. After a beat, he lets out a big joyful howl. Up at the sky, he yells at full volume, "Oh my God, you look absolutely amazing!"

Did Melanie pay a gorgeous local actor to perk me up?

"Oh shit, too good. You got me." When I don't reply, he continues, "I can tell you, from the back, you've absolutely nailed it." His smile is white and lovely as he drags his hair back. "I love costume parties. Can I come?" His slender-muscly body shakes from laughing. It's a full-body workout. He's standing so close, for a moment I don't process the words. Then I feel the slice.

"Excuse me?"

He is staring at my chest with open appreciation. The glasses that I wear for computer work are still hanging from a chain around my neck. "Perfect," he says reverently before dissolving into laughter again. "Are you going as one of the Golden Girls?"

"No—"

"You just need a string of pearls and a walking stick. Look at those granny shoes." He says it like a fond scold and taps my toe with his. "You've even got the old-person car to match. You've thought of everything." He wipes a tear from his eye. "You look like Tweety Bird's granny."

"You don't need to be rude." The prim words are out of my mouth before it occurs to me that I should just say, *Sure, I'm headed to a big party, I hope my costume wins.*

I don't think I've helped someone who really needs it. Tattoos are expensive and he's covered himself in a fortune. His unusual biker-guy jeans have a lot of seams and diagonal lines, the result of skilled craftsmanship. My thrift-store eyes spot a tiny logo on his pocket: BALMAIN. Very, very pricey.

He's noticed my attention and the corner of his mouth lifts in a mischievous way. "So how old are you? Are you an eighty-year-old with a facelift?"

"How old I am is none of your business." The words I've ached to say to all the residents at Providence, and I blurt them in the face of a tattooed guy with a motorbike? "I paid for your gas because I thought you were in trouble. But I can see you don't really need it."

"I was just psyching myself up to call my dad." This guy scratches his jaw and I can't read the word printed across the knuckles. "I try to fuck up during business hours, so I can speak to his assistant instead. Less of a lecture that way."

"I'll give you my PayPal address. You can pay me back and I'll find someone who actually needs the money." I can't write on the Parlonis' receipt. I have one of Sylvia's business cards in my pocket. I cross out her email and write mine. The gas station attendant gives me a grinning thumbs-up and I burn red with humiliation.

He studies the business card I put into his palm. "A retirement villa?" His eyes spark. The irises are mixed colors—familiar, but I don't know what they remind me of. He is holding a new laugh in. "What's going on with you, anyway?" I cram myself into the car and lock it. "Wait, wait," the guy shouts. Now his *I'm sorry* is muted and far away. I'm sorry too. Funny how fast a good deed can turn bad in the outside world, like time-lapse footage of rotting fruit.

While I wait for a gap in the traffic, I look in my rearview mirror, praying he doesn't try to follow. The heel of his palm pressed to his temple is universal language for, *I fucked that up.* At least he realizes it. Most people who hurt my feelings never have a clue they did. I just invested twenty dollars for a reminder of why I stay at Providence and tucked in my safe little forum in the far corner of the internet.

Outside World Shields Up.

"YOU'VE BEEN SO quiet today," Melanie says behind me. "Did I say something, or . . . ?"

"I got my feelings hurt a bit last night. Not by you." I keep staring at the parking lot, watching for a car.

After I sorted out the Parlonis and left them asleep on the

27

couch, holding hands, I stood in front of the mirror in my bedroom. Then I used a second makeup mirror to look at myself from behind. That guy was right: From most angles, I am an old lady. I messaged my forum admin friends Austin, JJ, and Kaitlynn. The group chat was a big chorus of outrage—*what a dick, that's so RUDE, of course you're not old*—but the reassurance didn't feel authentic because none of us have ever actually met in person.

"Here's what I know. You're a good person, Ruthie," Melanie says so kindly. "And you don't deserve hurt feelings. Tell me who did it and I will kill them."

"A complete stranger. Someone I'll never see again." I recheck the time and sidestep the tight squeeze of emotion in my throat. "I need to focus on the meeting. I wish I knew what it was about."

"I'm sorry," Melanie says. "I know I screwed up big-time."

When I was up a ladder replacing a blown bulb outside the recreation center this morning, Melanie took a message for me. All she wrote down was:

- *Jerry Prescott*
- *Today @ 3 P.M.*
- *Maintenance something?*

"Jerry Prescott owns Providence," I told her, with sheer terror coursing through my veins. "You spoke to his assistant?" She shook her head no. "You spoke to the owner of Prescott Development Corporation? PDC? PDC?"

"He sounded nice, I think," she replied.

I have tried everything—even an improvised hypnotism session in the darkened office—but Mel swears she can't recall any more details than that. Jerry's assistant never called me back.

A motorbike turns into the parking lot.

"Nope." I'm looking for a rental car. The rider takes off his helmet, shakes his head back, and looks up at the office. I'd know that phenomenal head of hair anywhere.

CHAPTER FOUR

A sensation I've never felt before unfurls in my chest and now my heart is throbbing in my ears. Angry, thrilled? The guy from the gas station is here to repay his debt, or apologize for laughing at me, or to ask for more cash.

"Oh great," I say out loud. I don't have time to deal with him on top of my shredded nerves. "Mel, I need you to run interference on something."

"I live for that," she confirms instantly. "Can do. Point me at it."

But . . . my mouth doesn't open and I don't want to delegate just yet. The breeze picks up his hair and swirls it artfully. Just like at the gas station, he sits sideways on his motorbike and is in no hurry. There's that bulging backpack again. I wouldn't think riding around with everything but the kitchen sink strapped to your back would be very comfortable.

"Who's that?" Melanie says, coming around to look. "Do you know him?"

"He owes me money. Don't ask." I enjoy being mysterious, who knew?

"But I have many, many questions," Melanie argues. "I really wish we had the Sasaki Method agreement in place, because then I could give you some serious advice. That one's out of your league, girl."

Why'd she have to say that? I am a dork. He is on a motorcycle. High school wasn't that long ago, and I know what combinations are impossible in real life. I've got that familiar hurt feeling somewhere near my heart, like Melanie's dug her thumb into a soft peach.

"In a million years I would never—"

Melanie advises over the top of my protests, "You've been walking around with hurt feelings over—actually, I have no idea what. I'm not letting you get hurt by this one. He is a Lamborghini, and you're a learner driver. You'd tap the gas and drive into a wall. Hurting yourself."

"It's really not like that. You've got the wrong idea."

"I see a bad boy. Do you see that too?" I have to nod. "You need a nice suitable man who won't destroy your heart. Never loan money. Never get yourself hurt." That last bit is a protective scold. Melanie links her arm through mine, squeezes, and holds tight. "Suddenly I'm glad you never go anywhere."

Embarrassment and the friendly lean of her shoulder on mine makes me gruff. "I'm not stupid, Mel. I can't even imagine trying for a guy like that."

What a liar. I can imagine everything.

I feel the crunch of gravel under my shoes. I'm stepping between his knees, twisting my fist gently in his hair. I tip his head back. His eyes spark with surprise, a new laugh on the tip of his tongue. He allows me to hold him in place. I make his cheeks burn with color as I tell him something honest, and I drop my mouth down to his and—

Melanie interrupts. "I wouldn't blame you for fantasizing." (I try not to squirm.) "Wow, that's some pretty hair. Maybe prettier than mine. Ugh, I hate that guy." She drops my arm and threads her ponytail through her hands. Like he can feel her attention, he twists his black mane into a knot with an elastic from his wrist. It's safer for the general public if he holsters a hair weapon like that. "You're really not going to tell me how you know him? At least tell me his name."

"I can't."

The nameless guy sits there, yawning big lion roars. A tortoise lump gets closer to his boot. He picks it up, talks to it, dances it gently on his palm, then puts it in the garden. That tortoise's thought process is something like: *He's so big, beautiful, and funny, but why did he do that to me? I'm not actually injured, but I'm also . . . not okay?*

Maybe he's rehearsing what he'll say. A good speech, combined with that torso and the repaid sum of twenty dollars, and I might just get my faith in (young) humanity back. I can't seem to take my eyes off this person.

The clock is ticking, bringing Jerry Prescott closer and closer. I need to get myself together. "I'll run out quickly. Just to get rid of him."

Melanie replies, "I'll do it."

Before I reply, a late-model sedan comes into view. This is the rental car I've been watching for. The driver accelerates fast into the space beside the motorbike, braking with a screech. That tortoise would have been pancake-flat. A man hops out, and it's Jerry Prescott. (I have done some extensive online research/stalking, so I can say this for sure.)

He speaks to Tattoo Guy and gives him a slap on the shoulder. Hey, man, how's it hanging? Men are all part of one big penis club. Poor phrasing on my part. Now I'm looking at Tattoo Guy and I'm thinking the words *big penis* . . .

I force myself to move away from the window and rearrange water glasses on the tiny meeting table.

"They're coming in together," Melanie narrates. "Young Guy is picking up a different turtle now. He's showing it to Old Guy, who's mad about it. They're walking up the path. They're having an intense conversation. A chest poke. Can't see them now, but they're almost at the door—"

"Knock, knock," Jerry Prescott says in the doorway and I still jump. He comes inside, and Tattoo Guy leans in the doorway, an air-paddling golden bonnet tortoise in one hand and his backpack hanging heavily from the other.

"Hello, Mr. Prescott. Nice to meet you. I'm Ruthie Midona." I weave through the tight office space to shake his hand. "I'm holding the fort in Sylvia Drummond's absence." I sound plummy and old-fashioned, a good solid secretary type in my cardigan and loafers. Oh man, I'm still wearing my reading glasses on their chain. And they've been noticed.

"Oh hey," the young guy says with easy recognition, like we're old friends. "I had a real interesting dream about your glasses last night."

I decide I didn't hear that. "And this is Melanie Sasaki, my temp."

"Ruthie, Melanie, good to meet you both." Jerry pumps our hands vigorously. He's the older version of Tall, Dark, and Handsome. He has an expensive smile. To me he says, "I've heard a lot about you from my team back at HQ. You're a lot younger than I expected."

"I get that a lot."

(Tattoo Guy grins broadly with his own expensive teeth.)

I lock eyes with him. "I have a meeting at the moment, I'm sorry." Read: *Get out of here.*

"This is my son, Theodore," Jerry says, turning to the young guy. "Come in here, introduce yourself."

"Hello, I am this man's son," Theodore says obtusely, making his father frown. "I am the infant child Prescott."

"Could you possibly take something seriously? Just once?" Jerry scolds him. "Put that turtle down, for goodness' sake. I'm so sorry," Jerry apologizes to us in a desperate hush as Theodore wanders back outside to release his captive.

The only explanation for this visit is that I've majorly messed up somehow. I audit every memory of the gas station incident. I was curt and rude to Theodore, but I'd also been called elderly. Is it against PDC rules to loan strangers money? Did I scratch his bike with the car when I pulled out?

I'm fired. That's what this is.

I'm fired and homeless in one deft stroke, and Theodore Prescott and his hair are walking back into the office at this exact moment to see it happen. "It's okay," he says, reading my murder-victim body language. "No, it's okay, Ruthie, don't freak out."

"Sorry, this is all a bit irregular." Jerry laughs, false and bright, and it occurs to me that he's nervous too. "We're just dropping in to see how things are going here."

"Would you like to sit?" I gesture to the tiny round table and fill water glasses. Theodore hands one to me like he's concerned.

Melanie sits and pelvic-thrusts her office chair over to the table. "I'll take notes." In a sparkly notebook, mentally eating popcorn. Her brown eyes flit to Theodore approximately once every five seconds, chipping away at segments of him until she's seen everything available. It is deeply annoying, because I wish I could do that too.

"I like that one." Melanie points to a tattoo on his arm. "That's a dai-dōrō, right? A Japanese stone lantern," she explains to me and Jerry. "They're really beautiful when they're lit up at night."

Theodore replies, "This one never lights up, no matter what I try. Are you Japanese?"

"Half," Melanie says, warming to the subject (herself). "My dad is from Kyoto and my mom met him when—" She falls silent when she feels my glare. "Sorry. Back to business." She

35

writes today's date. I have the strangest thought: *She doesn't know about that rose on the back of his arm. That one's mine. And I bet his lantern glows all night.*

"I'm sure you must be wondering what all this is about," Jerry says.

"I think I know," I reply, and I make prolonged, unblinking eye contact with his son for the first time.

Theodore Prescott has:

- Hazel eyes
- Little-kid freckles across the bridge of his nose
- A lot of empathy in his expression, for a thoughtless jerk

He says, "You've scared her shitless, Dad."

I explain myself. "At the gas station, I was just doing my good deed for the day."

"What does she mean, gas station? What did you do?" Jerry turns on his son, his voice taking on the kind of growl-tone you'd use on your golden retriever that's standing in the dirt of an upturned indoor plant. Theodore is clearly used to it; dopey grin, tail wag.

I must be charitable, because I try to cover for the younger Prescott. "I was filling one of the residents' cars with gas for them. I thought maybe, from an insurance point of view, I shouldn't have driven it."

Theodore won't allow me to take the fall. "She happened to find me in a tight spot and loaned me twenty bucks for fuel.

Dad, you are looking at my Good Samaritan." I can read the word printed across the knuckles on his left hand: *TAKE*.

"Teddy, you can't ask total strangers for money." Jerry is horrified. "You should have called me earlier. What if someone knew you're a Prescott?"

"Teddy," Melanie echoes in childlike wonder. She writes it in her notepad, repeating like a magic spell, "Teddy Prescott."

"What? Don't I look like a Teddy?" He's got humor in his eyes now, and that question is for me. I doubt he has it in him to be serious for more than thirty seconds at a time. He prompts me gently, "Well?"

Does he look like a Teddy? "Uh . . ."

I actually have a stuffed bear from my childhood called Teddy in my room right now. They both have a lot of experience sitting on girls' beds. Bright-eyed, adorable creations made for hugging and finding in your sheets in the morning. The spark in Teddy's eyes intensifies; he's biting his lip, holding the laugh in. I brush some hair away from my face; my cheek is hot.

Melanie can be relied upon for honest feedback. "Teddy is silly, you're too old. What about Theo instead?" She's wrong. When I'm faced with that alternative, it suits him down to the ground.

"He's been my little bear since he was a baby," Jerry says, making his adult son dissolve with embarrassment. It's luscious to witness this moment. "But yes. He's too old for a lot of things now. Definitely time for a haircut."

(Melanie writes down, *little bear = baby Teddy*, in her note-pad, and now it's me who's trying not to laugh.)

"But girls love my long hair." If he released his bun, Melanie and I would be blinded, but it's irritating that he knows it. His eyes flick back to me like a reflex, and I realize he wants to know if I agree. He's messing around with me. Am I a Teddy? Am I irresistible? I huff and straighten up in my seat.

Jerry continues like he hasn't heard that. "I've been a bit hands-off Providence since we acquired this place. I've been focused on another project."

"I only just found out about PDC and this place," Teddy tells me. "I really didn't know." The melodrama of sitting on your bike not wanting to call your rich father who owns *so many things* is just something else. I look over at his backpack again.

When Jerry notices that Melanie and I are looking worried, he says cheerfully, "Don't worry, we haven't made a decision on how we'll proceed with the site yet."

That's the summary I'm going to be emailing to Sylvia? No bulldozers, yet? I whisper, "Okay, well, that sounds great." I'm supposed to be taking care of this place, and that's the loudest I can get?

Teddy sighs. "Why can't you leave things how they are? This place seems fine."

"Life is change," Jerry says, and I suspect he repeats that often. "If I wanted to sit in an office and just buy and sell, I'd do that. I like being out, on-site." Here, he bangs on the table solidly. "Talking to people and making a difference. Giving things new life. Caring about something. You should try it."

Teddy's eyes blaze and his jaw squeezes. "You know that I care about something a lot."

"Oh, sure. Your latest brain wave," Jerry begins, but the glance he gets from his son ends that train of thought. Too bad for me, because I was edging forward in my chair to find out what could make Teddy glow incandescent in this one moment.

I instigate a subject change. "I've been following your acquisitions, Mr. Prescott."

He's surprised. "Really? Call me Jerry, please." In the background, Teddy exhales and gives me *thank-you* eyes.

"That old golf course must be a challenging site. Is getting labor difficult? I have enough trouble getting our maintenance contractors to stop past here."

Jerry nods like he's amazed. "You're exactly right. It's a nightmare."

"You hate golf," Teddy says cynically.

"It's going to be a day spa with sixty-five self-contained cabins. Horseback riding, hiking, meditation, the works. It makes more sense to create accommodation and employment than to try to bring those fairways back to life." Jerry looks at his son. "You could come out and see it."

His heir doesn't take the job-offer bait. "Can't wait. I need a facial."

"You need a residential address, period," Jerry replies.

Again, I step in. What is it about Teddy that has turned me into a human shield? "I can print off a dashboard for you, showing our occupancy and financial position as of Monday, eight A.M."

"Could you do that, Teddy? Run the financial data on a site?" Jerry says to his son. "Can you use accounting software?"

"Of course I can't." Teddy is getting riled up, almost crackling with blue-black sparks. "But I won't need to know how. Alistair does all that."

"How is that fair to him? If you're starting a business, you'll need to learn." Jerry is pleased to have made a point. To me he adds, "No, that's fine, Ruthie. Just send your usual reports to the office."

I need some way to impress Jerry. "We work very hard to ensure that Providence maintains its reputation, which of course goes without saying."

"You may need to explain it for Teddy's benefit," Jerry says, but I detect a faint whiff of face-saving. Perhaps Jerry can't remember why he added PDC to his sold-sticker collection. I click into brochure mode.

"Providence has been consistently listed in the country's top ten retirement complexes since it was built in the late 1960s. We really pride ourselves on the boutique feel. In this area, there's a saying: 'With any luck I'll retire in Providence.' They're saying that this is the ultimate goal to aspire to."

Jerry isn't really listening. "And you live on-site here, correct?"

"Yes, sir. It's part of my salary package. There's a dual-occupancy cottage that used to be for on-site security and maintenance. I am here twenty-four, seven for the residents."

"For how long?" Teddy asks.

Is he not very bright? Oh dear. Beauty fades. "Sorry, how

do you mean? All day and all night." I shimmy out of my hot cardigan.

Teddy says, "No, how long have you been living here, twenty-four, seven?"

"Oh. The whole time. Six years."

Teddy is as dumbstruck as that moment when I turned around and revealed my true age at the gas station. "Do you go anywhere?"

"Providence is a great employer. I visit my parents when I take my vacation. And I go to the gas station," I add with a pinch of dryness. "It doesn't matter where I go. It matters that I'm always here."

"That sounds absolutely—" Teddy is silenced by his father's sideways look.

"It sounds like true long-term commitment to a job," Jerry finishes. "It sounds like someone who chose a role and stuck with it. Someone who doesn't go chasing after the next shiny thing."

Teddy argues back, "I'm not doing that. I'll prove it to you when we open."

"Sure, we'll see." Jerry looks at me with a small smile. "It's rare I meet someone as dedicated as you, Ruthie. I can always tell when someone's only in it for the paycheck."

I am sick with pleasure from this praise. I'm also conflicted, because Jerry's blunt dismissal has hurt his son. "Thank you. I love it here. Would you both like a tour of the grounds?"

Jerry says, "Teddy needs somewhere to stay for a month or two. He's been kicked out by his roommates and has run out of couches. It wouldn't look great for a Prescott to be sleeping in a cardboard box. He's going to take the other half of your cottage."

"It's a little musty." My stomach flips over in surprise. We'll be sharing a wall.

"I'm stashing him here for a few months. Just enough time for him to get back on his feet. Save some money. Sort yourself out, Teddy. If you could get me the keys, Ruthie, we can walk up and find it. Maybe you could give it a little once-over with a feather duster for him."

This morning we were completely off the radar to PDC. While swooping in to rescue his hapless, walletless son, Jerry has remembered we exist. And now I have to clean. I manage to say blandly, "Sure, that's no problem."

Teddy is affronted, possibly on my behalf. "I can clean it myself." He holds out a hand for the cottage key, but his father does too. I know who my boss is.

Jerry takes it and says, "While you live here, Teddy, you're going to help out here in the office."

I keep my eyes neutral. I can't transmit how deeply, desperately I do not want this.

"She doesn't want me to," Teddy says. Am I a completely open book to him? Scary.

"Of course she does," Jerry rebuffs. "I think learning on the site will be a good way to get you interested in our business. You can adapt it to your latest venture, if you want," he adds unconvincingly.

Teddy sighs. "I'm not a property developer. I'm a tattoo artist. I'll never be on PDC's payroll." The compulsive inking is explained. Tattoos, motorbikes, floating on the breeze, completely unconcerned about his next meal or next bed? No wonder he keeps staring at me like I'm microscopic.

Jerry eyes Melanie thoughtfully. "Have you signed a contract?"

I answer for her. "Yes, two months, and I've already trained her." No way am I sitting across from the boss's son while he dicks around doing quizzes online for eight hours a day. I've got Mel for that. She blinks at me, expression grateful. Teddy's looking roughly the same. "We've got a maintenance contractor, a gardener . . . we're all set."

"Anything else?" Jerry refocuses like a laser on me. "Any other odd jobs around here he could do?" Jerry really wants to put a big tick in his Teddy Project column. "Ruthie, you just mentioned filling up a resident's car with gas. That sounds like a job."

I feel like my brain's cogs are clunking too slowly. It's the stress. I can barely remember my own name or pull in a deep breath.

What to do? A job for Teddy . . . what could be done . . . ?

"That was for the Parlonis," Melanie offers helpfully. "They need a lot of help. Wait a minute," she begins slowly, turning to me. Her young cogs are faster than mine. "They're hiring for an assistant. He can work for them."

I felt small and ridiculous at the gas station, when Teddy Prescott roared with laughter over every single aspect of my appearance. Now it's time for a little payback. "Perfect; well done, Mel. Would you like to see the job ad, Teddy? It's mainly driving, errands, and cleaning." It will also be the strangest, most demeaning experience of your life.

"Perfect," Jerry echoes, and I think he's feeling some Teddy payback too.

Teddy is regarding me with suspicion because I'm filled with evil glee. "I think these residents should interview me first. I don't want special treatment."

Jerry can't argue with that. "Put in a proper effort. I'll take a walk. Always nice to actually set foot on one of our assets." When he steps out onto the path and turns away, I see that his profile is just like his son's.

I wish Jerry wouldn't walk around here without me. He's going to get ideas, I just know it. Life is change, after all. But I have to make him understand how important this place is, and I have to report to Sylvia that I tried really hard.

On impulse I follow him out and say, "Mr. Prescott? Sorry, Jerry? Would I be able to join you?"

"I'd rather you go with Teddy to the interview. I know you want some job certainty," he adds. He looks exhausted now as he looks up the hill. "I can't even remember when we acquired this place."

"You're a busy person."

"Too busy. My daughter Rose is ready for more responsibility. I'm going to ask her to conduct a full site review and recommend to the board how we proceed. I'll ask her to call you." He seems pleased with this solution.

"I'll provide her with any information she needs." I know

that it's going to take more than reports to convince them to leave Providence as it is. What opportunity do I have to showcase what an impact we have on our residents? How can I make him fall in love with the place? "I don't suppose you'd like to come to the Christmas party this year? I do the fund-raising for it and we have a lot of fun. We have a theme, and . . . it's just a great example of what we do here."

Jerry is charmed. "Send through the details to my assistant. If I'm available, sure. Why not? Sounds like a good time." He sets off up the path. "Send an invitation to Rose as well, please. She needs to learn to get out of the office and meet people. I doubt Teddy will still be here then. But until he leaves, can you keep an eye out for him, and help him settle in?"

I have to reply: "Of course."

CHAPTER FIVE

Back inside the office, Teddy and Mel are getting along like a house on fire. I dial the Parlonis and when it's eventually answered, there's a loud TV blaring in the background. "What?" Renata yells so loud that Teddy hears her from where he's standing. "Who died?"

"I have a new boy here for an interview." Applying the word *boy* to these tight muscles is laughable. But then again, he did just come in here with his dad like he was applying for a paper route.

"I thought we were going to get our diapers changed by a nurse," Renata barks. "I was about to start wetting myself. What's he like?" I hear loud chewing. "What category?"

She means, is he:

- Droopy Goth
- Brain-Dead Skateboarder
- Prima Donna
- Talentless Musician
- Idealistic Youth

- Many other categories I can't remember right now because a handsome man is staring at me like I am interesting

What category? All I know is, his eyes are like a golden bonnet tortoise shell. Brown, green, and yellow. Exceedingly rare, found only right here. My gaze starts on his T-shirt sleeve, and before I know it, I'm moving down that forearm to his wrist. I'm ravenous to see more of this perfectly executed living art. Under my eyes, his hand flexes like I've touched him. Without much air, I say, "He's in the tattoo category."

"You know that's only a subcategory," Renata says.

"He's the son of the owner of Providence. He'll be living on-site in the other side of my cottage for a little while. It'll be very convenient—he can just pop up to your place whenever you need him."

Renata whoops in delight. "So we've got ourselves a Richie Rich for my last-ever boy. I've been training for this." There's a short pause. "The owner's son, did you say? Do I have to behave myself with this one?" It's the first time she has ever paused to consider how her high jinks might impact me.

"He doesn't want any special treatment," I tell her with barely concealed relish. "Just do the usual interview."

"I'm going to do the White Shirt Challenge. Haven't done that one in a while. Send him up. What am I going to wear?" She hangs up.

To the dial tone, I reply, "No problem. See you soon." I hang up. "Let's go."

"Can I come?" Melanie grabs her notepad.

"You need to stay here and answer the phone." She wheels her chair back to her desk and slumps into it. "You really didn't need to take notes, by the way."

"I was just copying you and all your lists. Anyway, I hope you get the job," Melanie says to Teddy. "It'd be nice to have someone young around here to talk to."

His gaze flicks to me. "I think I'm older than Ruthie."

She realizes how that sounded, covering it up with huffs and blustering. "There'll be three young people here, of course that's what I meant. So have you ever heard of the Sasaki Method? Of course you haven't, because I invented it."

"Based on the name alone, it sounds very legit." He's interested and grinning, leaning over to poke around in the junk on her desk. "I hope it's not a pyramid scheme. I'm broke and gullible. Ah, what the hell? Sign me up."

"You will not tell him about the Sasaki Method," I counter-instruct.

Teddy picks up her notepad. " '*Baby bear*'? Oh my God, kill me now." He picks up a pen and scribbles that out. He reads out more of her notes. "'*Haircut. Crowning glory. Golf course facials.*' This is a useful record, good job. Wait, what does this mean? '*Warn Ruthie off this one again.*'"

Mel shrugs. "Just making sure my boss doesn't get blinded by the hair."

Teddy's eyes cut to me and he strokes his head with his fingertips. His gaze holds mine. *Stay bland, Ruthie. Hold steady.*

With zero shame, he smiles at me and crosses out that "Warn Ruthie" line in Melanie's notes.

Melanie doesn't notice all this somehow. She continues in her previous train of thought. "We have a maintenance dilemma here at Providence. Deciding whether Ruthie is high—or low—maintenance, for her dating profile. What do you think?"

"Dating profile?" He stumbles over this, but recovers and pretends to inspect me. "Hmm, let me think."

Great, two giggling employees. The thing about being the butt of a joke? It's funny at first. But after an entire childolescence being Truthful Ruth the Reverend's Daughter, it's worn thinner than a contact lens.

Melanie says, "With the Sasaki Method, I will ensure that Ruthie—"

"That's enough, Melanie," I say in a voice that would make a golden retriever piddle. "Please get back to work."

"Roger," she replies, uninjured. To Teddy she says, "I hope you weren't the one who hurt Ruthie's feelings."

He turns to me, surprise in his eyes, but I walk out. "I sometimes do that," I hear him tell her with what sounds like genuine regret. "I've been told I can be a careless little asshole."

"Just don't do it again," Melanie replies with steel in her tone. "Or I'll kill ya."

"Come on, you've got an interview," I call out with dark glee in my heart. I hope Renata Parloni absolutely breaks this one.

Teddy keeps pace easily with me as I almost run up the path. "What's with the wildlife situation?"

We come across two golden bonnet tortoises. They are mating. I mean, I'm happy for the species, but, sheesh. In my effort to give them some privacy, I knock into Teddy and pinball into a hedge. He puts his hand on my arm to steady me. We stop and face each other.

"Careful," he chides, like I'm the clueless visitor. Like I haven't been here, working my ass off preserving his family's investment. Now I'm steaming mad. Providence was under the radar. We were forgotten. Now Jerry Prescott is on the other side of the lake right there, taking photographs, delegating, and making new plans.

"Maybe they're playing a game," Teddy says, gesturing down at the path where the tortoises are rocking each other's worlds. "Maybe it's not what we think." He wants me to be playful with him.

"The ones with yellow on the shell are endangered golden bonnet tortoises. Please don't step on any, or I'll have to scrape them up and fill out a form."

You wouldn't even know where to locate that particular clipboard, buddy.

Teddy blows out a breath, looking back down at the office. "That was probably the most humiliating thing I've ever sat through. 'Little baby bear,'" he groans, remembering afresh. "Hey, is that the faintest ghost of a smile at my expense?" He's still holding my arm and squeezes me gently.

I'm sort of . . . gently panicking? Is that what this flutter-sensation inside is?

He notices my reaction and folds his arms slowly across his

chest like I'm a spooked critter. The knuckles peek out—his right hand has GIVE across the knuckles. GIVE and TAKE, oh gosh, why is that making it hard for me to find actual normal words to say out loud?

"I know you've been put in a real difficult spot by my dad. Sorry about that. I promise I'll be out of here as soon as I've saved enough. Just a couple of months. This place is kind of something, huh?"

"This place is really special. Come on, let's get going."

"Yeah, wait," Teddy says, in no rush like always. "Let me take it all in."

Providence is built around a natural lake, fed by streams running down from the steep hill to our right. The dark, scribbly-looking forest isn't good for hiking or picnic-blanket daydreaming; I've tried both. It's nothing but mosquitoes and Bigfoot manure in those trees. Tortoises slowly graze the banks of the lake, and in the spring the banks have nodding drifts of bluebells and white tulips that I planted myself.

But Teddy's not taking in the view—he's looking at the town houses.

"Looking at these houses makes me feel like I've got something on the tip of my tongue. Like déjà vu." He steps over the copulating tortoises and begins to stroll, looking troubled. "Maybe I dreamed this place." He looks at the glasses hanging against my chest. "I've been having a lot of dreams lately."

"I'm sure you have." The dryer I am, the wider he grins. I gesture up at the houses. "Once I tell you, you won't un-see it."

Teddy stands in front of the first town house, number 1,

home to Mrs. Allison Tuckmire, and he tucks a fist under his chin. He looks cute when he's thinking. He should do it more often. "Give me a clue. The architectural style."

"You're into architecture?"

Shrug. "I like design." I suppose. He's completely covered in them.

"Colonial Revival. The double pillars on either side of the doors, the arch motifs over the windows. The shutters and the slate roof. I already gave you a hint earlier, in my brochure spiel. This place was built in the late 1960s."

Teddy twists his body back to me with a groan. "I can't take it. Tell me."

I say, "Graceland," and he looks at me like the ground has dropped out from under him.

"Graceland," he repeats with genuine wonder. "Graceland had a litter of kittens."

I laugh at his perfect description. "The architect who designed Providence was Herbert St. Ives and he was a big Elvis fan. There's a total of forty kittens here." I sweep my arm at the huge square of houses surrounding the lake. "This was, once upon a time, extremely modern and glamorous. Now it's just . . ." I try to think of how to spin it. "Preserved to the best of our ability."

He rubs his neck and looks contrite. "I'm sorry if I hurt your feelings at the gas station. I have an incurable case of verbal diarrhea. I get really carried away and you just sparked my imagination too much. But that's my fault, not yours. I'm sorry."

I'm speechless that I could spark anything in him at all. We stare at each other, and I realize the part I'd hoped for the most is not coming. The bit where he says, *You really don't look old at all.*

The silence becomes too much for him to bear. "I'm guessing everyone here is super rich."

I've heard a variation of this statement from many, many candidates. Resident Protection Shields Up. I walk off. "This way."

I'm learning that some guys can make you intensely aware of their . . . maleness. I feel like I'm being followed by a *T. rex*. The pavers make audible granite squeaks underneath his boots. His shadow stretches out in front of us, eclipsing mine. And I don't know how it's possible to *feel* someone's interest, but the hair tie holding my bun feels loose and my tights roll down my waist a few inches.

In his man's voice, all deep and husky, he asks, "Can I ask about my duties?"

"I think it'd be best if you just brought them up in the interview," I say, sidestepping both the question and a tortoise. "The Parlonis will be your bosses, not me."

"But I'd do anything you asked me to." I don't know why, but the way he says it flusters the absolute hell out of me. When I don't reply, he continues in his normal voice, "You're not going to even give me a clue of what's coming."

"I want to see how you work under pressure."

He lengthens his stride to fall into step beside me. "Don't worry. My specialty is walking into rooms and making people love me."

"And do you have a hundred percent success rate?" I expect

a grin and an outrageous claim in return, but instead he just looks rattled. I see that his confident mask has slipped. Maybe he's thinking about his father.

He notices my attention. "You do fine under pressure, too. I know it must have been stressful to have Dad barging in."

I straighten up my clothes before I ring the Parlonis' doorbell. "Your dad's asking your sister Rose to conduct a site review."

"Oh man, I'm sorry. Pack your bags." He draws in a deep breath and blows it out, and I know for sure he's nervous. He's just a good actor.

The door opens, and it's Aggie, natty in a pewter pantsuit. Only armchairs and wealthy old women can pull off that kind of thick jacquard fabric. "Renata's selecting a new costume. Hello, young man."

I take charge of the introduction. "Theodore Prescott, meet Agatha Parloni."

"Teddy," he amends with a smile. They shake hands in a brisk, business-like way. "Nice to meet you, Mrs. Parloni."

"Call me Aggie. This way, young man. Are you going to sit in, Ruthie?" She's noticed my notepad.

"I will, if that's okay." I trail along behind them. Around us, the house is in slight disarray. There's a four-foot stack of garments in their dry-cleaning bags across the back of the couch. The bench is covered in mugs again. Only last night I stacked their dishwasher, fuming that I paid twenty dollars to be laughed at by a guy. The memory galvanizes me. I am not helping him out from this point forward.

"A bit untidy," Aggie says with a weary sigh. "Did you have any trouble finding Providence?"

"No. And Ruthie was very kind to walk me up."

"That's Ruthie," Aggie says, a faint smile on her lips. Little does she know I'm dreaming of some ritual humiliation. "So kind."

"Kind of uptight," Renata deadpans from behind us. What a treat to get a free master class in comic timing. She walks toward us. A bonus fashion show.

Teddy is wonderstruck. "So green."

It's an entirely green ensemble. She's wearing very wide pants, a silk blouse, a bejeweled fanny pack, and a visor that has MONEY printed across the brim. Her little flat shoes sparkle. To top it off, she's got on the emerald-green wig she calls "the Pisces." She is wearing makeup that could be seen from the back row of a Broadway theater. Blending makeup is for "young people with time on their hands."

If she's gratified by Teddy's jaw-on-the-floor reaction, Renata doesn't show it. Instead, she strolls around him like he's a fridge that has just been delivered. "What make and model is this?"

Aggie sighs at her dramatics. "Teddy Prescott, this is Renata Parloni."

"Unfurl that hair, Rapunzel," Renata orders Teddy, and there's a genuine shampoo-ad gloss-and-tousle moment when he does. "What a wig that would make. Would you consider selling that to me?"

"Sorry. Without it, I'm nothing."

Renata replies, "Worth a try. Do you ever cut it?"

"My sister Daisy trims it at Christmastime, out on the back patio. She's the only one I trust. The others would shave me bald." He grasps it now for comfort.

Renata will not give up easily. "I'd pay top dollar. Think it over."

Aggie clears her throat. As always, things are off to a weird start. "Let's sit in the sunroom."

"My least favorite room," Renata replies dourly, positioning herself out of the pool of warm yellow light. "If I had my way, we would have the shutters closed permanently."

"But you don't have your way," Aggie replies mildly, and I realize I've missed something in their dynamic. Renata is loud as a foghorn and half as subtle, but Aggie is the boss. "Take a seat," she encourages, and we do.

"Teddy Prescott, your first task is to ensure sunlight never again touches my skin. You two don't know what you have: SKIN." Renata makes both Teddy and me jump in our seats. We look down at ourselves. She intones like a creep, "Nice young skin."

Teddy asks, "Am I going to end up in the bottom of a well, applying lotion to myself?"

"What you do in your spare time is none of my business," Renata advises him. "Oh, let's take a look." She means the tattoos across his knuckles. "GIVE and TAKE. Are you left- or right-handed?"

"Left."

"So you admit you take more than you give." Renata is locking into a mode I have seen many times before: a serpentine argument based on the applicant's self-perception. We barely have sixty seconds on the clock.

"Depends on who I'm with."

"Elaborate," Renata instructs crisply.

"If I'm down in the well, alone with the lotion, then yes. If I'm not alone, then I definitely mix it up." Those multicolor eyes flick back to me now, maybe checking how I'm handling this risqué line of reply. He sees I'm amused, and now those eyes are sparkling.

"One point to Teddy," Aggie umpires.

"What a blank canvas we've got here." Renata reaches over and takes my wrist, unbuttoning my cuff and pushing up my sleeve. "We could take her to get a tattoo. I'll pay. What should she get? I know, a big Virgin Mary." She's shockingly strong and I inhale as her nails begin to press.

"Ow," I protest.

For the first time, Teddy looks truly uncomfortable. "That's the first interview question? What tattoo would I, a licensed tattoo artist, give Ruthie? Whatever she asked for. Let her go, please." His voice has dipped down into that particular register men use when they want their way, now. We three women suddenly remember what he is.

Renata releases my arm, which is now marked with crescent nail indentations. She makes long eye contact with Aggie, who remains impassive. They conduct a wordless communication. Then Renata says to me, "We're going to have to invent a new category, aren't we, Ruthie?" This is her apology.

"What are some of your common categories?" Teddy asks, like he is not dealing with a strange person. "Maybe I can tell you which one I fit into."

Renata begins ticking off on her fingers. "Country Bumpkin. Little Boy Lost. Too Dumb to Live. Fake Grandson—they're the ones hoping to inherit."

Aggie adds, "Environmental Man—no deodorant."

"I wear deodorant."

"Another point to Teddy. I think sometimes I still get a whiff of Matthew," Aggie says. "And it's been years."

I try to join in. "Tortured Artist?" If these are his designs, he's talented.

"I'm feeling mildly tortured right about now," Teddy agrees.

Renata looks out the window like she's remembering someone special. "My favorites have been Insomniac Potheads. Ones who can get me a good supply, and we sit up all night talking about which celebrity is going to die next."

"I'll pretend I didn't hear that." I must be getting mellow. It's the late-afternoon sun shining through onto my back.

"When you're this old, weed and takeout is all you have left to live for. And love, of course," Renata says, patting her sister's hand. "Ah, je suis très romantique . . . Quick. Give me a compliment." That's a test lobbed at Teddy.

Teddy replies, "Your house is nice." The view from this room is lovely: Manicured lawns roll up to an English box hedge. Beyond that, there is a birdbath and a stooped wisteria.

Renata scoffs. "Boring attempt, minus a point. If I wasn't a million years old, I'd be back in my old loft in Tribeca." Not this song again. Her eyes narrow dangerously. "I meant a compliment for me."

Teddy steps up to the plate. He squints his eyes against the sunlight. He lifts his bat. "You are," Teddy says with emphasis and absolute sincerity, "the best-dressed person I have ever met."

The crowd leaps to their feet. We shade our eyes. He knocks it clean out of the park. That compliment is denting the windshield of a bus two suburbs over.

"Oh," Renata says, looking down at herself. "You mean this outfit?" A smile is on her mouth and she strokes a hand down her rail-thin thigh as if it were a treasured pet. "This old pair of Dior cruise collection 2016 palazzo pants? This vintage Balenciaga blouse? He's pretty good, that's ten points," she says offhand to Aggie, who is starting to doze in the warm room.

He doesn't gloat. "What's the job involve?"

Renata asks, "Can you drive? That's all I care about. One time, a boy told us he didn't drive because of the carbon footprint. I put a footprint on his ass."

Teddy grins, and it's a lovely thing. "I ride a motorbike. But I'd love to take your Rolls-Royce out for a spin."

Aggie rouses herself from her sleepy sunlit dozing. "Tell us more about yourself." At the exact moment, Renata says, "How tall are you?" Why are elderly women obsessed with knowing how tall young men are?

"I'm twenty-seven. I'm six four. Like I said, I'm a tattoo artist, but I've also been a delivery driver."

Aggie considers this. "Why are you not working in your chosen field?"

"I might try to get some freelance work. At night, so it won't interfere."

"We are very demanding," Renata interrupts. "I want you always available to pick things up or drive us around. There's a lot of dry-cleaning. It's an easy job, I don't know why young men have such a hard time with it. Get us flowers. Pizza. Restaurant reservations. Hmmm, what else?" Renata looks to me.

"Maintenance, cleaning, laundry, spontaneous compliments." It's an expansive role, based around swallowing one's rage and pride. "Lots of running out for snacks and helping them order things online."

"I can cook a bit too," Teddy says. He keeps looking to me. Is he expecting me to ask something? Am I his safety blanket? I shield my page from him on the side of the table and write down:

- *Tattoo artist/Delivery driver*
- *27 yo, 6'4", That Hair*
- *Can cook; sincerely rendered compliment*

I've also been keeping track of the points allocated and subtracted. Melanie can't be faulted for thinking I expected meeting notes to be taken. Add *Kind of uptight* to my dating profile.

I put my hand into my hair, checking for unwinding strands. I bite back a yawn. I smush my lips around to redistribute my lip balm. Why is everything silent? I look up. Teddy is still looking at me. The sisters are looking at Teddy looking at me.

Aggie is smiling. "Doesn't she look so pretty sitting in that sunbeam?" Teddy jerks his eyes from me in surprise. So that's what it feels like to be visible for a few long moments. Like touching a live wire.

Renata adds, "There is an expression. Still waters run deep. Do you know what that means?"

"I do now," he replies, again with that sincerity. "I really think I do."

Just as I begin to get hot with embarrassment, Aggie says, "I take it that this job will be a stepping-stone, back to tattoos." She is the Patron Saint of Merciful Subject Changes. I will light a candle for her tonight.

"One of my friends is setting up a second tattoo studio in Fairchild and I want to buy in. I'd manage that location. But I need the money by Christmas or he'll sell the share to someone else." His eyes come back to me like a reflex, and his next words are humble. "At least, that's the plan."

I know his father seemed to doubt his sincerity in pursuing this, but let's get real. This is a person who could sell ice in a snowstorm. If he focused his charm and effort, he could have anything he wanted. Before Renata can shoot him down, because she does like taking potshots at simple goals and dreams, I reply: "Well, of course you'll do it, Teddy."

He's surprised by how certain I sound.

"I've never been to Fairchild," Aggie says. "How far away is that?" We are all already trying to calculate if he'll be *gone-forever* gone.

He confirms that he pretty much will. "Five hours away. It's a really nice town. Kind of like here, actually. But best of all, there's no studios there. I researched it for my business case. There's a community college campus and a military training base there, and they have to drive hours to get work done on their tattoos." Sounds like he's got a bigger stake in this than he first let on. My perception of him shifts a little.

"Why don't you just ask Daddy to stump up the cash?" Renata asks with saccharine sweetness. It's actually the question I wish I could ask. "Get an advance on that inheritance. Cash in, sonny boy."

"I'm fairly sure there's no inheritance."

Renata asks, "Are you the only son?" Teddy nods, but he's very uncomfortable. I'm just about to interject when Renata keeps going. "You're probably hitting the jackpot eventually."

"I have four sisters ahead in the queue. Anyway, I don't take money from him. And he doesn't give money to me. It's an arrangement involving no money."

Aggie says, "So, Teddy will have his studio. Do you have a goal, Ruthie?"

The question is asked in that slow kind way that people ask kindergartners what they want to be when they grow up. As a kid, I had an improvised veterinarian uniform made out of my father's old white shirts, plus a toy ginger-striped cat with bald front legs from my rebandaging. Aggie's just being polite, and this interview is not about me, but I find I want to answer anyway.

"I'm hopefully going to—" I'm about to explain about Sylvia's retirement and my more realistic office manager aspirations when Renata speaks right over the top of me like I don't exist.

"Now, time for the practical component of your interview."

"Okay," Teddy says, looking reflexively to me.

Renata snaps, "You're on your own. No clues, no hints. This is why young men have always infuriated me. They stopgap their inadequacies with competent young women." She's getting very angry now. "Early in our careers, we were like donkeys that the men in our offices loaded up with work. No more, never again. You're the donkey now."

"Of course. Sorry." He is suitably chastened. "Hee-haw."

"Here is three hundred dollars. Go and buy me a white shirt. Let's see how clever you are, little donkey. You have one hour, starting now." The money is slapped down. "Ruthie, sixty minutes, if you please."

"She hasn't done this one in a long time," Aggie says to me. I go to their oven and set a timer. Just looking at how late we are in the afternoon, I don't think he's going to make it. Panic and glee are rising inside me.

If Teddy is surprised by this task, he hides it well. "Am I allowed to ask any questions about what sort of shirt?" He's looking at the timer and setting his own on his phone.

Aggie shakes her head at his attempt. "Of course not, young man. Do your best." Her eyes gleam with deep amusement, and for a split second I think she's every bit the puppeteer that her sister is. "All you can do is your best."

He looks outside across the manicured lawns. His father technically owns everything framed outside that window. It's a degrading task for someone with the surname Prescott. He's going to tell her to shove it. He'll find another job.

"Easy," he says. As his running footsteps depart, Renata lets out a howl of pure elation and we all grin at one another. It is luscious to make a young man run for his life. And just like that, no matter what he brings back, I am absolutely certain that Teddy got the job.

CHAPTER SIX

No one would guess my penchant for evening nudity by looking at me in my daytime wool knits.

My usual evening routine is to close all the drapes, take off my clothes, and walk around my cottage for a few minutes before my bath. It didn't start in any kind of deviant way. Six months after I moved into this cottage, I had to walk out naked into the living room to find a towel in the laundry basket. It was the exact moment that I realized I have my own house and can do whatever I want, and now I'm addicted to that air sensation all over. But for however long Teddy hangs around here, I'm going to have to remain buttoned up.

It's amazing how life works. You can wake up in your current existence and then go to bed with everything changed.

After a kitchen fire in the mid-1980s, this large cottage was converted into a dual occupancy dwelling, with a wall put right down the middle. I can hear my new neighbor shuffling around in his new home. There's a sneeze, a banging cupboard door, a barked expletive, gentle fake sobbing.

I am gallantly committed to keeping to my routine. I'll do the same thing I do every night, just with this new shimmer in my stomach. I preheat the oven. I go into the bathroom and light the row of candles on the back ledge. I drop in a blob of bubble bath and release my hair from its bun prison.

I'm exhausted from the email I sent to Sylvia. It was an impossible tone to achieve: *Hi, how are you* mixed with *don't panic but* and a smattering of *I have a bad feeling*. A three-paragraph email took me almost an hour of redrafting and arguing with myself. I've never needed a bath more. I put one hand on the top button of my blouse and there's a tap on the door.

"Sorry to bother you," Teddy says when I open my door.

I'm still holding the button in a half in/half out purgatory and it's pretty obvious I was about to undress. For a moment, my heart is in my throat. I don't know him, and in this low light he's positively vampiric, with sharp-looking teeth and an interested gleam in his eye.

He reads me and steps back, facing away. "I can come back."

"No, it's fine. What's up?" I redo the button. And the one above it for good measure. I'm tortoising.

"Where's the hot-water unit?"

"We share one. Sorry, I didn't think." I walk a few yards inside and he isn't following me. It occurs to me that vampires need to be invited in. "Uh, enter."

He comes in and looks around slowly. "I love your wallpaper. It's a repro Morris pattern, right?"

He really is into design. "Yes, it's called Blackthorn. I hung it myself." I bought one roll per paycheck for an entire year.

Sylvia cackled at my folly, decorating something that isn't even mine. I've enclosed myself in this dark, flowered forest and I'm glad I did. Especially right now.

Teddy takes out his phone and begins to pick out details and sections to photograph. "It reminds me of the endpapers of a fairy-tale book." Now he strokes down the wall, and I swear, I feel his palm down my back. "You did a perfect job, Ruthie. The pattern's lined up so well."

His fingers marked GIVE find the line between the sheets and slide up. Forgotten parts of my body tighten in response.

Wallpaper gets more action than me. "Thanks. Do you like flowers?"

"The guys at the studio give me shit, but I've got a real thing for flowers. I love doing them on clients." He exhales, dramatic and shivery. "Can I put your walls all over me?"

I wonder what it's like to just say whatever outrageous thing is in your head. My voice is tight with frustration at myself when all I manage to parry back is, "Go right ahead."

He mistakes my tone for censure. "Sorry. I always seem to say the stupidest stuff to you." Now the moment is over and he's in my linen closet. "I knew you'd have a label maker. So what am I looking for here? I can't see it."

"The hot-water unit."

"Where?"

It is an ancient metal drum, it takes up half the space, and is taller than me. I'm looking up to check if he's a very unobservant person when I see his eyes are sparkling with fun. He says, "Oh, there it is. Ruthie, why didn't you label it?"

A joke where I'm the punch line. My favorite kind. "There's a big lever on the back of it. I'll get it—"

I haven't finished my sentence when he's knelt down, reached back, and said, "There."

"Oh. Wasn't it hard?"

"Nah," he says, back on his feet, wiping his palm on his knee. Having biceps and strong hands must be nice.

"Now you can have a hot bath."

"A bath," he repeats, eyes sideways to my bathroom, where the tap is pouring gallons of our now-shared water. What a dumb suggestion. Do men even have baths? But then he says, "I never thought of that. Maybe I will."

I walk in and turn off the faucet. "I'll try to not use all the water."

To my back he says, "Don't change your routine on my account." Funny, that was just what I was telling myself, right before he appeared and interrupted it. He leans on the bathroom doorframe, rubbing his face. "I would kill to have a routine."

"I take it your life has been a little unstructured lately."

"That's an elegant way to describe it. Unstructured." He hesitates, then apparently decides to confide in me. "When you were a kid, did you have a bedtime? Strict parents?" I nod. "I want a label maker, but I think it's too late for me."

"It's not too late." I want his smile to come back. "I can give you a bedtime if that's helpful."

He's looking at me, then away, cataloging the room.

Now back to me.

Is seeing me out of an office context weird for him? The candles glow in his eyes, his dark hair is cloaking him, and I think of old-fashioned illustrations of the devil. What would my parents say if they knew I was in the same room as this man? They would say a prayer.

I should feel unsafe and scared. I don't. "So you got the job for the Parlonis."

"I did."

"What shirt did you buy?"

"I went to the thrift store on Martin Street and found a vintage blouse. I think it was a kid's shirt. Seemed about her size. It was a cream color, so I wasn't sure if it counted. I wanted to call you and cheat." He grins and I swear, the candles all flare. In a voice like velvet he adds, "Can I have your number?"

It's a rookie error to give your number to a Parloni assistant. "That's actually my favorite store. Who was working? A young guy?"

Eyebrows down. "Yeah. Does he have your number?"

"No, that's Kurt. He puts aside things in my size he thinks I'll like, but he's usually so off base. He picks out some really short skirts." My current hemline is more on the ankle end of the scale.

"I'll bet he does." Teddy's eyes blaze brighter. He resumes his catalog of the bathroom until he's run out of things to look at. Now I'm getting a long perusal. "Your hair is really pretty."

I put my hand up to it automatically. "I'm about to do a keratin treatment. Let's just say I'm feeling inspired."

He doesn't notice my hidden compliment. Fondly, he says,

"Women. How do you handle all the upkeep? You know you don't actually have to do all that stuff." He drags a hand through his own hair.

I gesture to his tattoos. "I would bet my hair treatments took less time than those."

He takes the point with a one-shoulder shrug. "What were some of the other outcomes of the White Shirt Challenge?"

The room's getting too warm. Every inhale is full of steam and fragrance. I'm fogging up like a mirror. "Some wasted time going somewhere like Chanel or Gucci."

I squeeze past him in the doorway. He smells like a sweet tea bag; how obnoxiously nice. He tags along beside me, extending our claustrophobic squeeze. "Going to Gucci is a waste of time?"

"It's like a trick question. You'll never find a shirt there for only $300. That's a mistake that has pushed some young men to the brink." I walk through the living room and click on a few lamps. "Some go to Target. Some take the $300 and never come back. You did good," I admit grudgingly. "Vintage is what I would go for, too."

"No, she absolutely hated the shirt. My first task in the morning is to bury it in the garden, I quote, 'a minimum of three feet deep.' I think she's serious."

"I guarantee she is."

"Despite the fashion fail, she appreciated the lateral thinking, and the $298 change." Now he's standing in the doorway to my bedroom. He puts his hands on his hips. "Don't mind me, I'm a very nosy person. Ruthie Midona's bedroom."

(This is said with completely unearned awe.)

If he slides a toe over that threshold, I am grabbing him by the scruff and throwing him out. "You shouldn't just look without being invited to. What if there's . . . mess?"

He makes a soft noise, like *tsk*. "I've already established that you're a very tidy person. I love looking in women's rooms. I learn a lot."

"I'm sure," I reply so dourly that he laughs. "Go on then, roast me. Tell me how boring I am." Taking control of oncoming teasing is an advanced technique.

"You're very, very interesting." He's utterly sincere. I need to remember that's his countertechnique. "You always seem so concerned. Relax. You'll get a wrinkle. It's all good."

I know he's got a reason for hanging around here, and it isn't anything to do with how interesting I am. If this was high school, I'd suspect he's got a forgotten essay due tomorrow. Please get the heart stab over with. "Look at those baskets on top of the wardrobe. They're all labeled. With my label maker."

He shivers like a goose has walked over his grave. "Hot."

"Oh, very." I always thought of my bedroom as cute and cozy, but I think it looks very childish to him. My eyes drop to my bed and I feel heat rising up my neck.

"Hey man," he says to the ancient teddy bear on my bed. "What's up. I'm Teddy. And you are?" He looks at me sideways. I seem to feel his smile low down in my body. Really low. He says, "Please, please tell me it's called what I think it's called."

I barely survive the voice and the eyes. "His name is Rupert," I lie with dignity.

71

He doesn't buy it. "Sure. So who sees this room?" What odd phrasing.

"What do you mean? No one sees it except me. And now you." This makes him smile again and dislodge his shoulder from the doorframe. "Scoot, Teddy. I've got a bath to take." I almost get him out.

"I have a bit of a problem." His hand wraps around the door, and I see those knuckles. TAKE. A timely reminder. The lingering is about to be explained.

"Tell me about it in the morning." I begin to peel each finger loose. T, A, K . . .

"I have no sheets. Or towels. Or . . . anything that isn't clothes. Not even a bar of soap, let alone a scented candle. I think I need help."

Maybe I should be hospitable to the boss's son.

"I'm sure there's some emergency supplies in there. Let me take a look." I follow him into his new home and wince. Cold, dank, and barely furnished. Okay, I do feel bad for him. "This is the thermostat. I'm not sure it works."

"It has all the charm of a Soviet missile testing facility. Can you please be my interior decorator?" Teddy bumps my shoulder with his in a friendly way. "I'm on a budget, but I know you can work miracles."

"Sorry, I'm not taking on new clients."

"I'd much rather be in there"—he nods at our shared wall—"with you."

My heart unstitches itself from my rib cage and bounces

across the floor. Just as I'm about to start scrambling for it, he adds, "Kidding, kidding. I only want you for your TV."

Translation: *Don't get the wrong idea, dork.* I open the linen cupboard. "I could have sworn there was a set of sheets around here." There's not even a roll of toilet paper. Very hard times.

"Ruthie," Teddy says all husky and persuasive behind me. That wallpaper-stroke sensation slides down my back again, but he didn't lay a finger on me. "Could I have your Wi-Fi password?"

"You are dreaming, Theodore." I have to be a bit cruel to this tomcat, or he'll be mewing at my door all night. "Well, the supermarket is still open. Off you go."

He's glowing at me now. He's got a special smile with perfect teeth, somehow increasing the intensity the longer I stare up at him. "What is it you think you're doing right now?"

He blinks and the force field dims. "What?"

"You're attempting to charm me." I'm gratified to see he's now quite embarrassed and he now can't meet my gaze. "Your magical powers probably work on girls a lot, but they won't on me." I hope I'm right. I go back into my cottage and he slides in behind me before the door shuts.

"It's so warm in here." He rubs his hands together like he's come in from a blizzard. His pink cheeks add to the effect. "I'll just sit awhile." Now he's on my couch, unfolding a health magazine. "Let's see. Yeast infections. What the hell does that mean? What's yeast?" There's an excruciating pause as his eyes move side to side. Sorrowful, he says, "How do women endure it all?"

I find words. "I'm not having a bath while you sit out here."

"Why not?" He looks back at the oven, still preheating. He's thinking about how to score an invitation for dinner. He pats the TV remote. He snuggles into a cushion and sighs. "I think I'm in heaven."

There's no lock on the bathroom door. "I don't know you."

"I feel like I've known you forever," Teddy replies, with an earnestness that takes a bone-crushing amount of effort to resist. But to borrow Renata's words: *I've been training for this.*

When he leaves for good, I'll be left remembering how lovely this moment felt. Effortless, instant friendships don't come along every day. Everyone who's needed my help has eventually vanished without a backward glance. The fold-out sofa in my parents' basement is remade with fresh sheets. The residents change their address to heaven. The Parloni boys leave in a fury. Melanie's contract will end. Sylvia hasn't sent me a postcard.

Sadness has a good grip on my throat. "Out."

Teddy heaves a big sigh. "Well, hurry up and have your bath so I can come back in and you can know me." Like that's a perfectly reasonable thing to tell your new neighbor/virtual stranger, he walks out—with my magazine—and closes the front door behind him.

Being naked feels wrong now, but I persevere. I sink down in the bath and wait for the heat to sink into my muscles and slowly unpin me. The angry return email I'll get from Sylvia about today's developments feels further away. She can't get me here. I melt into a pink marshmallow, every single stress I've had throughout the day just gone—

"Ruthie."

I jolt upright, sloshing water over the edge. A candle goes out. I cover myself with my arms, top and bottom, and I have to recheck that he hasn't wandered in. "What is it?"

His voice is crystal clear through the wall. "I'm lonely."

I'm glad he can't know I smiled at that. It would only encourage him. "Go away, Teddy, I am in the bath."

"Fuck, these walls are thin. We need to make a toilet roster. I have this medical condition where I cannot take a shit if a pretty girl might be listening." I hear a tub-squeak on his side of the wall.

My mouth opens and I cackle at the ceiling. "Oh my *God*." I blaspheme loud enough that God's going to call my father personally. *Reverend Midona, it's about your daughter.* Wait. Did Teddy say pretty girl?

I can hear the grin in his voice as he continues. "I'm just sitting here now in my empty bathtub, fully clothed, so keep your mind out of the gutter. None of the luxuries you're enjoying right now. Definitely no kerosene hair treatments."

"Try keeping your inner monologue inner." I'm grinning too. "I bet you've used handwash as shampoo."

"I have, is it that obvious? I don't deserve this amazing hair." A big pause is left, perhaps for a compliment. "I need to buy a toothbrush." Another pause is left dangling for a small eternity. "Come help me choose one. You're tidy, I'm a mess. Label my life for me."

This isn't the first time a new Parloni hire asked me to help with something. My smile fades and I remember how Jerry

Prescott tried to task me to clean Teddy's new quarters. "Was I put on this earth to be an assistant?"

"I don't even know how to work out what size sheets to buy. I texted a picture of the mattress to my sister Daisy, but I had nothing to use for scale."

The word *scale* makes me think of bananas and ChapSticks. "And?" I have to sluice water over my face.

He has a fond laugh in his voice. "She said to ask a grown-up."

"Does the cute helpless thing work on everyone?"

Cheerful: "Most people. Ever been on a motorbike?" He's actually serious.

"I'm sorry to say that I am done for the day." Tonight's routine will continue. Oven timer ding, today's *Heaven Sent* episodes, and a bit of lurking around in the forum. I'll do some stretches, write in my journal, and then I'll be tucked up in bed with my sweet old Ted . . . I mean, Rupert. My childhood bear, *Rupert*.

He says, "Pretty early to be done for the day. It's six thirty."

"In Providence time, that's midevening."

In a way that makes me think he is trying to be careful, he says, "You know there's a world outside Providence, don't you?"

He's too close to a nerve there and I feel the twinge. "I don't have to explain my routine to you, Complete Stranger." I inhale deep and slide all the way under the water, exhaling bubble after bubble.

When I resurface I hear, "We're neighbors. We share everything."

I pick up a bar of soap from the ledge and regard it dolefully.

Everything? "I really don't remember that being part of the deal."

"The deal?"

I'm confused. "Huh?"

"Did my dad say something like: If you can get my baby bear interested in the family business, I'll give you a ten grand bonus?" Teddy does a good impression of his dad. I also think he's worried about my answer.

"I wish he did say that." I splash water on my knees to watch the suds slide. When he doesn't react, I add, "I'm kidding. No bribes were taken."

He agrees: "My sparkling company is more than enough compensation."

"You know what would be nice compensation? The twenty dollars you owe me."

"Oh. That. Yes." There's the sound of empty-tub-squeaking; he's either getting comfier or extracting himself. "I will absolutely pay you back as soon as I find my wallet. My next scheduled Good Samaritan is taking their time on that."

Must be nice to put your full faith in the universe. "Did you cancel your cards?"

"Ruthie, they canceled themselves long ago." He groans something that sounds like *urggg-I'm-a-mess*. In his husky voice now, he adds, "Ever maxed a card out, Tidy Girl?"

What a ludicrous question. "I take all forms of payment. Bank transfer, PayPal, Venmo, Western Union. Gold bullion. Pennies." When he doesn't reply or laugh, I ask, "Your dad owns this place, but you don't have twenty bucks?"

"Please stop bringing up what my dad has. He and I are two different people. He has his things. I have mine."

(It really sounds like Teddy has no things.)

How weird that it's the son of a rich guy who is making me appreciate all the luxuries I have. Soap and towels. "Why aren't you working at your tattoo studio now? What happened?"

"Alistair told me I can't go back until I buy my share in Fairchild, one hundred percent, in full. It was one of those all-or-nothing ultimatums. I've never seen him so mad before." He falls silent.

I can feel his changed mood through the wall and my water has gone cold. What he said is true: We are the kind of neighbors who share everything now. "Are you still there?"

"Hmmm."

I try to picture him now, lying in that dusty ancient tub. "I'll make you some dinner. And I've got a spare toothbrush."

"No, I've realized you've done more than enough for me. Good night, Tidy Girl." What kind of person tattoos TAKE on their own hand, anyway? Apparently, someone who's acutely aware that that's what he does.

Every bath I've ever had, I've lain here listening to the lick of water on the edges of the tub and my own pulse. I'm back to where I've always been, just floating, completely alone.

CHAPTER SEVEN

'm surprised to find Teddy slumped over the tiny table in our shared courtyard when I open my front door in the morning. "Good morning."

"Morn," is the slurred reply. He's drawing in a sketchbook, but he flips it closed when I approach. He notices my mug. "Oh, my, fucking, God."

"Would you like some coffee, Theodore Prescott?"

A bleary eye blinks through his tousled hair. "I would marry you for coffee."

I absolutely itch to go inside for my hairbrush, to bring this mess back to glass-shine perfection. But that's his strategy, right? He's attracting females with his plumage. "No proposal necessary. How do you take it?"

"Black and sweet." He's drawing again, but closes the book again when I return.

I spent a long time thinking about how he retreated last night. It's important that from now on, Teddy earns everything he gets. "I want one drawing for this cup of coffee. No freebies."

"Sure." He opens to a fresh page. "What do you want?"

"A tortoise." I set the mug down.

"That reminds me." The pen goes to the page, and he begins a long, flat curve. "I did a terrible thing last night. I'm just working myself up to tell you."

I wait, but he won't volunteer it. "Were you comfortable last night?"

"If my Fairy God-Neighbor hadn't looked out for me, I would have cried myself to sleep. Thank you so much."

"That's okay."

Full disclosure: I tried to leave him alone to fend for himself. I finished my bath, ate my chicken Kiev and vegetables, washed dishes, and spent time approving new Heaven Sent You Here forum members. I took my late-night walk around the grounds, flashlight in hand, completing the checklist I've got in my phone.

I finished up, as I always do, at the western edge, where I hung from the chain-link fence with both hands and listened for motorbikes. I probably looked like a prisoner.

As I was brushing my teeth, Teddy still wasn't back. I felt terrible about my lack of charity, especially to the boss's son. Like a model Fairy God-Neighbor, I left on the courtyard table a stack of the following items:

- One set of sheets (cloud print)
- One towel and matching bath mat
- One quilt
- One toothbrush (red)

- One roll of toilet paper
- One spare pillow from my bed (how strangely blush-worthy)

Like a mom, I say, "Your mattress is queen size. Anyway, have a good day with the Parlonis. I'm sure you'll do great." I go to leave.

"Wait. Something bad happened last night when I was walking back from the parking lot. I knocked but you didn't answer. Were you asleep?" He drags a hand through his hair. It shines like a raven's wing, blue black, slightly evil, totally beautiful. With a groan, he reaches under the table and brings out a torn Kleenex box. Inside is a golden bonnet tortoise that doesn't look so great. "I stepped on it, and now you'll have to fill out a form."

"I had my headphones on." After I'd left the bundle of supplies out for him, I'd had a sudden paranoia that he'd interpret it as a love token. I swaddled myself in bed with my laptop and turned up the volume of my *Heaven Sent* episode. I tried too hard to not hear him return.

"I took it to the after-hours vet clinic, but they only stabilized it with painkillers and told me to find a reptile specialist." He nudges a lettuce leaf closer to the tortoise's disinterested face. "The crack it made under my shoe. I still hear it and feel it."

I'm sure no one has ever felt so rotten about stepping on a tortoise. "I'm sorry, Teddy." His expression falls. "No, it's not time to call a priest just yet. We can fix it."

I'm grateful for the practical task. I get my kit, put on gloves, and we lift the injured tortoise out. It's a small one, the size of a deck of cards. "Well, it can move all its legs. That's good."

"That's what they said last night. But here." He indicates the cracked shell. "They've put a gel in there to stop infection, but it's not fixed. They didn't have the stuff they need. Lucky I live next door to a reptile specialist."

"I know a couple of things, but I'm not an expert." I follow the crack and try to visualize the damage, based on past x-rays I've seen. "The shell needs to be repaired with resin. Maybe wire for this section."

"Can you do that?" He's impressed when I nod. "You really are like a vet. Is that what your goal is? Renata talked over you yesterday in the interview." He picks up his pen and recommences sketching. The tortoise is coming to life on the page. He runs the pen along, maybe like a tattoo needle, linking lines, filling in texture.

I tell the tortoise, "My childhood dream was to be a vet, once upon a time. But not anymore, obviously. I'm a babysitter. These guys are valuable on the black market, apparently. It's part of my reason for living on-site."

"Your setup here looks pretty professional."

"I just give them a place to rest and recover." I go to the edge of the low enclosures I've put together in the courtyard. "I think number 44 has to go to the Reptile Zoo. We'll send this one along for an x-ray and they can do the repair. They come through town pretty regularly, and they don't charge us."

"Wish I'd known that before I flirted the vet's receptionist into giving me an account." He grins at the memory.

I feel a pang, but it also injects a little resin into my heart. This is what he does. I've got to keep these Teddy Shields Up. "I know you didn't get your money's worth. Sorry I didn't hear you. I'm not used to having anyone else around."

He frowns over his tiny victim. "I knew you'd be really disappointed with me for this." He's got eyes like a little kid when he looks up, expecting a scolding. "You've never stepped on one, I bet."

"I've been walking around these paths in the dark for years now. I'm sure you'll watch your step." I take a red lipstick out of my kit. "This one is number 50."

"You rescue them and let them have a soft landing. I've never identified with a tortoise so much in my life." He picks up his pen and writes a number 50 on the back of his hand. "I don't think it's too late for you to be a vet."

I'm flustered. "I'm just an office assistant. Anyone can do this." I turn to a fresh sheet and give him the clipboard. "You can do the form. Write his ID on his shell. Before you ask, I've tried the label maker, but they don't stick. Long wear lipstick is perfect."

He takes the lipstick and initials the shell TJ. "Teddy Junior. Where are you going to put him?"

"Just with the others."

When it's time to hand both the creature and the paperwork over, Teddy looks at my outstretched hand like he doesn't trust me. Now he's squinting up at the sky, checking for rain. He looks around the courtyard. It's not good enough for his little prince.

Maybe like my sketch-for-coffee deal, it would be better if Teddy had to fix this himself. Besides, he invested a lot in this creature. "If it makes you feel better, you can keep him until his ride arrives. Just keep the box very level, don't jiggle him around." We put some bedding material in the box.

Teddy checks the time on his phone and does one of his huge lion-roar yawns. "Shit, I've got to start work soon. I have not been awake this early in years."

I'm perplexed enough to recheck my watch. "It's eight A.M." I'm so early for work myself, I give myself a break and sit down on the cold metal chair beside him. Another thing I've never done? Actually sat in this courtyard in the morning sunshine.

"I can't function this early. How bad is today going to be for me? Here's your drawing," he adds offhand, scribbling his initials in the bottom corner. I take the page he's torn out for me. How was this detailed tortoise rendered with so little apparent effort, with a one-dollar biro? I expected a cute cartoon and I now own a one-off piece of art. I need to frame this.

His ego will be inflating but I don't even care. "Teddy, this is amazing."

Careless shrug. "So's this coffee." He turns over to a fresh sheet in his notebook and begins drawing with loose, easy motions. The outline of a long wool cardigan emerges, shaped onto a female figure. She's rounded nicely at the breast and hip, and there's an arch to the back and a flattering slim line to the waist.

I ask, "Where'd you go last night?"

"The bowling alley. Memory Lanes has got this insane thing

84

on the bar menu called Frankenfries, and every now and then I can't say no to the craving."

"What are Frankenfries?"

"It's a chain, so each location has its own version. At this one, it's french fries, topped with macaroni and cheese"—he's layering his hands now, TAKE-GIVE-TAKE—"then they put gravy, then a layer of breadcrumbs and it goes under the grill. Before you get it, they put a hotdog frank into it like a torpedo. It looks like dog food. We go there most Friday nights after we close up." He means his tattoo buddies. Scrolling through his photo album he says absent-mindedly, "I need to look up if there's one near the new studio."

He shows me a photo of a hideous pile of food. His friends all crowding over it, pretending they puked it up. Tough guys with piercings and tough girls with presence. "See?" He uses two fingers to zoom the photo. "Yummy dog food." One of the girls is looking at the camera, and the silly boy holding it. The look in her eye reads loud and clear. He's divine.

I mean it when I say: "How disgusting."

"When you need to eat your feelings, it's the only thing that'll do."

"Your feelings must have been pretty gross and mixed up."

"Yeah. You get it." Sketch, sketch. "Anyway, that was my sad night. I came back late, imagining myself alone in the world. Then I found your care package and I remembered that there's nice people everywhere."

You may have noted that I only gave him one towel.

"I probably should have mentioned this, but I'd appreciate it if you didn't bring guests on-site. During the day when they're signed in at the office . . . that might be okay if a friend wants to visit you. But I need to know every single person on-site. In the event of an emergency."

"Who would I bring to a retirement villa?"

I can't bring myself to say it. *Don't bring any of those people from the photo here. I've cracked a hole in the wall of my little world, and it's only big enough for you to squeeze through. Don't make me hear a woman's laugh through our wall.*

His eyes flash to my face, tortoiseshell vivid. "Ohhh, I get what you're saying. Not with our thin walls. I wouldn't traumatize you like that." He resumes work on his cardigan artwork. He thinks I'm just a kid.

I defend myself like a kid would. "I wouldn't be traumatized."

My brain guesses at what I might hear in the dark. A mattress squeaking, the bed headboard nudging rhythmically against the wall. A girl gasping from uncontainable pleasure, the kind you'd feel from his body, his touch, but mostly the intensity of being his sole focus. I imagine his hair curtaining around her face, pooling like black oil on the pillow as he dips down for a kiss.

What would a filterless person like Teddy say in the moment? How carried away would he get, how would his imagination be sparked? He'd apply all that charm in just the right way. I think Teddy would laugh a lot in bed.

And all this would happen on my cloud-print sheets.

I manage to joke, "Okay, maybe I would be traumatized."

I close my mouth to contain the pressure building inside me. There will be zero girls experiencing that here, or I swear I don't know what I'll do—

"But since Melanie tells me you're about to start online dating, maybe you could do me the same courtesy." He is detailing buttons onto the cardigan sketch and doesn't look up. "I'm easily traumatized myself."

"I really don't think that's going to be an issue." I gesture to myself with my thumb.

He starts guessing at what I mean. "Your . . . cardigan won't come off. There's another cardigan under that cardigan, just hundreds of them like a box of tissues. It's a chastity cardigan. An enchanted cardigan."

On the page, he dusts a few blue-ink sparkles around the shoulders and hemline. He sees shapes when he looks at me?

His teasing hasn't riled up my hedgehog prickles like I thought they would. I must be getting used to him. I take my breakfast muffin out of my bag and break it in half. It is almost tearfully received. We sit and eat, and I think about this wafer-thin wall between our cottages.

"Tonight, when I'm in bed," I start, and it changes him. He's gone from sleepy-yawns to glittering, narrowed eyes. The flickering candlelight is back in them now. "And when you're in bed"—(oh boy, his eyes are even worse now)—"we should say something out loud. To see if the other can hear. Not for any weird reason."

"I'm interested in weird stuff, big-time." He's checking the time on his phone. His lock screen is a photograph of a neon sign that reads: ALWAYS AND FOREVER. He clicks it away to blackness and hands me his empty mug. "Thanks so much. Better go."

"Have a good day." I feel a little guilty because I know what sort of first days the Parloni boys have.

"I might come down for a visit later, if I get a lunch break." He's gathering up his things now. He blows out a breath like he's nervous. Maybe his survival instincts are kicking in. "Any last hints or tips for me?" He's using the same velvety voice he probably used on the veterinary receptionist last night.

"The Parlonis usually have a siesta. If you make it until then, you can have lunch. Come and visit us at the office."

"If I make it? Of course I will." He laughs like I've made a joke. "I'll have you to look forward to. Can't wait."

I'm almost down the path to the office when I realize I can't wait, either, and therefore I'm possibly in big trouble.

CHAPTER EIGHT

All morning, I keep trying to guess when the Parloni sisters might take their siesta. Perhaps tormenting Teddy on his first day at work has given them an energy boost and he won't come down to visit at all. I tell myself that I'm glad to have a little peace and quiet.

Mrs. Petersham called the office earlier and asked us to go to the store for some new magazines. "I am well qualified for this," Melanie assured me, grabbing a fist of petty cash. "Choosing magazines is a strength I should have put on my résumé. I'll be back." Eventually?

I'm catching up on my to-do list. It only took two clicks off the PDC home page to find the new site manager of Providence. Rose Prescott, Junior Management Associate, is a blue-eyed blonde with a strong stare. She would get picked first for team sports at school. She would blast a hockey puck into your face. There is absolutely no similarity to Teddy at all, from her coloring to her fierce aura.

"Teddy would be smiling properly," I say out loud to the

empty room. The photographer would have one hell of a time just getting a shot of him where he wasn't laughing, blinking, yawning, or moving. I'd love to see his passport. I print Rose's corporate profile out and add it to my PDC folder.

The next thing on my list, I've been procrastinating on.

Dad answers the phone on the second ring. "Reverend Midona." Put it this way: If God calls, Dad can't be accused of not taking this seriously.

"Hi, it's Ruthie."

He presses the phone to his chest and I hear him calling: "Abigail. Abigail." This goes on for a while and I just sit there waiting. "She's coming from the garden." He goes to lay down the receiver.

I rush out, "How are things with you?" Put a tick in the dutiful daughter column.

"Fine, busy, fine."

"I hope you haven't gotten that flu that's been going around." I completely make that up. I wouldn't have a clue what germs are filling up his church, but desperate times call for desperate conversation topics.

"I don't have the flu," Dad says, and now we both just sit, phones to our ears.

I break first. "Did Mom tell you that I'm the manager here at Providence while Sylvia is on her cruise?" As soon as I hear the hopeful boast in my voice, it feels like an error. This feels like that moment when you've set up a joke perfectly, and the other person has a killer punch line.

He delivers it. "I hope you're remembering to lock the office. Here's your mother."

"Okay then. Bye." I hold the receiver away to exhale. I'm shaky and tears are threatening. I'm careful now. Aren't I?

I open my checklist app to make sure I performed my lockup routine properly last night. One item—the recreation center door—is unticked. Did I actually do that? I know I was there, but I think I got distracted. I close my eyes now and visualize myself, out there on the path, the door handle cold under my palm. But my ears were listening for faraway motorbikes.

Mom interrupts my miniature meltdown. "My little Ruthie Maree. You know, I was just thinking about you. How are you?"

Even though I called her, I'm irrationally annoyed. I need to go. "Good, thanks, Mom. How are you?" I sound too brisk. "Want to do speakerphone?" No one can say I don't try.

"Your father has disappeared." She's vaguely amazed. "I wonder where he went."

"Maybe he climbed out of the window." Slid down the drainpipe. Jogged away. I take a second to close my eyes and rebalance all the mixed-up feelings I've got right now. It's the sensation of being repelled, then clutched too tight. This is why calling home is always a chore on my list, rather than something I want to do.

"Well, that's very creative." Mom is bland about the situation between me and my dad. For all I know, she hasn't noticed it.

I think of a topic. "How's the young mom with the new baby—what was her name? Are they still living with you?" I

91

can't count how many haunted-looking strangers have sat at our dinner table and slept in our basement emergency accommodation. There's always a fold-out sofa bed made up with fresh sheets and a towel folded on the end. Charity begins in the home, after all.

"Oh, Rachel and Olivia. You would have loved this baby, Ruthie. She was the sweetest little thing. Barely a peep out of her all night." Softer, she adds, "Even though that baby was so quiet, the house feels silent now."

"When did they leave?"

"Last week. It was rather sudden. Rachel left us a voice mail on the office phone, though."

That's a lot more than most people do. Most are grateful for the assistance given, but once they're on their feet, they keep walking. I know that's how it's always been, but my mom's hurt and I've got an indignant *how rude* building up inside me. "Sounds about right."

"It's a good thing she's left," Mom reminds me, choosing to ignore my bitter tone. "Thanks to how generous our congregation is, they've both made it across the country to her grandmother's place. I can rest easy."

Until the next one knocks on the door during a midnight rainstorm. Mom gave a piece of herself that someone else took. I have no idea how she replenishes herself. I don't think she even lets herself have a bath and a nostalgic TV show. As I ponder that, she moves on.

"How's life in Providence?"

"Nice and quiet." As soon as I say this, I see Teddy walking down the path to the office. "I mean, actually, there's been a few interesting things happening while Sylvia's away." My parents have known Sylvia for years through the church.

"She must be having the time of her life. I've been checking the mailbox every day. Remember when she went to Tahiti?" Mom probably still has that Tahitian church postcard on the fridge and it's been years.

I press refresh on my in-box. "I haven't heard from her, either, and she hasn't been replying to my work updates. She swore she'd be online every day. Maybe there's something wrong with the cruise ship's internet."

"You know what Sylvia's like. She'll reply when she can."

I wince. I do know Sylvia. "Anyway, we've got a couple of temporary staff here. They're my age. It's been pretty fun, having them around." I write on a Post-it: CHECK REC CENTER. I stick it on the back of my hand.

"Wowee," Mom says with real excitement. "That sounds like new friends. You won't know yourself, Ruthie Maree."

"One lives next door to me now. He's my age, he's pretty nice."

"A boy." She's doubtful. She still thinks of me as fifteen years old, not twenty-five. "Oh, I don't know about this, Ruthie."

"It's completely fine. He's the son of the owner."

"As long as this boy doesn't come inside your place," Mom says slowly, turning the concept over in her mind. "Then it should be all right."

I picture Teddy leaning on my bedroom doorframe with a smile on his mouth. He'd curl up on the end of my bed if I let him. If I disappoint her, too, then Dad again, who am I left

Sally Thorne

with? "No, of course not, Mom, he's just a worker here. He's not my friend or anything."

When I look up, Teddy is standing in the doorway and he's laying his hand over his heart in a theatrical display of hurt.

Mom says, "Are you being nice and careful, sweetie? Locking up the front door at night?"

"That was a long time ago."

I don't know what's worse, her careful question or the sarcasm in Dad's voice. Sometimes, in my dreams, I'm just checking a door handle, over and over. "Sorry to have to hang up, but the . . . maintenance guy just walked in. Can I call you back tonight?"

"I've got pickups tonight, silly billy." She's been out driving her van picking up donated food from restaurants and grocery stores since I was a kid. "But I'll talk to you tomorrow morning. I want to hear everything you've been getting up to." We hang up and she's unaware that I'm a loser and she's gotten my full update.

Teddy pulls up a chair and sits across from me. He plucks the Post-it note off the back of my hand and sticks it to his chest. "Hi," he says, closing his eyes. "I am your friend, whether you like it or not."

If that's true, maybe I'll walk out first. Someone can see the back of me as I walk away. I start to push my chair back, but he just says with so much need: "Please stay."

He's tousled and tired and I have to admit it: he's someone I want to look at. While his eyes are closed, I can. His dark navy T-shirt is stretched tight across his body, and I've got some new tattoos to look at. I'll let myself have a few from the midbicep

94

region. Goldfish. Swan. Jar containing one (1) human heart. He's moving his arm now, and I get a couple of bonuses. A stiletto shoe, a dagger, a black feather. And it's when his arm is extended out from his body, turning his wrist up to me, that I realize his eyes are open and he's showing himself to me.

"Sorry, sorry." I'm sure I go red. "So what have they had you doing?"

He folds his arm back across his stomach. "My first mistake was to say I'm not a morning person."

"Oh Teddy. Very foolish."

"My new start time for the rest of the week is six A.M." He gives me a look of genuine resentment. "You could have trained me, so I knew how to play this. But you just threw me in the deep end on purpose. What did I ever do to you?"

The gas station hysterics come to mind. Ditto getting Providence on his dad's bulldozer list. He's blissfully unaware of either crime. Here's the most annoying part of this: It's impossible to maintain the irritation I wish I could have with him. He's my friend, whether I like it or not.

"I knew you could handle it."

Big grumbling sigh. "After I buried the white shirt under a lemon tree, Renata told me I'd buried it under the wrong tree. So I dig it up, rebury it, and I think I'm done. But then she decides maybe it wasn't so bad after all, so I redig it, and have to hand-wash it in the laundry."

"Sure. Okay."

"You are not remotely surprised. What crazy shit have you seen?" His eyes have gone wild.

"I've seen everything. And don't forget, every time one of you quit, it's me digging and reburying. Anyway, I'm sure you need to get back to them." The pull to walk up to the rec center is almost overwhelming. He waves me down.

"I'm not done venting. That only takes us up to a quarter past nine. Ruthie, the things I've done this morning are just illogical. Is she . . . of sound mind?" He shakes his head. "I did the Cupboard Cake Challenge."

"Ah. I've done that." (Make a cake with what you can find.)

"They had no flour. I ended up making this weird peanut flour in the food processor."

"The point is, you tried."

"Renata made me set the table for a tea party, with all the good china and a tablecloth, and serve them like a butler. I had to invent a tragic backstory for my character, and the cake was . . ." He tries to find a word. "An abomination. She made me bury it under the lemon tree in the original hole." His bleary eyes catch onto mine. "I have to do this again, every day, from six A.M.? It'll be like purgatory."

"Has Aggie talked to you about your salary?"

He perks. "It's this strange arrangement," he begins, then hears himself and shakes his head. "I mean, of course it is. She says she's devised an incentive scheme. Every week I'm working for them, the salary doubles, to a capped amount that is some CEO-level shit. I could be at Christmas dinner telling everyone I'm officially a part owner of my studio." He looks sideways, daydreaming.

"That's great." I smile encouragingly even though inside, I'm drooping.

"But I'm not going to make it. You were right." He leans forward and drapes himself facedown across my desk. His cheek is on my calculator and the screen fills with numbers. "I should have known. You're always right."

"You're very professional. Not at all dramatic." I'm smiling anyway.

I don't know what to do with this lax male body. His hair is twisted into a knot, held with a grim rubber band, and it's depressing how much I wish it was loose, washing over me like a tsunami.

From this side of the desk, all I can see is the big rounded slopes of his shoulders cling-wrapped in cotton. The vulnerable shells of his ears. I can only see the side of the rose tattoo inked on the back of his arm, but I know it is pretty enough to be printed on wallpaper. All of him is.

"Daisy." I tap my finger on one of many flowers inked on the inside of his wrist. "Ah, I see."

Every time he was bored, he added another daisy for his sister. The girl in me wants to sigh *that's so sweet*. The woman in me wants to know exactly how many other females are indelibly marked all over him. If he has a big heart somewhere with a name in it, I'm going to be pissed off. How did that big surge of hot air fill my lungs? "How many sisters do you have?"

Despite his deadness he replies, "Four. They all think I'm useless."

"I'm sure they don't."

"It's true, I am. They tell me a lot."

"You know what my mother always says? You've got two hands and a heartbeat. You're not useless. I really should go check the rec center door. I was careless last night." I laughed in the bath and I walked around in the dark with my head full of him. It's frustrating how handsome men scramble up the people around them.

His hands are curled over the edge of my side of the desk. Right there, inches from me. GIVE and TAKE. They're really beautiful hands, and I've seen what they can create.

"I need you to help me get through this." His eyelashes are dark on his cheek. "Do you hear me? I need you."

On the back of his right hand is that temporary number 50 and I'm glad it's there to remind me. A few lettuce leaves, a rest, and Teddy will be swimming off without a backward glance.

I am too honest in my response. "And what happens to me, when I get you through this? Ever think that maybe I need help too?" I hear him inhale in a way that makes me want to rewind time.

"I'm back," Melanie singsongs, dumping her bag on her desk and giving me something to focus on besides my increasing pulse rate and mixing emotions. I'm sure the guy facedown on my desk is relieved he doesn't have to answer me.

She grins. "Uh-oh. Is the Teddy-Bot broken?"

"I think so. I was just going to try to prize open his control panel. I think I'd have to cut his hair off to get to it, though." I pick up a pen and lift his hand. It drops back, loose.

Melanie is explaining about traffic and tapping on her phone, and Teddy's dead, so I can do this next thing. I use the tip of my pen lid to trace the G on his first knuckle. I keep my breathing steady, because he's close enough to hear it.

Under Mel's chatter, I tell his corpse, "Sometimes, at night, I feel like the last person on Earth." He doesn't flicker an eyelash. Next, I draw over the letter I. "Sometimes, I work through the whole weekend. Twenty-four, seven is a long time. I'm getting tired."

Melanie booms, "And then I realized they were porno magazines. Can you believe that?"

I laugh dutifully at her and when I drag my pen on the sexy down-up lines of the letter V, his hand flexes and he shivers all over. I toss the pen across the room and pretend I never, ever did that.

Melanie is at the end of her stories. "Is he still dead?"

"Yes, sadly. Vale Teddy. Let's put him where all the other Parloni boys are. Concrete blocks around his ankles, then into the lake."

"The turtles need to eat something," she agrees, walking around. "You take his arms, I'll take his legs."

"I'm alive," Teddy decides and sits back upright. Anyone who doubts the presence of a spirit or soul hasn't seen his hazel eyes spark back to life. There's the faint outline of calculator buttons on his cheekbone. He's so lovely, I couldn't speak now if I tried.

Something's changed now. My words and my touch have put something new in the way he regards me. He says to me, fingers flexing: "Could you do that again?"

99

"Do what?" Melanie's eyes are flat and suspicious.

He regards me for a moment, reads the DO NOT in my expression and lolls back in his chair, rubbing his knuckles. "What's going on, Mel?"

"Living my best life. I just went and bought magazines for an old lady. She made me stay for a cup of tea. It tasted like orange peel, but I drank the whole thing."

No more hiding in the bathroom from our residents? "Mel, I'm so proud of you."

"Don't be too proud." She's pink-cheeked and smiling as she begins unfolding a receipt and change, stepping in behind my desk to get the file. She then seems to remember something and looks down at me with fear in her eyes. "I have to confess. I kind of spaced and got Mrs. Petersham a magazine that said Fifteen Ways to Make Him Scream on the cover."

"Never too late to learn," I say, and they both laugh like I'm actually funny.

"Teddy, you are a good influence on our Ms. Midona, she's loosening up nicely. Maybe I should have saved that article for you." Melanie pats my shoulder. "I could incorporate it into my Sasaki Method."

"I keep hearing about this method," Teddy grumbles. "I hate being left out."

"I don't think making anyone scream is in my near future." I can't believe I said that out loud, in an office. Neither can they; they're both open-mouth-delighted. I look at the Post-it on his chest and ask Melanie, "Did you unlock the rec center this morning?"

"Why are you so obsessed with it?" Teddy is so bored with it he yawns. I've seen every arctic-white tooth in his head by now.

Melanie says, "It was already unlocked. I thought you did it."

Under the background of Mel's relentless chatting as she begins filling out the petty cash record, Teddy asks me, "Ruthie, what's going on?"

"I screwed up." All I can do is regulate my breathing. I've never been so grateful for a Melanie interruption.

"Magazines are so pricey these days. I've got a new renovation project that would impress even PDC. Want to guess what it is?"

Teddy's unwilling to take the interruption, eyes still on my face. "You're okay, you didn't screw up," he promises me fiercely. And my body believes him. Each breath is easier, until I'm back in my body.

Melanie says with a flourish, "Ruthie Midona is my project. I'm fixing her right up."

Teddy seems offended for me. "My old motorbike in storage needs fixing up. Ruthie doesn't."

"She needs to rev her engine all right," Melanie parries back smartly.

I interject. "Ruthie has not agreed to this plan yet."

(Ruthie is also privately amazed to be talking to people of her own age like they are her friends. Maybe Ruthie should lean into this?)

Melanie continues, "I am creating a dating program designed to get her out of her turtle shell. Fun and dates and meeting new people and romance. We need to do something important from the movies." She likes leaving dramatic pauses, and this one is a doozy. ". . . Makeover."

Annnnd I'm leaning back out. "That's a no."

"But look at her," Teddy says to Melanie, like she's going to be fighting an uphill battle. I begin to recoil inside like a big painful spring until he finishes with, "Why mess with perfection?" He holds my gaze in a way that feels like a steadying hand.

Melanie says, "I agree, of course. She's an amazing person. But I think if she could just jack up her confidence, she'd let other people see how funny and smart she is. Cue soul mate, and me in a lilac bridesmaid's dress."

I stare at her. "You are getting so far ahead of yourself it's insane."

"But is that what you really want?" Teddy asks me and the question feels too intimate to reply. He perseveres anyway. "If it's what you want, then I'll help you too."

Melanie's pleased. "Ruthie, we're both helping you, that's settled. Please let me have my makeover montage. I have been dreaming of plucking your eyebrows from the moment we met." This is said with sweet ardency.

"I tried to be cool in high school and it didn't go so great for me. I don't want to date someone who meets me when I'm hot from my Melanie Makeover. I want someone to actually be into . . . this."

"And how do you describe 'this'?" Melanie has her notepad again. "I didn't get too far in the profile draft. You gave me nothing to work with."

"A tidy girl," I borrow Teddy's phrase to make him laugh, but he just stares deeper into my eyes and I cannot look away. The room goes black and the flecks of gold in his eyes are my only light. My other senses heighten and I can navigate this new world purely by touch. I try again. "Buttoned-up tidy girl seeks . . ."

His eyes put images and thoughts into my head. Tidy girl seeks a tall messy man to press her up against things. She wants to get messed up, flat on a bed, on the edge of desks, walls, moonlit lawns. Every door unlocked, always. All she wants is skin, the satin heat of it all, a thick rope of black silk hair coiled in her palm . . .

A chair squeak breaks my train of thought. Teddy's leaned forward. He wants to know my next words so badly his knuckles are white. "What?" His voice has a dare in it.

I think about what the word *give* means and how much I want to take.

Melanie, the creator of dramatic pauses, can equally be counted on to fill a silence. "Cute twenty-five-year-old professional seeks same." She hesitates, eyes sparkling, then goes for it. "You must know fifteen ways to make her scream."

Dead serious, Teddy says, "I know thirty ways."

If Teddy Prescott came into my bedroom and showed me what he knows, it wouldn't matter how thin our walls are or how much noise I made. He'd be the only one at Providence who'd hear me.

"I know fifty ways to hide your dead body," Melanie scolds, tapping Teddy on the top of the head with a ruler. "Ruthie is looking for a soul mate, not a genital mate. Get that through your thick skull."

CHAPTER NINE

On Day 2 of Teddy's employment, he walks into the office and sets down the Kleenex box containing TJ on Melanie's desk. She regards the box with suspicion. "Yuck. I don't know why you want it, Teddy. Let Ruthie keep it."

"That's my son you're insulting," he returns.

"He's looking okay, all things considered," I remark as I watch the tiny creature munch on a dandelion. "I'll find out when the Reptile Zoo people are coming for him."

"I have an invitation for you. It's got terms and conditions, of course, but don't worry. The strings are only attached to me." He reaches under his butt and unearths a warm envelope with my name on it. "Why is everyone waiting for me to quit, by the way? This job isn't that hard."

He's got a smudge of something black on his cheekbone. There are cobwebs in his hair and his shoulders are powdered gray. He sneezes and says, "I've never had such an easy job."

"Why are you so dirty?" Melanie asks him as I open the envelope.

"They made me go up a ladder to tidy the attic."

I look up. "The town houses don't have attics."

"Well, duh, that would be too easy. I just pretended the crawl space was an attic full of antiques and dead bodies. They laughed their asses off. I had a power nap on a big cushion of insulation." He grins at the memory. "I'm going to dream about ghosts tonight."

I give the invitation my full attention. It is a square card with a border inked dense with vines and roses. I bet he did it in an absent-minded couple of minutes. He wears his talent like a dirty five-dollar T-shirt.

"This is pretty enough to be a wedding invitation," I tell him. He shrugs like it's nothing but his eyes flare bright with pleasure. "Maybe you could help us with the Christmas party decorations."

I read the invitation out loud because Melanie is almost hurting herself craning to see. "Ruthie Midona is formally invited to an all-expenses paid fancy lunch and afternoon of goofing off with the Parlonis, Friday at 12 noon. RVSP yes verbally, immediately, to T. Prescott." Melanie releases an anguished howl. Her name was nowhere in those words. I'm not that overjoyed myself. I put it aside. "Okay, so it's not really an invitation. It's a summons."

"Not exactly," Teddy tries, but he's unsure of what the afternoon has in store. I've known the Parloni sisters for years.

"It's fancy jury duty. I'm going to have to sit on a white couch in a boutique and watch Renata try on outfits with Aggie asleep on my shoulder. I've got work to do tomorrow."

"I should tell you that declining isn't really an option," Teddy says apologetically. "Renata said I'll have to carry you to the car if you say no."

Mel says to him, "Seriously? I'm not invited too? I'll carry you if it means I get out of this place."

"I need you to babysit TJ," Teddy tells her in his special persuasion voice. "I don't trust anyone but you." She colors up, pleased and honored. I probably have a face like a toad. He refocuses those charming eyes on me. "Might be fun though, right? Fancy lunch? Just think about it. I'm sorry, Mel, I'm just the messenger."

While she abuses him, I sit and think. It takes me a really long time to get my foot off Providence soil some days. I know that's not exactly normal. And to be in a car that I'm not driving—no control, no way of coming back immediately if I'm needed? I feel like I need to go sit somewhere and take a few deep breaths.

"Trust me, it'll be okay," Teddy says, gathering up his Kleenex box. He holds it so carefully. "I'm gonna be with you. I'll hold your hand the whole time."

And I find myself saying in a doubtful tone, "Okay."

On Friday morning, Teddy arrives at the office, unsure of what to do. The Parlonis gifted him with a gold watch for his hours of faithful service. (Apparently Aggie called their "watch guy" who personally couriered it over. Oh, to be that wealthy.)

"I tried to make them return it. Is this even allowed?" He

holds the box to me and I see what the issue is. A Parloni Checkmate: It is engraved on the back. Unreturnable. Unpawnable.

The engraving reads: *Teddy Prescott, Remarkable Boy.*

"I'll say," I say out loud by accident. As his mouth lifts in a delighted smile, I try to remain professional. "I know you didn't manipulate them into buying this for you. I think you can keep it." I've used a plunger on the Parlonis' powder room toilet but you don't see me getting engraved keepsakes. Instead, I get Renata's cackled jokes about putting me in her will, if I just do this one more thing for her.

Teddy puts it on his wrist. "I haven't had a watch since I was a kid." He's admiring it as he walks out to return to work.

The phone rings a while later and Melanie answers it. "It's Jerry Prescott."

I look at the flashing light on my phone and take a deep breath. I pick up and we do pleasantries for about thirty seconds about weather and busyness. Then he gets to it. "Just calling to check in on Teddy. How's he settled in?"

"He's doing fine. You just missed him, actually."

Jerry replies, "He's behaving himself?" I hear a young woman's voice in the background, talking to Jerry. Something about *at night.* "And he's staying on-site at night? Not off partying?"

"No, he's been home at night. He's working really hard, and he has a six A.M. start time. Today is Day Three and everything's going great." I sound like I'm bragging a bit.

Jerry laughs. "Six A.M. I didn't think he had it in him. Rose, pay up. Twenty bucks." They bet on whether Teddy was screwing up? How horrible.

"He's doing a great job. He's already gotten involved with some of the endangered tortoise rehab we do here."

(There's no need to mention that his size twelve boot was also the cause.)

"Don't let him dazzle you," Jerry says, tone dry. "He tends to do that."

"Dazzle?" My face is surely turning pink. Melanie mouths back at me silently, like a magic incantation: *dazzle.*

Jerry continues in my ear, "He dazzles people. I love him, but it's his personality flaw. He charms his way through life. There is a row of broken hearts stretching back a long, long way."

Rose: "Is he messing around with the office girls?"

I assure Jerry, "That's absolutely not going to happen."

Melanie holds up a notepad: **SPEAKERPHONE PLEASE**.

Jerry's struggling on how to explain this. "I don't mean to make him sound like a con artist. In his own mind he's very genuine, but he takes a few liberties with people who are too charitable."

In the background, Rose says, "Theodore has never cared about anyone more than himself. The universe orbits around him. He's the sun. Just like his mother," she adds with maliciousness.

"That's unfair," I blurt out loud. Then I cover my mouth and shut my eyes. I hear Melanie's shocked gasp. Oh my God, what is coming over me? Thankfully for me (and possibly my job), Jerry has held the phone against his chest again.

Jerry's back. "Give him an inch, he'll take a mile, that sort of thing. I wasn't kidding that he's run out of couches."

I take a moment to consider my own couch. He lay on it last night, complaining and laughing about his day. Renata made him cut up her Big Mac into bite-size bits, and he had to feed her like a baby.

"I'd hate for him to hurt a nice girl like you. Let's face it, you're not his type." There's a big laugh from Jerry now. "But I'm sorry to say, it won't stop him trying it with you and your temp. Making girls adore him is a reflex he just can't control."

"Good to know," I manage to reply even though it feels like my tongue has swollen from mortification. "I hear what you're saying and I appreciate your concern." The next couch I think about is the fold-out sofa bed in my parents' basement, ready for the next needy soul.

"He's a lawsuit waiting to happen," Rose warns.

Muffled conversation again. "Yes, I'll tell her," Jerry says, then returns to the call. "I mentioned when we met that I've got a lot going on at the moment. Let me tell you, Ruthie, that golf course site is no hole in one."

I laugh because he pays my bills.

"Rose has just finished her current project and is now ready to ramp things up and make Providence her new baby." Jerry says it like I should be delighted. I try to pretend.

"Will she be coming out to see Providence in person? I'd be glad to have her here, so she can see how special it is." I will make her fall in love with this place if I have to train a string of tortoises to pull her uphill in a sleigh.

Jerry covers the handset and puts this option to Rose. He explains the importance of a site visit, but she cuts him off.

Now I hear nothing and my heart is sinking. Rose doesn't want to see my sparkling lake. She wants this place to remain abstract. Jerry confirms it.

"She prefers to do her review remotely. It's better to keep her and Teddy separated. Now remember," Jerry says with humorous mock-sternness, "don't get dazzled. Anyway, Rose will call you soon."

He's not wrong. Rose calls four minutes later and briskly tasks me on running so many reports that the ink in my pen goes scratchy. I'm nervous. Sylvia told me before I left that she specifically didn't want me messing around with the accounts. *I don't want to come back to another Ruthie disaster*, she'd said, and I knew exactly what she meant.

I tell Rose now, "Sylvia checks everything before I send it through to PDC. Everything you have will be right."

"I want it all again. Now, what Jerry said is really important," Rose says in her flat, business-like way. "If you are ever made uncomfortable by Teddy, I want you to call me. He'll move on to greener pastures soon, but in the meantime just stay professional."

I've been really, really unprofessional. The absolute certainty of this makes my chest tight. "Of course. I'll start work on those reports for you. Could you tell me, though, what is the purpose of a site review? I think you've got a lot of this from when PDC acquired Providence."

"I wasn't involved in the acquisition and I want to start from the beginning. And before you ask again, I don't have time to visit. I'm not like my father, traveling coast to coast, wasting time. Everything can be done remotely. I need the login details for the Providence banking accounts, if you can give that to me now." I think she's got a pen poised.

"I don't have that. Only Sylvia does."

"Only one person has access to the accounts?" Rose finds that strange. "How long has that been the arrangement?"

"Always." I feel like I'm snitching on Sylvia. I asked her about it early on in my employment, but she told me that she'd tell me when I could be trusted with them.

Rose interrupts my stressing. "I'll sort out my own access. I also want an understanding of the hiring practices on-site. Take you, for example. Were you thoroughly vetted? Police check, things like that?"

"I'm not sure. It was a long time ago." There's a file marked R. Midona in Sylvia's bottom drawer but I'm scared of it. "I knew Sylvia when I was growing up. There was a vacancy, she talked to me on the phone, and here I am, six years later." I'm meaning to demonstrate that my hiring was a success.

"Sounds very informal." Rose does not approve. "I'm going to need to take a look at every policy document you have. Are your systems ISO Quality Accredited? Look, I've got another call coming through. My assistant will be in touch with yours."

"So what did you find out?" Melanie asks as soon as I put the receiver down.

"I found out that we need to tread really carefully."

I have a meeting reminder pop-up: I am supposed to give Melanie an answer on the Sasaki Method this afternoon. With Rose's voice still in my ear, the unprofessionalism of this hits me afresh. I click away the reminder and wonder how disappointed Melanie will be when I say no.

"We're going to be busy these next few weeks. I'm going to be pulling some long hours. I don't think I'll have time to even—" Another reminder pops up. They're buzzing around me like gnats. This one is about lunch with the Parlonis. "I don't have time," I repeat in a hiss.

Melanie knows what I'm doing, and she's not having it.

"You'll be doing some long hours, but I will be helping you," she assures me with her dark eyes intent on mine. "We will get all our work done, and what we do in our own time is our own business. And you're going to the fancy lunch with Teddy and the Parlonis. Call it a client lunch. Case closed."

CHAPTER TEN

Teddy arrives fifteen minutes prior to the Fancy Lunch, and he's wearing the chauffeur outfit that I have seen on many Parloni boys. It's never looked quite like this, though. "That looks hot on you," Melanie says like she's struggling with her tongue. She's only human. "You look like a stripper-gram."

He glints the name tag ("Hot Stuff") at her and I think she's dazzled by it. "There's a good reason for that." He puts his hat and the box containing his tortoise on her desk then looks over at me. "What do you think?"

Someone so gorgeous doesn't need a compliment from me. "Say goodbye to TJ," I say to him. Then to Melanie, "Mark from the Reptile Zoo is coming, he knows where my courtyard is. Sign him in and out. No unauthorized—"

"I know how you feel about the visitors' book," Melanie replies with an eye roll. "You should have been a security guard. It's your true calling."

This hurts because that's not backed up by my past, but

before the memory takes hold, Teddy says, "Just like that, huh." He's touching a finger to TJ with a stark expression.

I realize what the problem is. "Don't worry, they'll bring them back."

There's an upward flush of color and energy in him, lighting his smile up white and his eyes tortoiseshell brilliant. "I'm glad to hear it," he says. "So, so glad. Thank you, Ruthie."

His relief means my relief. How do I feel the emotions and changes in him, and will I ever resist the urge to fix things for him? To get the smile back on his face, like right now? The warning I received from his dad was far too late. I needed to hear it about five minutes before I arrived at the gas station dressed as a grandmother.

Stretching his shoulders like a weight has been lifted, Teddy says, "I'm taking your boss, Sasaki. Let's go, Midona. Lunchtime."

"I cannot believe I'm not invited," Melanie huffs, using a pen to touch the tortoise. "Huff," she further enunciates to drive the point home. "I am not a valued member of this team. I'm left out."

"It's so hard to get a decent sitter at short notice," Teddy pleads and she reluctantly nods. Poor thing. She really deserves some fun more than me. I have a tin of perfectly serviceable soup that I've had a hundred lunches before.

"I've just gotten my task list from Rose so I'm probably busy for the rest of the evening. Mel, you can go in my place." I ignore the sad lurch in my stomach as she beams and claps. "Have fun, you two."

"Uh-oh, you know what that means," Teddy says. "Didn't I

warn you? My strict instructions were to carry you out of here, kicking and screaming."

"No? What?" I roll back in my chair as he rounds my desk with purpose. "No, wait, I'll come—"

"Rules are rules," Teddy says and takes both of my hands in his to pull me to stand. His eyes are sparkling.

I've got to heed the warning about being dazzled, but it's too late. He bends and puts his shoulder into my stomach, there's an upward push, an arm around my knees and I'm facedown, a long way off the floor, looking down at his butt. I repeat: *dazzled*.

My foot knocks over a cup of pens. Melanie is screaming with joy.

"No, no," I beg, but now I'm looking at the carpet, the in-tray on Melanie's desk, TJ's astonished blink, the potted plant near the door. "My bag. My jacket."

I'm hoisted, which feels like a bob and a bounce. Melanie brings both things to Teddy, hooking them onto his free arm. I say into his back, "I've got to start work for PDC."

"When's it due?" he asks Melanie.

"Her assistant emailed me already. We have time. One long lunch won't ruin anything. We also had an accounts receivable meeting locked in, but I think we can reschedule that. In fact, I won't expect her back this afternoon."

I argue, "I'll definitely be back."

Upside-down, she says to me, "I know you're planning on working all weekend. I'll come in tomorrow and do a half day with you, so you won't have to be alone." Her hand combs through my hair. "Have fun."

Melanie's Saturdays are sacred. She sleeps in until two P.M.

"Oh, Mel, you don't have to." I'm having difficulty having a work conversation while folded over a man's shoulder. In an even, normal voice I try to handle this situation. "Very good, Teddy, you've made us laugh, now put me down."

"I don't hear you laughing." His arm squeezes my legs.

Melanie says, "Turn her more this way so I get her face in the shot."

I screech like a pterodactyl. "You're both dead. Do you hear me? Dead." I try to grab at the doorframe when we pass it, but no luck. All I can think of is: What would Rose Prescott say if she could see me now?

Teddy says, "See ya, Mel. You're on your own this afternoon. I'm keeping her." Off we go, down the path. The pavers scroll underneath me. "Look after my boy," he calls back at her. "He's gluten intolerant."

I bellow, "There's an instruction sheet in the black binder I made for you with the lockup procedures. Set the alarm. Lock the door. Text me when you lock the door."

"What? I can't hear you."

"Lock the—"

She bawls back, "I'll waste company time and work on the Sasaki Method. Don't do anything too naughty. See you tomorrow, not too early."

Life is now this hypnotic swing and the sound of his footsteps. I'm possibly lying in the coma ward at the hospital having the best dream of my life. This ass. How is he carrying me so easily? How do I fit onto one of his shoulders? "Please don't drop me," I clutch at the waistband of his pants when he steps around a tortoise.

"Don't grip too tight, you might tear them off. Relax, I'm not gonna drop you. I got her," he yells down the path. "Look at me, Caveman Teddy. So . . . Rose has been giving you a hard time. I'm sorry." He apologizes very earnestly. "She's fairly terrifying."

"You haven't met Sylvia." I don't know their family situation, but I am guessing Rose and Teddy are children from different marriages.

The coldness in her tone when she spoke about Teddy was incomprehensible. He's so . . . warm. Figuratively and literally. When he pauses to bob and bounce me up again, my hands slide. I'm technically just holding on. This hill is going to end and I shudder in sorrow.

"Like a sack of taters." Renata is upside down when Teddy pulls to a halt. I resent her, this flat ground, the nearby car.

"I always thought girls liked being swept off their feet," Teddy replies to her as he lowers me down. "But this one doesn't."

"Oh, they like it, all right," Renata says knowingly. "Look at those pink cheeks."

"Sorry about these two," Aggie says to me, dignified as always. "I really do think they're a bad influence on each other. Shall we go to lunch? We need to stop along the way to service my addiction." I think she means she needs to check her lottery tickets.

"Ladies," Teddy says, the sun glinting off his "Hot Stuff" badge. "Allow me." He runs to each back door, helping the old ladies in. My door is opened too. "Hey," he says near my ear before I get in. "You smell so nice. Must be from all that marinating in the bathtub."

I drop so heavily into my seat that the entire car bounces. The feel of his shoulder is still pressed into my stomach.

"I think that was fun," Aggie translates. I glance back to her; she's holding hands with her sister, how adorable. I'm relieved to see her looking quite bright and awake.

"How have your hands been?" I ask her. She shrugs, like, *what can you do?* In response, Renata picks up the one she's holding and begins to rub it tenderly.

I have thought this many times during my employment: how nice it must be to live with someone who loves you when you're old. The thought is chased by a sudden sense of urgency, and I reflexively think of Melanie's dating plan for me. I really need to make a decision on the rest of my life. No pressure.

During the whole car ride to lunch, we laugh at Teddy. He improvs several different characters:

- Eddie the Livestock Trucker ("Keep it down back there, you rowdy l'il cows!")
- Tedderick the Nervous Driver ("Oh my hubcaps, oh shivers, oh Lordy.")
- Prescott Providence the Bodyguard (I think he quotes Kevin Costner, but I'll have to look it up later.)

"I was born for this," he declares, tipping his chauffeur hat suavely at a pedestrian at the traffic lights. "I want to thank you for helping me find my life's purpose."

(His long thighs in that tweedy gray fabric are my new life's purpose.)

"Our absolute pleasure," Aggie tells him. Renata just grins and looks out the window.

Happiness fills the car, and it hits me that leaving Providence wasn't hard at all; not when I was carried out, kicking and screaming. I've known so many Parloni boys, and this is the only one who cared enough to do that. I look over at Teddy's profile; he's looking in the rearview mirror, smiling at his bosses with unfakable fondness.

He put me back on the ground a while back now, but I feel like my heart has remained draped over his shoulder. It can't beat in a normal way now. I hope he doesn't notice my inconvenient crush. I will pray on my knees tonight that Melanie doesn't notice it, because I'd be dead meat.

He looks over at me and a record player needle skips in my stomach. "You okay?" I have to laugh and shake my head, because the answer is: probably not.

Teddy stops the Rolls-Royce in front of an intimidating-looking restaurant. It's in a building smothered in creeping ivy. "We have arrived at our destination, Snobsville," he declares. Like the good little chauffeur he is, he jumps out swiftly and extracts Aggie first and she hangs on to his arm until she's safely up the curb.

"Me now," Renata yells at him. I open my own door and get out. From what I can see of the restaurant, I'm underdressed. Maybe Teddy and I can find a burger around here. "Famished," Renata adds as she straightens her clothes and runs a veined hand through her hair. "Absolutely parched, too." Hooking her arm into Aggie's, they walk straight in, not looking back.

Teddy sheds the waistcoat with the "Hot Stuff" name tag and Frisbees his hat into the passenger seat before handing the car key to the valet. Now he's standing there in those sexy trousers and a white shirt. As he loops a tie around his neck, he looks like a trendy young professional heading in for an expensive client lunch.

It feels like the light is reflecting off his new gold watch, straight through my chest, blinding my heart. He gives me a playful eye roll when he notices I'm watching. "I went to private school, I know how to do a knot." The next knot he performs is on his hair.

"Being good-looking really does transition you into any situation." I shake my head at the unfairness of it. I point through the glass. "Look at Renata making the staff panic. Whatever table they have for her, she won't want it."

"What's the point of being old and rich if you can't flex it?" He makes a fair point. We push through the front door. Behind my ear, he says, "Could you expand on how good-looking you think I am?" His hand slides on my waist.

"Theodore," I yip and he just smiles like I told him anyway. There is definitely a table for four with a reserved sign, but two tables of two are being hastily reset.

"We're sitting here. You two have to sit by yourselves," Renata booms across dozens of well-dressed people eating their meals. "How very romantic." Every single person lowers their cutlery and looks at me. I feel like every single loose thread in my outfit is visible. Renata isn't done. "Ruthie, you can practice having a date before the real thing comes along."

"The real thing?" Teddy repeats. "Pinch me. Last time I checked, I was real."

"You know what she means." I am neon pink with embarrassment. The entire silent room of diners watch, cutlery still lowered, as we weave through to our designated table. Teddy pulls out my chair and I ease down into it.

"This menu has no prices," Teddy observes. "That's not a good sign."

"Your friends have advised us that they will be ordering for you," the hovering waiter says. "Any dietary restrictions?"

"Just basic poverty." Teddy is gratified when I laugh. He rubs his hands together. "Free lunch. Everything's coming up Teddy. Is it weird that I'm kind of obsessing about my tortoise?" He sends a text. "Mel promised me updates."

"Sometimes when I have a really sick one, I make excuses to go up and check it."

He nods. "You're the only one who knows how it feels. How come we can take them to the Reptile Zoo for free?" He nudges my foot under the table. "Who came up with the forms?"

"I just knew that they were endangered, so I made some calls and the zoo sent some people up to Providence. The forms were me, of course. Any excuse for more paperwork," I joke, but he shakes his head at the self-deprecation.

"So you created the entire rehab program for an endangered species. By yourself. I bet your horrible Sylvia doesn't approve." He sees the answer on my face. "Mel told me you have to fund-raise. These Providence people have enough money under their couch cushions to fund the Christmas party ten times over."

"It doesn't matter."

"It should. People take too much from you. Make sure Rose doesn't trample you too." He holds up his phone to change the subject. Melanie has sent a selfie of herself staring into TJ's Kleenex box most diligently. She's made a paper nurse's hat and decorated it with a red cross. "That girl is a complete nut," he says fondly.

For one shivering moment, I marry them in my mind. What a sweet story for their wedding. *And I told her, the only one I trust is you. A toast to my bride!* I bet I'll have to help their caterers clean up empty glasses.

Even while having a bad daydream, I can sound normal. "Even tortoise daddies need to take a break."

"I know it's weird. I've never had a pet." Before I can explore that with him—surely as a kid he could have had a pony if he wanted it?—he blinks away the sadness and smooths the tablecloth. "Well, this is very fancy. Did the other Parloni boys get free lunches?"

"I don't think so. I think you're special. I mean—"

"Very special, how kind," he agrees in a warm voice. Then he grabs at one of the tiny bread rolls and slathers it with butter. Scarfs it down. "What was the last boy like?"

I lean back in my chair and straighten my cutlery. "That would be Phillip. He was studying journalism and ran a blog about sneakers. He drew the line at ironing practical joke underwear."

"What, you mean that ratty leopard-print thong they keep pranking me with? I've found far worse in the bottom of my sheets." He says that too loud and our neighbors turn their heads. "I folded it in that Japanese way, down to the size of a matchbox."

I laugh. "Sounds like you're a tidy boy sometimes."

He replies, "Since I met you, I've been folding everything. I've lived in mess my entire life. I want a label maker. I want to tattoo my belongings. Tell me about the boy before Phillip." Teddy inserts a second bread roll into his mouth.

I'm distracted because I just saw something real and deep down, underneath his easy smile. I don't think being a Prescott is as easy as I'd assumed.

"The boy before Phillip was Brayden. Nineteen, chronically unemployed. He was shocked to be given the job. It was sad how elated he was. He hung around the front office, getting in my way."

I think he asks through his mouthful: "How'd she break him?"

I smile against my will. "She pretended to be dead and he ran away and never came back. For all he knows, she did die." I turn and watch Renata laughing with Aggie. "It was so unnecessary. Sometimes I wonder if she's actually evil."

"I think she tried that with me. I changed the TV channel; that restarted her heart. And before him?" He's buttered a third roll, but something makes him freeze. It's me. Do I have some kind of expression on my face? "Sorry, I was in a bread frenzy. Excuse my fingers."

He puts the torn, buttered roll on my plate. I can do it

myself, but I didn't have to just now. And that's why it's the most delicious bread roll I ever had.

In between bites I tell him, "Luke was about twenty. He skateboarded down the hill, hit a tortoise, and fell off. He tried to sue Providence. Luckily, I'd written down each time I'd warned him not to do it. Time and date."

"A lawyer's dream. A model employee," Teddy tells me in a praising way, but I still feel embarrassed. *Goody-Two-shoes*. "Want another one?" He hovers his hand over the breadbasket. "You need some carbs. Thank God I saved you from your tin of soup."

"Yes, please. I saved your dad from a lawsuit. More inheritance for you." I accept a glass of wine from the waiter but I won't drink it.

"Drink it," Renata shouts across the room.

Teddy shakes his head. "That's me. Just killing time, waiting for that inheritance of mine that I'm definitely entitled to." He butters the next roll with a bit of violence. "Over Rose's dead body."

I need his smile back. "Cheers, Teddy. Congratulations on probably being the longest-serving assistant to Renata and Aggie Parloni." We clink glasses and I take a sip of the sour wine. It's awful, but I have to grow up.

I remember what Mel said about this being a client lunch. Maybe I should be trying to have a professional meeting with Jerry's son.

"PDC hasn't known we existed before now. I don't know what this review is really for. We were totally forgotten." Resentment colors my tone and he probably hears it.

"I ruined everything when I showed up, huh?" He waits. When he sees me trying to choose my reply, the light in him goes out. "She'll do a review of the assets and liabilities and make a presentation to the board. She'll tell them what will make PDC the most money. If that hill is worth more covered in high-rises, she'll do it."

I wonder what other inside knowledge he has without realizing it. "And is she a lovely person who has a soft spot for the elderly?"

"She probably had a toy bulldozer as a kid." His expression is blank and I don't like it. He picks up his phone and yawns, effectively exiting this conversation.

"Probably? You don't know for sure?" I sip more wine. "Maybe you could convince her to come and visit. If she just sees it in person—"

"I'm going to tell you a fact about me," he says, and when his eyes meet mine again, I get a sharp, scared drop inside. He's now a zero-nonsense adult man. "I always know when someone is hoping I can be useful in some sort of Prescott way. I like you a lot, so I'm going to give you a spoiler on how this turns out. I can't get involved. If you're imagining I have some kind of influence, you are miles from the truth."

I respond with emotion. "Don't you care that Providence is home to so many elderly people who don't deserve to be uprooted at this time in their lives? The stress could kill them."

He looks over at his employers and I see true regret. "I do care. But I can't help you. Even if I wanted to, Rose wouldn't allow it."

CHAPTER ELEVEN

The waiter interrupts to present us with pale, unappetizing salads. The plates are dotted with enough dressing to coat one taste bud, plus garnish flowers I've seen growing on roadsides. My stomach makes a noise like a disappointed Melanie.

"Is this a tomato?" Teddy's holding up something on his fork, begging for a subject change. "Is it a see-through beet? A dead onion?"

"It's the ghost of a tomato," I decide, and we scrape around our plates for something edible. "I don't mean to be ungrateful about a free lunch, but so far, the buttered roll is the standout."

He asks me now, "Your parents still together?" I nod in reply. "What do they do for a living?"

I guess I'm going to have to cross this bridge now. It's an unsexy bridge, which makes people think it's a shortcut to understanding why I'm like this. "You are having lunch with the Reverend's Daughter." I take another wincing sip of wine.

"Don't drink it," Teddy says.

"Not even one second after learning I am a reverend's daughter, you've decided I'm too sheltered to drink wine?" I open my mouth and gulp it all. I breathe out wine fumes and feel like I swallowed a lit match.

"No, I was saying don't drink it because you clearly don't like it. You don't have to do everything Renata says. She's less than five feet tall. What's she gonna do to you?" Teddy sips from his water glass. He's a chauffeur, after all. "Do you still go to church?"

"If I'm visiting home, I'll go to avoid a fight. But I don't have a church I go to here. My dad is disappointed in me." It's quite frankly amazing how I've managed to KonMari those feelings into a matchbox. I've lost faith in the church, and my dad has lost faith in me. Which came first? I hold up my glass to a waiter. "I need another glass, please."

Before I can answer, Renata's voice cuts through the room, making patrons around us wince. "What are you two little lovebirds talking about?"

Teddy lets me field this one. I can't even stage-whisper, because her hearing isn't good enough. "Daddy issues?"

"Carry on," she says waving her knife airily. And because Teddy's eyes are bright with amusement when I turn back around, the stares from the diners around us don't affect me in the way I thought they would. Who cares.

The wine has curled up inside me, warm and snug. I should probably try to soak it up. I point at the bread rolls and Teddy begins to butter another one for me. "You just do them better than me," I explain and he doesn't think it's strange. "I'm hungry and somehow already drunk?" The waiter gives me my second glass with perfect timing.

Teddy assesses me. "You've only had two bread rolls and the ghost of a tomato. Can I ask what's for mains?"

"Spatchcock," is the waiter's listless reply. "But soup is coming."

"We're too hungry for mini chickens. Could we change our order? Let's go for the steak. That okay, Ruthie?" The waiter is very irritated and walks off. Teddy is pretty pleased with himself. "I'll be in trouble for that later."

"Thank goodness the Parlonis are paying. I'm broke." I could use that money Teddy owes me, but I don't care about it anymore. He's a day out at the carnival and I'm happy with the price I paid.

"I haven't forgotten." He digs around in his back pocket. There's the unmistakable sound of Velcro ripping, and a nearby woman looks over at his lower body in alarm. "Oh please no," he groans, patting his hip. "Not now, not here."

I try to see under the tablecloth. "What's happened?"

He's puzzled. "You're kidding, right? Didn't you see the 'Hot Stuff' name tag? This is a stripper's costume. It's all held together with Velcro."

"I've taken it to the dry cleaner so many times. What must they think of me?" As I pour the second glass of wine into myself, the looks I've gotten now make sense.

"That you know some pretty hot guys." The look he gives me is devilish as he carefully fishes out his wallet with only a small amount of ripping noise this time. "My next Good Samaritan came through. This really nice lady found it at the Laundromat. It's always ladies. Dudes are garbage." He opens it and a cartoon moth flies out. He scrounges out battered notes. "Twenty dollars. Thank you."

Our debt is cleared. I find I don't like having this link between us erased. His wallet is a squashed leather medieval relic, run over by horse and cart a thousand times. I want to open it and read every single card and receipt. I want to sleep with it under my pillow. Oh no, this isn't good.

He asks in an easy conversational way, "Who was the last person you dated?"

"My boyfriend's name was Adam. Yeah, I know, I went pretty literal with what kind of guy I thought my dad would approve of." The waiter takes away my uneaten salad. "We dated, or I guess you could call it dating, from sixteen to . . . the morning after prom night."

"That sounds like an interesting story right there." Again, we are interrupted. A small bowl of pink soup is presented to each of us. I touch the side of the bowl; it's cold. Teddy asks, "Excuse me, what is this?"

"Lithuanian cold beet soup." The waiter manages to say this with a straight face. Teddy wisely keeps the agony out of his expression. His employers are always watching.

"May as well try it." He spoons some into his mouth and looks up at the ceiling, eyes narrowed in thought. What comes next: yum, yuck? Why do I care? I need to take Jerry Prescott's advice before it's too late. I'm not sure what *too late* will look like, but it won't be a good thing for me.

I should focus more on my own experiences, not just wait on tenterhooks for his. I try some of the thick soup. "Like sweet crayons?"

"Tastes like a tub of beetroot dip got left out on a patio then it rained," Teddy replies. He's eating it anyway.

"Nailed it." I grin into my bowl.

"I love it when you smile. It makes me get a little flipper here." Teddy bumps a fist on his solar plexus. "So do you want to tell me what happened with Adam? Did he break your heart? Do I need to hunt him down?" He reminds me of Melanie.

The wine makes me confess. "Prom night went badly. I was his moment of bad judgment. He went to my dad for counseling in the morning. It was pretty bad." My voice breaks. I felt sick looking at my father's closed office door, knowing what they were talking about.

"He shouldn't have done that. Going to your father? That's a violation of your privacy."

"I don't know about violation—"

"They thought your feelings and experience and privacy were worth less than his. It makes me really angry. What did I just tell you? People take too much from you."

"I never thought of it that way." I finish my wine. "So that was my last . . . encounter. Working at Providence, it's been a chore on my to-do list that I've never gotten around to. Find a boyfriend. Until Melanie showed up."

Wine reeaally works. I'm day-drunk and sitting opposite a guy I have an ill-advised crush on. I'm probably as transparent as glass right now. "I have to give Melanie an answer this afternoon about—"

"The Sasaki Method," he finishes for me. "She's asked me to convince you to do it. But I don't want you to. It's a jungle out there." He makes a face. "And I will tell you again, dudes are garbage."

"You're a dude."

He repeats, "Garbage."

"If I don't want to be alone in a retirement villa from the ages of twenty-five to ninety-five, I need to do something. I want you to be completely honest. If this was a real date, how would I be doing?" That sounded so neutral and platonic. I amaze myself.

"You're being yourself, and that's all you need to be." When he sees that vague answer doesn't satisfy me, he thinks on it more. "You're a good listener, you're funny, you're smart and honest . . . any guy would be lucky to be sitting where I am." His eyeline moves over my face like a sketching pencil. "You're completely beautiful."

I don't let myself feel the full impact of those words, because he said them so easily. He's always got a compliment preloaded, that's all that was. "That's really kind of you." For a boy who's rather self-obsessed, he's been doing the majority of the listening, not me. When we make eye contact again, I get a zip in my stomach.

He asks, "Anyone on your radar?"

"Literally no one." It's a bald-faced lie, but I see him wilt like

I've delivered very bad news. What an annoying question. Of course Teddy is on my radar, in the same way that you might track the progress of a hurricane heading toward your part of the coast. Just take a moment to appreciate the special electricity that runs through him, turning everything about him bright.

I may as well get a crush on a hurricane. I'd be covered by insurance.

"No one at all on your radar." He's giving me one more chance to get the answer right. What does he want from me? To admit that I love the citrus yellow chips in his hazel eyes— and how they only show when the light hits them just right?

"My radar is broken."

He's not happy with that. He expects everyone to be in love with him. "We'll tune it up. What's your end goal? Mel has shown me her dream bridesmaid's dress."

"Lilac, I know." What I really want can't be said out loud. I want to sit on my couch with *Heaven Sent* on in the background, making out with a guy who employs just the right amount of give and take. "I can't tell you what my end goal is. You once told me you're easily traumatized." It feels good to say something so bold. It inks out his pupils.

"Traumatize me." He reaches out a hand and lays it flat on the tablecloth. It's a request. Touch it. Give. "I want you to."

Is this one of those moments I'll look back on later and wonder what would have happened if I'd had the courage to just slide my own hand into his, in the middle of a fancy restaurant on a weekday? If I had, would those fingers curl and tighten on mine?

Give, give, give.

"I wanna find a nice normal guy and kiss him on my couch," I say to see how he reacts. Not well. A frown forms, the hand is pulled back, and I never get to know if I had that kind of skin courage. I smile to cover my nerves. "What? That was pretty tame."

He frowns. "There really aren't that many guys dating online that'd be happy to stop at that."

"Who said I wanted to stop?"

I look up as two plates are set down in front of us. Steak and potatoes sure beats a can of soup. Being forced out of my shell can end up being something more nourishing than I'm used to. And Teddy just stares at me. If he suspects I have a teeny-tiny ill-advised crush, I think he'll start to look at me with gentle pity. "I'm doing it."

"Doing what?"

Overly bright and confident, I take my phone out. "Let's do the thing I can't take back, once I agree." I begin to text her and read aloud. "The Sasaki Method? I'm in."

Teddy says, "Are you really sure? Mel is not a quitter. You're going to find someone."

"I want some semblance of a work-life balance, and if I don't take this chance, nothing changes for me." I stare into his eyes and decide that he's my straightforward neighbor friend, and that is okay. I hit send.

On my phone there's some reply-dots, and the screen explodes into emojis. They're coming thick and fast, diamonds and hearts, rings and champagne bottles. Ridiculous GIFs of dancing babies and swinging gibbons. Joy is cascading down my screen. All at once, I'm so touched I could cry. She cares enough to be excited about helping me?

Lunchtime wine is a beautiful thing.

I'm sitting here in a fancy restaurant, with a kind, handsome man, and he'll help me too? I reach over and have enough courage to sink my fingers between his and squeeze, releasing before he can react. "I mean, what have I got to lose?"

"I didn't order you steak," Renata screeches across the room. Now we're at risk of losing our lives.

CHAPTER TWELVE

've set up the rec center for this afternoon's Stitch and Bitch.

It's becoming clear that Teddy is going to reach his second-week employment milestone tomorrow and I'm making him a tiny military medal to pin to his T-shirt. I can picture it; I'll pin it to his chest. He'll salute and laugh and ask me what's for dinner.

I think this is the closest I'll get to having a roommate. Or a best friend. I can see why the Parlonis enjoy having an affable young man around the house. He's created "The Good Neighbors Jar" a few days ago, with his first cash contribution toward my groceries. I think he knows I hate going off-site, because he goes to the store for me. He enjoys having a list.

He always buys me something sweet, as my treat for being so good.

While I wait for my Stitch and Bitchers, I'm taking a moment to test the rec center's doorknob, just to sharpen my muscle memory. Locked has such a nice full-stop feeling to it.

Unlocked is a sloppy looseness and I can't stand it. I've been practicing this drill for a while.

"How was your conference call?" Melanie asks as she strolls up the path. She's the old me, carefree and not required to attend stressful meetings, and I envy her deeply. Is this how Sylvia feels all the time?

I force my hand off the doorknob. "I think I sounded semi-coherent. Anyway, what are you doing here? You're meant to be looking after the office."

"You ran off before I could ask what heinous tasks they're giving us now. I could see your glittering sweat mustache from my desk." Melanie now gives a cheery smile to one of the residents passing nearby on a mobility scooter. "Hi, Mrs. D'Angelo. Relax, I've got the phone diverted." She waggles her cell phone at me.

I'd praise her increasing friendliness to the residents, but I'm distracted. "And it's unlocked down there, isn't it. Mel, go back."

She's too busy taking a photo of her manicure against the flowered hedge to listen. "What did Rose want this time?"

"Insurance details. There's also some advanced reporting they've asked for that Sylvia always does. I might need your help getting the packet together." Sweat mustache is putting it mildly. "I've got a bad feeling about this. They got access to the banking accounts. The way they were talking, you'd think this place was a sinking ship. I think I should try calling Sylvia."

Not one of my emails has been answered. She was the one

who insisted on regular updates, but I'm feeling like a harasser. Has she fallen overboard? She's not a woman I can imagine lying drunk on a deck chair, sunburned and asleep.

Melanie uploads the photograph of her #hand to her Instagram account. "No way. Prove that you handled everything. I have been temping for fifteen thousand years, and here's what I know. Everything that gives you a sick stomach is a great example in a job interview one day."

"You forget, my goal is to never do an interview again."

If Sylvia arrives back and I've screwed this up, she will fire me into next year. I think again of the fold-out couch in my parents' basement; maybe it's waiting for me. I take a rare moment to pray.

Melanie the Temp is never impressed by my company loyalty. "Picked out your Providence town house already? Prepaid that burial plot, too? Ew, Ruthie. We need to focus on the Sasaki Method pronto and get you back out into the land of the living." She turns to leave.

"Hey, wait a second. I want all of the Sasaki Method stuff to be just between us after work. There's no way I want them to find out we're goofing off. So I think we need to keep a line between us and Teddy."

"I agree. I think he's a test."

"A test from PDC?" I never thought of that.

"No, a test sent by the dating gods. It's like when you go to the grocery store really hungry. If you don't have your list with you, you'll end up in front of the cake cabinet, picking out a Black Forest to eat in the car. What's on your shopping list?"

I know what kind of answer I'm supposed to give. "Granola and toilet cleaner."

She hoots. "Exactly. We'll apply the same lesson to men. Some are yummy but just no good for you. I know he's been hanging around your place. You come up an awful lot in his dreams, by the way."

I want to know, but I don't even blink. "He's not a test. We're neighbors."

"I talked to him in the office the other day when you were up visiting Mrs. Tuckmire. I asked him if he's ever been in love." Melanie looks away, nibbling her bottom lip.

I now seem to have a rusty hacksaw slid between some of my major organs. If she says another sentence, it's going to wobble and slip sideways. "It's none of my business. Or yours for that matter, Melanie Sasaki."

"It was the way he laughed at the question that made me feel really . . . sad. He said he didn't have it in his DNA to love someone properly and forever." This sounds a lot like a warning and I prickle with embarrassment. She begins walking back to the office. "Remember your shopping list," is what she calls over her shoulder. "No bingeing."

It's a timely reminder because a car cake is now all I want. I'd make it real romantic, up at a lookout, the city lights sparkling below. All my buttons and zips loosened. My moans would fog that car UP.

Fast footsteps approach. Teddy is jogging along the path, trailed by Renata on her scooter. I walk out to greet them.

"What's happening?" Teddy gives me a friendly eyebrow raise and jogs right on past, my heart hot on his heels.

"He got sassy with me, so I've decided he needs to get some energy out. Do a lap of the lake, I'm watching you." Renata watches with evil satisfaction. His back is straight and the entire effect is of light ease. His hair gleams like a black cherry. I need to stop noticing any of him. But: Teddy's in good shape.

"I don't know about that," Renata says. (I said that out loud? Oh no.) "He makes an awful lot of fuss about his morning start time so I'm overhauling his lifestyle. He's making himself a kale and tofu smoothie after this."

"Such cruelty."

"I'm a wonderful employer," Renata defends herself. When she says, slow and sly, "Well, well," I realize I've been watching Teddy for probably an entire minute without replying.

Even with Renata's speculative eyes on me, I can't stop myself. He's so interesting. An eye magnet. He's the only thing worth staring at. He's come across a pair of residents walking on the path; now he's jogging backward slowly as he talks to them. His laugh rings out across the water, right through me.

"Well, well," Renata repeats. "I don't know how I feel about this."

I wrench my eyes off him and wave at Mrs. Penbroke as she passes us on her scooter. "Don't forget, Stitch and Bitch is on soon."

"I won't, Ruthie," Mrs. Penbroke calls back. "I'm bringing my needlepoint. And something to bitch about." She gives Renata a hard stare.

"Two dollars for the fund-raising tin, too, if you can please." Knowing how much the residents drink, my fund-raising for the Christmas party starts on New Year's Day.

"Focus," Renata snaps at me, tapping the arm of her sunglasses on her scooter. "I heard from a little bird that you are putting yourself on the meat market shortly. She's asked me to create a look-book for your makeover." Renata looks me up and down. "How do you feel about the design direction at Valentino?"

Dammit, Melanie. Renata will spill everything to Sylvia.

"Yes, it's true, I was thinking of starting to date, but the new owners of Providence are conducting a big review of our management processes, and Sylvia is away almost until Christmas. I'll be focused on the review PDC has asked me to do." Listen to me, being responsible. "I've also got the Christmas party to organize. You've never come to it, but it's a huge event. I don't think I can handle everything." As I say it out loud, I realize it's true. "I've got no experience in trying for a work-life balance."

"You're a smart girl. You can do everything, and besides, you've already got a crush. Here he comes."

"Let me guess, another lap," Teddy says and jogs past before she can reply. I feel a shimmer of energy when he passes me.

"You cannot imagine the satisfaction one feels in moments like that," Renata says as she pretends to hold binoculars up. "It's like my horse is out in front at the Kentucky Derby. I raised him from a foal, and now look at him go."

"I don't have a crush on Teddy. He's nothing like what I'd go for, or vice versa." I'm scared to ask this. "Is he going to last?"

"He might need to walk if he gets a stitch."

"You know what I mean."

Renata says with a deep sigh, "Unfortunately, I think he may complete two weeks of employment."

"Isn't he doing your chores and laundry?" I have to hold the words in: *He's helping you. Accept the amazing thing dropped into your life, you silly old woman.* I suppose the same could be said for me, being blessed with Melanie.

"He's depressingly competent at all that," is all Renata will say before she changes gears. "May I give you an elderly person life lesson? Good. Life is only bearable if you have someone attractive to complain to. If I didn't have my Aggie, I would not have survived the 1990s. Karl Lagerfeld, I will see you in hell."

I laugh. "Okay. Thanks for the advice."

She nods over at the lake. "You remind me so much of Aggie. She's made of the same stuff as you. That's how I know you will have very hurt feelings when this one gets the keys to his tattoo studio and rides off five hours in some direction without so much as a backward glance."

"I hope I find someone who suits me. I'd like to have someone attractive to complain to when I'm your age. Which is not old," I rush to clarify.

Renata pats my arm. "I am as old as dirt. Here he comes, sounding very unfit. He's put in the effort on his so-called last lap. Little does he know—"

Teddy says as he passes, huffing athletically: "One more, I'm getting a runner's high."

Renata is equal parts impressed and annoyed. "I really need to get smarter with this one."

"And I really need to get ready for the Stitch and Bitch," I say, but of course it's no use. She rolls the cuffs of my shirt up to each elbow. Tug, the skirt is pulled up higher. She's accepted her role as fashion adviser in Melanie's Sasaki Method. She releases two of my shirt buttons.

"Buy a size down. And this is your natural waist. Get some big belts, cinch everything in here." She draws a line on me. "What do you have against new things, anyway? Don't they pay you here?"

"I worked in a church thrift store so I know brand-new stuff gets donated. It's better for the environment. And yes, I'm on a budget."

Renata tugs at my hair elastic. It's difficult for her and in these moments of struggle, I feel her frailty acutely. It's the only reason I submit myself to her like this. She's a tiny little loudmouth, but she's also stuck in a ninety-one-year-old body against her will.

With more tenderness than I ever thought her capable of, Renata says, "Look at yourself. Any young fellow would be lucky to have you. And when you find him, he'll never let a good girl like you go."

I turn and see my reflection in the window of the rec center. Renata can work small miracles. Maybe I can picture myself, standing outside a bar, raising my hand in greeting as a man walks toward me. *Ruthie? Nice to meet you at last. You look nice.* "Thank you. I think so too."

Teddy is now in front of us, hands on knees, panting.

Renata instructs him: "I want specifics on the physical sensations you're feeling. I haven't jogged since the eighties. Or the seventies. The sixties." She racks her brains. "Ever."

"Like a warm burning, but it's so good," Teddy puffs, rubbing his hands on his thighs. His clothes are steamed onto his body now. "Like I can't get the air deep enough. I'm all hot, I can't see straight." He's talking down to the pavement. My presence is still unacknowledged.

What an unexpected treat to see color in his cheeks and glittery specks of sweat on his brow. Is this exact kind of breathing what I'd hear through our wall? I have never thought as much about sex as I have in the past few days. I try to pull my shirt back into place and Renata spanks me with her sunglasses hard enough that they break.

"Get that," she says to Teddy, and he seems only too happy to collapse to his knees. "When we get back, I'm going to dictate a letter for you to type up. We'll address it to the current creative director at Céline. Dear Sir. Quality is down on your sunglasses."

"Sure," Teddy says, gathering the pieces. Then he finally looks up.

All I can think of to say is, "Are you recovering?"

He's really not. The makeover has astonished him. His eyes are on the deep triangle of breast skin exposed to Renata's solar nemesis. Arms, waist, hair, he's not even blinking as he moves from one part to the next. His chest is rising and falling.

Right in this moment, I'm extraordinary.

CHAPTER THIRTEEN

've been hanging for five o'clock all day," Melanie tells me as I lock the office door behind us. "Finally, I get an invite to your place. Time to get this show on the road."

"My place isn't exciting," I warn as we walk up the path, but she's not interested in my boring caveats and excuses.

"Hello, I still live down the hallway from my mummy and daddy. You're a grown-up lady in your own house. And I. Am. Excited." She jumps into the courtyard, spends a bit of time looking at the tortoises in their enclosures, then knocks on Teddy's door.

"He won't be there," I tell her as I unlock my own door. "And he's not invited, remember?"

She turns his door handle and pokes her head inside. Great, so now I've got to worry about his lack of security on top of everything else? She calls, "Hello? Teddy, are you decent?" We hear nothing but silence.

Teddy has been . . . nesting? He's got a battle-scarred leather armchair with an afghan throw on it. There's a coffee table that he definitely found on a roadside somewhere. He's put my *Women's Health* magazine on it and has a plain white bowl filled with candy. Has he copied my furniture layout? I take a few steps in. On the crumbling plaster wall, he's drawn a huge flatscreen TV with a marker, complete with brand logo: TEDDYVISION.

"Lucky his daddy is the landlord," Melanie observes. "What a dump."

"Believe it or not, this is a big improvement." The way he's folded his little blanket makes my heart feel weird.

Melanie leans in farther behind me. "Aw, look. There's his turtle tank. He was scared TJ would get pneumonia out in the yard when he gets him back."

It grates when she acts like I might not know something about him. I dug that tank out of the storage closet myself. "Yeah, I know."

"It's so cute how bad he misses his boy. Oh my God," Melanie gasps, and I'm sure she's seen something truly scandalous. She finishes with: "He's borrowed *Reptiles and Amphibians for Dummies* from the actual library. He'll be a cute dad one day, don't you think?"

He'd parade his baby around like his perfect little trophy.

"In the far distant future, when he's grown up himself." I tug Melanie out of his doorway. "Come away from there. Let him have some privacy."

When we go into my cottage, she says, "It's exactly like he described it. He said it's like Pooh Bear's house in a tree. No wonder he's always trying to slither in here." She knocks on the wall I share with him. "You are next-door neighbors with a hot boy. A silly, weird one, but undeniably hot. How does that feel?"

"It mainly feels irritating, but in a nice way."

"How?" Melanie is smiling and perplexed.

"Like when my oven timer goes off and he tells me through the wall that he had a dream that I was cooking him a lovely dinner."

"He dreams about your cottage," Melanie says blandly. I keep a bowl of candy on my coffee table—exactly where Teddy put his—and she takes one. "And he can keep on dreaming where you're concerned."

"I'll get some snacks." I stayed up late, pre-preparing a snack platter, all the while warning myself that Mel might cancel. After all, she's young and fun. I'm about to reveal a 1950s-housewife level of effort. "Want to sit in the courtyard?"

"Sure, after I take a look around." She practically zips herself into a full-body forensic suit. I'm not too bothered; there's nothing scandalous to find.

I put the cheese platter and crackers out in the courtyard on what I've come to think of as Teddy's table. Next, lemonade and some glasses. Friday evening and I'm actually doing something social with someone my own age.

"You're so neat," Melanie's voice calls from faraway inside.

"I guess," I reply right as Teddy skids into the courtyard on the heels of his sneakers, holding a walkie-talkie like he's a security guard. He takes one look at the food on the table and says, "Yessssssssssss."

(Here's a secret: I made a larger cheese plate than I needed to.)

(A bigger secret: My heart just skidded into my rib cage on the heels of its sneakers.)

"I am absolutely—" He's interrupted by his walkie-talkie's static crackle. "Starving."

"You left your door unlocked," I accuse him. "Melanie just broke in. What are you doing here? This is a private function."

"Nothing to steal in there." He shrugs. I am about to argue when we're interrupted.

"What's your 10–20, Panda Bear?" Renata's sharp voice says from the walkie-talkie. When he doesn't answer, she tries again. "I told him that this wouldn't work. Come IN, Panda Bear, what's your 20? OVER." A couple of seconds later, a flock of birds fly over us.

Teddy allows himself a soul-deep sigh then presses the side button. "Affirmative, Fashion Victim, that's a big 10–4. I might be a while. Babe Ruth's put out a big plate of cheese and grapes and crackers. There's even a third glass, just for me. Over."

Renata replies, "Cheese party in the courtyard on a Friday evening. Is there wine? Describe what sort of cheeses. Over, obviously."

I go inside as he begins describing them to her—*hard yellow doorstop, gooey white hockey puck, gross one with mystery bits*— then find Melanie in my bedroom picking through the things on top of my dresser. "Teddy's here."

"Good, good," she says, distracted. "Is this all your makeup?" She opens an eyeshadow tin with her fingernail like she's prizing the lid off a Petri dish.

I lie. "I'm not sure. Maybe there's more in the bathroom."

"Already looked there. Okay, so a lot of this is very old and needs to go in the bin." (She's not wrong. I used that palette for prom.) "I'll want to see your clothes at some point too. That's Week 3 of the Method."

I lower my voice. "We won't go into full details of the Sasaki Method while he's here. We'll let him sit with us until he gets bored and wanders off."

"Good plan." She goes outside. "Hello, Teddy, oh helllllooooo cheese." They begin cutting into the cheese, squeaking knives and banter aplenty.

"Renata's revving up the scooter as we speak," Teddy warns us, assembling a palmful of preloaded crackers for more efficient scoffing. He hands me one with a small flourish.

"I think it would be better if you left," I tell him as kindly as I can. He reacts like he's never been so hurt. "This is something that I want to keep private."

"Aren't we friends?" He's got me there. "If you're worried I'm going to tell my dad or Sylvia that you're doing this, I won't. I just want to help."

"Ah, just let him stay. He's impossible to get rid of." Melanie gives me a single sheet of paper. "I want you to sign this first."

It's something resembling a waiver.

"'In participating in the Sasaki Method (hereby referred to as 'the Method'), Ruthie Maree Midona'—ah, so that's why you asked my middle name—'acknowledges that she does so on a voluntary basis and is able to opt out at any point in the process.'"

"But I hope you don't," Melanie interjects.

I continue reading. "'She waives, releases, and discharges Melanie Sasaki from any and all liability, including but not limited to the following that may result from following the Method.'"

I read out loud the following events I am indemnifying her against:

- Hurt feelings
- Unfulfilled expectations
- Emotional turmoil or distress as a result of online dating
- Being murdered by a blind date (Teddy chokes on his mouthful)
- Costs associated with unplanned pregnancy (my turn to choke)
- Miscellaneous expenses incurred from any recommended physical presentation improvements, hereby known as "the Makeover"
- Any costs associated with the inevitable wedding that shall result from participation in the Method

"Initial each," she instructs.

I hesitate for a long moment on the *hurt feelings*. "You are a very creative person. Where'd you get this template?"

She watches my pen, halted on the signature line. "I found one online and modified it. The most important part is that you agree that this is voluntary. And down at the bottom you see that I copyright the term the Sasaki Method. I mean, I would if I knew how. What I'm saying is, don't steal my amazing idea, you guys. I'm getting rich from this one day."

"I'm happy to sign that," I try to not sound too dry. "But I want a confidentiality clause."

"I didn't make one."

I look at the son of Jerry Prescott. He's currently eyes closed, blissful and chewing.

I write an amendment: *All information regarding Ruthie Maree Midona's participation in the Method will remain strictly confidential.*

"We all sign. Whatever happens, I want it to stay between us. I'm also adding a clause here that says we will not discuss or participate in the Method during working hours. No resources from the office are to be used."

Melanie replies, "Whoops, too late. I've stolen nine sheets of paper and half a spoonful of ink. Sorry, Teddy, I'll pay your dad back. But the binder, I bought specially with my own money."

"Relax, I'm not gonna tell him." Teddy takes the pen and signs next to my amendments when it's his turn. It's a surprising signature, very adult-man, and would look right at home on real estate contracts. "Or am I? Maybe I'm a corporate spy, sent to investigate all the minor paper thefts going on around here."

I'm starting to notice that he always checks to see if I laugh at his jokes. When I smile, he lounges back in his seat and eats grapes like life is grand. Melanie and I sign the document too.

"Breaker, breaker," the walkie-talkie squawks. "Fashion Victim incoming, over."

"I don't mind this one," Melanie confides in me. "She makes me feel like getting old won't be too scary."

"I'd better get more cheese."

"There's more cheese? I don't have to hold back?" Teddy says with his mouth full and the word TAKE on his cheese-knife hand.

"That's you holding back?"

Serious-eyed, he swallows and says, "Will you marry me, Ruthie Maree?" And I hate to admit it, but my heart hears the words, and it's gaping-blushing-starstruck.

Melanie pretends to pack up her folder. "My work here is done. Remember, lilac bridesmaid's dresses."

"Even the cheese I thought would be gross isn't gross," he's telling her when I go inside for more snacks. "It's walnuts in cream cheese with honey. I'll get a lilac tie to match you all."

I lean on the kitchen bench to privately regroup.

"Don't you dare try to be Ruthie's husband," Melanie scolds him. "We're going to do a worksheet on it, but I already knew the moment I saw you. You're not the right type for her."

He smiles with wicked white teeth, judging by his tone. "I'm everybody's type."

"The fact that you think so just confirms you're definitely not hers. Maybe you're the next candidate for the Sasaki Method," Melanie fires back at him, and I feel a moment of real, actual fear as I look in the fridge. Teddy out in the world. Teddy dating, being funny and charming. I mean, he always has been. But I know him now, and I don't think I want him to. Oh no.

Then Melanie makes the feeling worse. "I just assumed you don't have a girlfriend. If you do, you should be ashamed of yourself."

"If I did, do you think I'd be curled up on a sixty-year-old mattress in the middle of nowhere? Eating"—*crunch, crunch, crunch*—"stolen handfuls of tortoise lettuce?"

I'm walking back out with replenishments when Renata rounds the corner with a bottle of wine in her scooter's basket and a single empty glass in her fist. "I'm here. Open this bottle," she tasks Teddy seamlessly.

"Hi, Fashion Victim. I think your wig's on sideways," Melanie says and she's right. Renata has wispy bangs over one ear.

"At my age, sideways is good enough." Renata edges her scooter up to the table, not planning to dismount. "This is most civilized. What have I missed?"

I reply, "You missed out on me signing a very creative waiver, and we're about to start on Week 1 of the Sasaki Method. If Mel will actually explain what that means."

Melanie seems to compose herself for a moment, taking a new sheet out of her secret folder. "Week 1, of an eight-week program," she announces like an infomercial, but then falters. Renata's presence has knocked her confidence. It's understandable. The woman could make a billionaire CEO stare into a mirror.

"It's okay," I encourage her.

Melanie turns through the pages. She says quietly, "Just a reminder that I've never done this before."

"Pitch it," Renata instructs. "Sell it." Big cracker crunch. In this moment, she's young again, at the head of a board table as her quivering staff present a mock-up of the next *HOT OR NOT* magazine cover.

I say to Melanie, "Just explain it to me."

She begins. "When I thought about Ruthie, I decided that she needs to ease into this. So with that in mind, we will do different weekly activities, with a real date with a guy being the goal at the four-week midpoint. By the end of the eight weeks, I'd like to see her happily dating a really nice guy who's into her, and she won't need the Method anymore. Look at my first worksheet." We all lean over it. "Ruthie will write down all the qualities she wants in a man, the sorts of things she'd enjoy doing on dates and any deal breakers. There's a bunch of columns and lists for her to fill out here. We know she's good at that."

"Four weeks? Eight?" Renata is unimpressed. "What about now?"

I make eye contact with Teddy. He's giving me that same feeling as I had at the gas station when he looked me up and down: like he's squeezing, pausing, assessing.

Melanie's printed out a calendar. "We're here. By Week 6, Ruthie should have a date to the Christmas party. And by Week 8, it will be New Year's Day. She might be waking up with somebody." She winks, smirks, laughs. All of the above.

I ask Teddy, "Well, what do you think? Is eight weeks achievable?"

"Too achievable." He scowls darkly and jabs a thumb over his shoulder. "What if you get ahead of schedule? Don't forget about our thin wall."

"You'll be long gone," Melanie says to him dismissively. "What do you care."

"I guess I will be." To have the actual timeline of our remaining neighborly arrangement laid out for me in project software is quite daunting. All the more reason to lean into this process with diligence. There's got to be one single guy in this entire town who isn't planning on leaving ASAP.

Renata is struggling to cut into the firm cheddar. "Eight weeks is ridiculous. Find your person today." The frailty of her arm stretched between us does give me a moment of pause.

To ignore her advice is fairly arrogant, given how long she's been alive. I'm just considering whether an all-in approach is the better way forward when she loses her temper and says: "For God's sake, someone with bone density cut this cheese for me. Now, what about the Parloni Method." (We all brace ourselves.) "Go down to the bar and find someone whose teeth don't repulse you. Boy or girl, doesn't matter. Go home, take all your clothes off, roll around together. It's how we did things back in the day."

She holds out a regal hand until Teddy places a preloaded cracker in it. "I bet Panda Bear has rolled around in a fair few beds."

"That's sexual harassment," I remind her. "He's your employee."

Teddy just shrugs. "She can't harass me with the truth." Is he expecting me to be scandalized? I already knew that. There's no way a guy with this face and nuclear charm hasn't been in every kind of bed, from sleeping bag to four-poster.

I don't let myself look away. If I do, he'll think I'm an inexperienced little kid. Right now, in this light, his eyes are neither brown nor green. What's this in-between color called?

"But not lately," he promises me. "I don't roll around in beds anymore."

"I'll translate that for ya." Renata's gaze slides sideways to me and she tips all her wine into her mouth. Gulp. "He wants to roll around in your bed, Ruthie. Christ, does that sincere tone actually work out for you, Ted?"

Into the walkie-talkie, Teddy replies: "10–6, stand by on that, over."

I know why they're all laughing now. It's funny because my bed is not very roll-worthy. I laugh, too, to show I'm a good sport, but I think I'm blushing just the same. Would he even fit in my bed? Who am I kidding. He'd fit himself in anywhere.

Melanie takes me through my worksheet. She's put a lot of effort into it. When the air is getting chilly and the first mosquito makes its descent, Melanie turns to me as she gathers up her things. "I was wondering if I could ask you for a favor in return. You can say no."

I nod as I help Renata into her jacket. "Go ahead."

"With my contract ending in December, it's made me realize I want to find my dream job. I've been temping for so long, I think I've just confused myself about what I enjoy. Can you kinda do a Midona Method on me?"

My heart squeezes at the vulnerability in her voice. She has this much faith in me? And she's scared I'm about to say no? I think I'd walk through traffic for Melanie Sasaki.

"I only wish you'd asked me earlier, so I could have been as prepared as you were. How about this. You complete this worksheet, too, but for jobs. Turn-ons—what do you enjoy? Turnoffs—what will you never do? I'd love to help you find your dream job, Mel."

My eyes settle on the tortoise rehabilitation zone in my courtyard. Six-year-old me would be horrified to hear that administration is my "dream job." Little Kid Ruthie would have marched right into Teddy's living room and snatched up that *Reptiles for Dummies* book.

CHAPTER FOURTEEN

I think I'm going to host a monthly cheese party, here at Providence," I say to Teddy when my guests are gone and I'm carrying the almost-empty platter inside. "Did you know that I run a full seasonal activity program?"

His tone is dry as he lies on my couch. "Yes, Ms. Midona, I did know that." I drop a flyer down on his face anyway.

"The Christmas party here really goes off. I'm not even kidding. We invite residents from Bakersfield Retirement Home and I drive a minibus of really old men up here to even out the numbers. I have to do a second trip back in the morning. A walk of shame when you're over eighty is really, really slow."

I've got the oven preheating. Once I start filling the bath, my routine will be perfectly unaltered. Nothing unusual around here, except for the six-four real estate heir lying flat on my couch with his belt undone. His gigantic sneakers are kicked off like he lives here.

"So do you like the idea of a cheese party? I think the residents will love it."

"Sure. Everyone loves cheese." He flips through the channels. There's no smile on his mouth.

"Tell me what's wrong, Theodore." I sit on the end of the couch near his black-socked feet. I've affixed the Method worksheet onto a clipboard. "Mel's put a blank space here marked *Name*. Like she's got other clients and doesn't want to mix up the paperwork. Well, who am I to disobey a form." I write in RUTHIE MAREE MIDONA. "I have to write a list. I can do that."

"I just like it best when it's only you and me." He knows there's only room for one guy on this couch. "I've never had a place where the same thing happens every day. This is it."

"Providence is a little like that."

"No, I mean here. With you, the oven timer, and the pipes filling your bath. When I was growing up"—here, he breaks off, and this seems hard—"I usually didn't know where I was spending the night. Mom and Dad didn't really work out a custody arrangement, it was pretty ad hoc. Just whoever lost the coin toss got me."

"I wouldn't have coped with that."

"I barely did." He pulls himself up to nestle his shoulders into the throw pillows. I turn and do the same, and my legs fit between his. "I know I come off pretty flaky. I've just lived like this a long time. And I want this to last awhile longer."

We're like two people lying together in a bathtub. It feels like we've sat like this for years. He pulls the elastic from his hair and the sumptuous black coil sits on his shoulder like a pet. He looks like a man, muscled and animal. He says to the clipboard, "I won't like your list."

"Because the list won't be about you?" The way he blinks tells me *yes*. "Teddy, you are skating very close to gorgeous narcissist territory."

I tap the page with my pen. I'm going to ignore the sensation of his eyes on me and the way his energy tugs like a hand on my sleeve, asking me to look up.

"Gorgeous?"

"Your Honor, I rest my case." His legs are snuggling closer around mine. I'm trying hard to not smile. "Choose something to watch, please. You're driving me nuts changing that channel."

"Put on *Heaven Sent*. I know you have it, I can hear it through the wall." He begins singing part of the theme song: "'Whenever you're alone, I call your name, whenever you're lost, you know you'll get home—'"

Is he teasing? Blood makes my face hot. "Did you actually press your ear on the wall? I kept the volume so low I had to put subtitles on."

He nods and continues singing in a lovely voice (of course he can flippin' sing, what is he even bad at?). "'Life's got ups and downs, we play that game, but when will you learn?'"

Even me, with my heart of stone, cannot resist singing the last line with him. "'When will you learn, you're heaven sent?'" We even harmonize. I grin at him. "You think I'm a huge loser, right?" *Please just tell me you do.* Pop this helium feeling.

"If you're a loser, then I am too. I fucking love that show. Put on the one where Francine goes bra shopping." He keeps humming the theme song, tapping his toe against my hip. I look at the blank worksheet. I feel like I'm not going to like anything I write, either. If I don't get ahold of myself, it could easily look like this:

Turn-ons

- Tall
- Tattoos
- Those magic eyes
- That insanely good hair
- Quick smile/perfect teeth
- Talented hands that give and take

Turnoffs

- Anyone who isn't him

I'd better use a pencil and an eraser.

I haven't answered him. "I'm three seasons behind that episode. I always watch them in order. And I wouldn't let you watch that one anyway, you perv. Francine's supposed to be in high school."

He shrugs. "Hey, I was in high school, too, when it aired. My sisters and I never missed an episode. That was one thing

I could count on in my week. So where are we up to? We wouldn't want to mess up the special *Heaven Sent* system."

(Little does he know that, thanks to the worldwide rewatch hosted by my forum, there literally is a special system.)

"I only do an annual viewing, and if I watch them in order, it makes it more satisfying. The bigger story arcs build up so well."

"I'm sure, Tidy Girl." He grins to himself. "Only an annual viewing. Such restraint. Is this what you want to do with your dream man? Snuggling up, watching a churchy TV show? Does it remind you of home?"

We're interlocking our legs like this is normal. Sort of snuggling, now that he mentions it. The feel of another person, resting against me, warm and heavy? This is genuine heaven. "This was what I counted on each week, too. This routine of mine? It goes way back."

"How far?"

"Since . . ." I trail off but he nudges me with his foot to keep going. "My mom picks up produce from supermarkets and restaurants in the evenings. She's been doing it since I was around eight years old. A local business donated a van, it's all pretty professional. The food is distributed to soup kitchens and community organizations, and she doesn't get home until midnight."

"She was gone all night, then. But your dad was home."

"This is going to make me sound like a bad person." I hesitate. "I hated her being gone. After his day, Dad's tired, mad, distracted. He recharges himself with silence, and it wasn't comfortable between us. He'd usually be in his office at night."

"So you created your own nighttime routine." Teddy looks around the room and back at me with understanding. "And you knew when *Heaven Sent* would be on TV. You could count on it. Like me." A nice feeling of understanding glows between us.

"The other thing was, we usually had a stranger living in our house. There's an emergency room in the basement, with a bed for whoever needs it. I was a fragile kid. I couldn't deal with that, but I had to, because charity starts at home."

A stranger brushing their teeth in the bathroom. A stranger sitting in my chair at the breakfast table.

"You asked me when we first met if I had strict parents. I did, but I think they expected me to know how to do the right thing and left me alone to work it out. I think we've got a bit in common there."

"Your sacred bedtime Ruthie Ritual makes complete sense now. Maybe I should have done that, too."

"It's not too late to create a routine. Self-care as an adult is really important."

He's still thinking—about me, I think, because his eyes are on mine. "I'll just keep sliding into your routine until you get annoyed and lock your door on me. So that amazing care package you left for me in the courtyard. You've done that a few times, huh? And this is why having me turn up out of the blue has been hard for you."

I feel a little ashamed of myself. On the inside, I've been nothing but grudging charity. "Not hard, exactly."

"It's okay, I get it. Things are less peaceful with me around."

"Who's told you that?" I ask, but he's finding the next episode of *Heaven Sent*. "You're not going to talk through the episodes, are you? Wait, I thought of something to put in the deal breakers column." I write on the form: Doesn't like *Heaven Sent*.

Teddy performs an ab-trembling sit-up, reads what I wrote, then lies back down with a satisfied groan. "My sisters used to slap my ear if I talked. You can do that if you want."

I press play and we sing the theme song together. I grab a knitted throw blanket for my lap and Teddy grabs the other end. We tug-of-war and laugh. How did this happen so easily?

One episode ends, the next begins. I put two chicken cordon bleus into the oven instead of one. I thought silence was all I would tolerate, but I enjoy talking during the episodes. He only offers good, funny observations at the right moment.

Including one observation I might steal as a debate prompt in my Heaven Sent You Here forum.

"I thought I was going to marry Francine Percival back in the day. She was my dream girl," Teddy says when the credits roll and I hand him a plate of food. "Oh wow. I could get used to this." Both statements ding a warning bell inside my brain.

"What is it about Francine you like? Other than the obvious." The actress is now the face of a French cosmetics brand. This is a test for Teddy.

"She's so neat and tidy."

"Oh." The same words Renata used to describe me, but now they're said in his lovely husky voice. I put my plate on the coffee table and pick up my clipboard. In the turn-ons I write *Honesty*. Then I write, *Good listener. Confident.*

"She's so reserved," he continues as he eats. "I feel like she's got so much going on below the surface, but nothing outwardly surprises her character. She's self-controlled. Messes like me find that really intriguing. She's funny as hell in that good, dry way that I'm addicted to. Almost every laugh in this show is because of her."

I'm surprised by his insight. "I like that about her too. There's this episode when she gets her wisdom teeth out, and her crush Ash Dangerfield visits her in hospital—"

"Oh yeah, and she's waking up from the anesthetic." Teddy grins. "Francine's telling him the truth. No filter. God, I should be so lucky."

"She's ridiculous in that scene, but she's still somehow dignified. Francine can handle anything. It's liberating to talk about this out loud. I haven't found anyone in real life who watches this show, let alone a guy."

I go back to my clipboard and try to think of nonincriminating things to write in the turn-ons column. *Reliable. Mature. Insightful.* All those things could still be applied to Teddy in various ways. He's jumped through every flaming hoop that Renata has set up for him, and he's been admirably dedicated to his new job.

"Guys like me," Teddy says, and my tummy takes a dangerous dip, "wonder what it would take to get a girl like Francine all . . ." He forks up a huge mouthful of food. "All messy," is what he goes with when he swallows. "Uncontrolled and kinda wild. What would it take to get her there?" He's got those hot eyes again.

"I'm sure you wonder about that all the time." I hold the clipboard away when he tries to reach for it. This clipboard will confirm his suspicions. "No. Mind your own business."

"What'd you write?" The paw marked TAKE makes another swipe. "We share everything, remember?" I left the front door open, so I can't be surprised to have this big black kitty curled up on my couch now.

"Never mind." I switch to the next column. "Might as well think of a few turnoffs."

"You were just sitting there writing turn-ons? Fuck me. Scandalized." He puts his empty plate on the coffee table and slides down to lie flat, his socked feet in my lap and a forearm across his eyes. "I love it in here. Let me stay."

"What, for tonight?"

"Forever." It's declared sincerely. He looks at my untouched plate and licks the corner of his lips.

I pinch the bridge of my nose. "You can't keep saying things like that to me."

"Why not?"

"I'll . . ." I can't think of what to say.

"What." He's daring me. "Say it."

"I'll get too used to you being here." I wonder how many other girls' cushions he's curled up on. "Who was your last Good Samaritan?"

"What do you mean?"

"In the meeting, your dad said that you ran out of couches. You also said Good Samaritans were usually female."

He blinks a few times like he's mentally changing gears. "Not always. I had to bounce off a couple of guys I went to school with until I swallowed my pride and called old Papa Prescott." He pulls his feet out of my lap. "I don't like thinking about this."

He sits up, takes my unguarded clipboard, and lies back to read it.

"Boring as shit," he declares after a second. "This is what you want? This is your dream guy? Give me the pen. I wanna make some amendments." His eyes read, back and forth, a scowl I've never seen on his face. "Now this is someone who's never been late for rent in his life."

"Me, and what I want, is a ridiculous joke?" I slash an imaginary line across my knuckles. "I mean, I know you've got TAKE permanently inked on your body, but it really isn't an attractive quality."

"Generosity is underlined twice. Your dream man is a model of charity and virtue."

When I wrote that, I was thinking about how generosity takes many forms. Teddy is lavish with his attention and care. I try to take the clipboard again.

"You should learn how to take." He holds up a finger to silence whatever retort I'm trying to formulate. "Saint Ruthie of Providence needs to learn how to get selfish."

"Well, you're the perfect person to teach me."

"You could always take the option Renata suggested. Don't pretend you don't know what I mean." He spirals a finger at the dark doorway at the end of the room. "I've been dreaming about snuggling under your patchwork quilt. Please wake me up in time for work."

"Don't joke about this."

"I dare you," he says and for once, his hypnotizing charm-voice penetrates the shield I hold up around him. "What does it take for your composure to slip? You feel this, I know you do."

"Is this what you normally do? What you've suggested is not very romantic."

"It's true, I've never been accused of being romantic, but I think I'll love kissing you. That's all we'll do. Just kiss and I get to sleep in your bed tonight. I think that's pretty romantic."

Is the entire dating scene like this? Brutal honesty and possible nudity? I think I am so far out of my depth it's crazy. I tap the clipboard. "I think I'd better stick with this. This is something I can deal with. It's a process, it's got bullet points."

His eyes are unreadable in the half light as he leans down to put on his sneakers. "Gonna ask you a question and I know the answer. But just tell me. Are you ever going to leave Providence?"

Reflexively without thinking, I say, "Of course not."

"Yeah." He says that so sadly. "I get it now. I'll leave you alone."

CHAPTER FIFTEEN

At the swimming pool, I begin the arduous process of unloading the residents from the minibus. I'm struggling up the front path weighed down by purses, gym bags, and, worryingly, two forgotten walking sticks. Teddy is leaning against the front wall in board shorts and a tank top. He's wearing a visor that has FRESH MEAT printed on it. Undoubtedly a gift from Renata. "Here . . ." He smiles, pushing off the wall. "Let me help."

"What are you doing here?" I haven't seen him much over the last couple of days.

"We," he emphasizes, "are joining in for aqua aerobics. Well, I am anyway. The Parlonis will heckle me. They're inside." As he untangles bags from me and I grow lighter, I try not to look at the new tattoos revealed on this fabulous set of arms.

We walk inside and I greet Jordan, one of the assistant managers. "We've got twelve today. No, wait, thirteen." I indicate Teddy. "Plus two spectators."

"Aqua aerobics?" Jordan says to Teddy, face scrunched in skepticism.

"Just trying to keep my shit tight," Teddy replies airily and walks in through the sliding doors.

"I need you to take this." Jordan fishes a folded twenty-dollar bill out of his shorts pocket as we walk together into the pool area. "The really rude old lady gave this to me on the way in. She acted like I was a fancy hotel doorman or something." Jordan's eyeline is on Teddy now. "Is he her grandson?"

"Personal assistant."

"Yeah, well, he needs to notice she's handing out cash left and right. It doesn't sit well with me." Jordan hands it to me. "Get it back to her, okay?"

"Sure." He's so honest. It pings my memory back to my worksheet I submitted to Melanie this morning. Honesty is a turn-on. So is the protective bristling he has over the elderly patrons. Is this what it feels like to have a radar? I let him hold eye contact with me, but I feel nothing inside.

I look over at Teddy and realize my radar is calibrated very specifically.

I ask, "Where's Sandy?" She's usually poolside, ready to teach the class. Jordan excuses himself to go and call her. Teddy is marooned by the bleachers, covered in purses. I make my way over to him.

All in all, today's going great. Teddy's going to take that tank top off and drench himself, head to toe. I'm probably going to watch. This is all happening during work hours. Life is a gift. I'm smiling when I join him, holding out my arms for the bags.

"Did he just give you his phone number?" Teddy's indignant.

"No, he gave me back the twenty bucks Renata tipped him just for existing." I shoulder the bags. "I hope she doesn't do that a lot."

"She only tips good-looking people. It's a rule she has."

"Well, great. She's never tipped me once." I hang the bags in the change room. We're talking like things are back to normal. Renata and Aggie are seated on the sidelines, both looking lively and distracted. I'm easily able to slip the money back into Renata's purse—a Hermès Birkin, tossed like a lunch sack on the wet concrete.

"I forgot how cold and hard bleachers feel," Renata tells me, in a tone like everything's my fault. "And what chlorine smells like. I wish I'd never come at all, but Theodore insisted. Well, what are you waiting for?" She points at the pool. "Go on, get in, show me your doggy paddle."

"I usually stay out. That way I can see if anyone's struggling." I fold up some towels into cushions for them both to sit on.

"What's this I'm hearing about Providence being developed? It's all the old folk are talking about." Renata does not include herself in that demographic. "Inside scoop, please. Gossip is currency."

"I don't know. The Prescott family owns the site and they're conducting a site review. Could you talk to Teddy? I've been really hoping he'd become an ally for Providence in whatever's coming up."

She thinks this over. "I don't know. Maybe it would be the push Aggie needs to get out of this place. Central Park views would make her feel years younger."

Aggie sighs deeply and does not reply. She is methodically scraping at a scratch card with her famous lucky penny that she's had since she was a child.

"I need him to fall in love. With Providence," I amend just as Renata's eyebrows ratchet up.

I turn right as Teddy's fist twists in the bottom of his tank and pulls up. A big cheer rises up from the dirty old pervs in the water. I guess I'm looking like I'm going through something, because Renata says to me, "I want an exact description of what you're feeling."

"I'm praying that his front isn't as nice as his back." Mainly, I'm just praying. He's honey smooth. Tattoos everywhere, cut off under the waistband of his board shorts, all of them silly and perfectly done. He is a fresh coloring book and I'm a neat, tidy girl who thoroughly stays between every line.

He turns around, balling up his tank. "You getting in?"

"Goddamn it," I blaspheme reflexively, because:

- The front half of his torso is good, I mean,
- So, so good,
- So, so, so *good*.

"Pardon?" Teddy walks over, and I'm shrinking backward into the bleachers. "Oh, I get it, Ruthie's fainting at the sight of my magnificence." (Yes.) "You getting in?" He hooks his finger under the peeking-out strap of my bland one-piece swimsuit. "This looks like you're thinking about it."

I am very close to falling face first into a kaleidoscope of tattooed skin so I puff up defensively. "Sylvia doesn't pay me to actually participate. I'm working." It had occurred to me when I was getting ready for today that this might be one of my last chances to come back smelling faintly of chlorine.

"Sylvia doesn't pay you to run an entire activities program, but here we are," Teddy counters patiently. "Get in. Experience something." It's so hot in here I envy his shirtless state. At least, that's how I've decided to label my intense torso-interest.

Jordan approaches. "Sandy's running ten minutes late. If you can get them to just start warming up, that'd be great. I've got to stay on the front desk. Just get them to tread water or something."

"Sure, I can do that. Okay, ladies. Sandy's running a bit behind, so we'll start." I could lead an entire half-hour class. Maybe I've been waiting for this moment. After the warm-up, will I transition them into flutter kicks or leg lifts? Before I can decide, I'm interrupted.

"Teddy can teach aqua aerobics," Renata says from behind us. "What do you think, girls?" A big cheer goes up. She cackles. "This oughta be good for a laugh."

"Stand aside," Teddy says to me as he twists his hair into a bun worthy of a cool magazine photo shoot. His torso moves and flexes with the movement and I need to lower myself onto a tranquilizer dart. "It's time for me to get these women warmed up."

"Already am," someone calls out and the screams of laughter almost deafen me.

"Okay, let's get started. Walk on the spot." They're all smiling, faces tipped up to him like sunflowers, water roiling. "Swish your arms like this." He demonstrates.

Of course he's good at this. I make a long echoing noise like *urgggggggg*.

Anything I can do with complete competence, a young man can do with less technical ability but more fanfare. I've never gotten a cheer, not once. I don't think anyone even notices a single thing I do for them. I've still got marks on my arms from all the purses they hung on me.

"Don't look so grouchy, Ruthie Maree," Aggie says to me when I go to sit with them on the bleachers. "What's wrong?"

"He's so annoying." I glare at his beautiful back and blot my face with my T-shirt. "I've arranged this entire thing and come to every session for two years, and he thinks he can just . . ." I lose my words when he begins to do that walk-like-an-Egyptian dance along the edge of the pool.

To stop myself from cracking a smile, I say with temper, "He's. So. Damn. Funny." I bury my face in my folded arms.

I peek up because Renata has been silent throughout this; she's captivated by the poolside shenanigans, bouncing on her tiny butt, imagining herself doing the moves. She walks like a seated Egyptian. It's heartbreakingly sweet and I think she loves Teddy to pieces.

Then she ruins it. "Why's everything a big deal with you?"

Renata ponders at her usual volume. "Just do it. You're a super-model next to all those saggy old hens."

(Some of those hens look as if they would drown her if they could.)

"Fine, fine." I pull my T-shirt off over my head, step out of my shorts, and plunge myself in before I have another thought about it. How long has it been since I stepped into icy water? Years.

When I surface, I try very hard to not objectify Teddy, but the fluorescent lights are giving the flat planes of his muscles a heavenly glow, and cutting darker shadows between them. It's inexplicable that such an unhurried, cheese-eating person has a body like this. But he does, and what a treat. I lose strength in my legs and I sink down to my eyeballs.

"Please welcome to the class Miss Ruthie Midona," he tells the group, and now I'm getting the smiles and cheers.

I get it now. Life requires full, up-to-the-neck participation. And for the next few minutes, we obey Teddy as our instructor. Every dance move he can think of, we're doing it. We're moonwalking. We're doing the twist. We're singing lyrics. The Parlonis are clapping along. We're all shrieking with laughter and half drowning, and I'm not as fit as I thought. But I'm having the most fun I've had in years.

"You must be Sandy," Teddy says when our regular instructor arrives all sweating and flustered. "I kept them all nice and warm for you." And with that, he performs an illegal cannon-ball that almost wets the ceiling and swims up to me. "Can you believe we're being paid to do this?" he says, scraping his hands up his face.

I really can't believe it. On a weekday midmorning, earning actual money, we do aqua aerobics.

I didn't know that guys could be so open to try new things. But Teddy is. He's either laughing, or earnestly concentrating with a crease on his brow. His arm curls are magnificent. We line up against the side to perform push-ups and he doesn't notice how the oldies angle for a space either side of him. No one needs to get jealous; he mingles and shares himself around. For anyone getting tired, he provides a shoulder to hang on to. I am almost needing it myself.

I know he's being paid for this, but really the bare minimum required of him was to drive the Parlonis here. The way he spreads around his energy and kindness is so generous. He's completely, deep-down lovely, standing there with elderly ladies hanging on his shoulders, just so they can feel that kind of youth and beauty firsthand.

It's sad that he doesn't realize how generous he really is.

We're allowed ten minutes of free time after the class and we hand around pool noodles for floating. I think I should get out, so I can get dressed and position myself to help, but Teddy might watch the extraction process. I wait for a minute, hoping he might haul himself out and wander off, but he's enjoying himself too much. He's got a floatation ring around his neck and is carrying Mrs. Washington piggyback through the water. She looks like she could die happy tonight.

I didn't think this through. I'd be climbing that ladder into the heaven-bright light, water streaming down my butt and thighs. I haven't worn this swimsuit in years and it's shrunk up my crack. The backs of my knees are really weird. I'm completely stuck in this moment I should never have stolen to begin with.

"What's up?" Teddy swims over to me, his passenger now dismounted. "You look like you need to pee. Hold it in, girl. Think dry thoughts."

"Come on, you know I'm not a rule breaker."

"I'd say I'm relieved, but . . ." He laughs until I worry for his own bladder. Now he swims around me in a circle. "But seriously, what's up? You're stressin'."

"When I get out of this pool, I want you to close your eyes."

He covers his face. A sparkling hazel eye peeps through a big gap in his fingers. My laugh turns up his wattage. His hand drops away, revealing saucy eyebrows. "What's the big deal?"

"Gravity's the big deal." We're very close, but there's something about floating that makes it feel okay. "Not everyone looks like you in their swimwear."

"You flatter me." We're now floating closer, our hands making circles in the water, knees sometimes touching. "Do you think I'm a bit pretty, Ruthie Maree?"

I'm starting to get out of breath. "What's it like being so self-confident?" I sink lower in the water.

"It's just how I feel when I'm with you. But then I can't seem to get the reaction I want from you, and I start doubting myself. Then I look at my reflection in a spoon and I'm an abomination. By dinnertime I'm a wreck and the ugliest man in existence." He seems to bite off this torrent midstream and closes his eyes for a second like he's exasperated. "I say the stupidest stuff to you. Why does this keep happening? I'm actually really normal and cool."

I nod sagely. "I want to believe you."

He goes completely still, because he's tall enough to stand on the bottom. He puts my hand on his shoulder like I need assistance and a rest. Accurate. His eyelashes are crisscrossed spikes. Under my palm there's a lit match inked onto him, and I feel that tiny spark.

His lip lifts in amusement. "Now you're making me feel pretty."

"As if you need little old me to pump up your ego."

"Oh, but I do."

Keeping the smile off my face around him is turning me into a medically certified killjoy. But if I relax, what will happen? He'll be unstoppable. He'll annihilate me.

"Hands where we can see them," one of the residents shouts at us, and the shrieks of laughter echo off every reflective surface.

"Okay," I hold my other hand up, and the laugh gets louder. "They honestly suspect me of feeling you up on a workday? Dirty old women." The cogs turn in my brain. "Oh. They were talking to you."

"You have a guilty conscience, don't you? Where were we. Oh yeah, self-confidence. You gotta start walking around like you're the shit, because you are," he tells me, gathering up my hand and walking me in an improvised backward water waltz. "Want to hear a secret?" Even before he opens his mouth, I see the compliment coming straight for me like a shark fin. "Neat and tidy is my absolute favorite kind of girl."

I don't know how he can switch modes so easily. He was just horsing around poolside. Now, he's got darkening eyes and that seductive husk in his voice.

I decide to try swimming for shore. "Okay." I'm twirled out to the length of his arm, the water churning around us.

"But you don't believe me." He pulls me back, closer this time. "Your eyes are . . ." He blinks away from me now. Why would he feel self-conscious? He does, and it flips my heart. "Magnetic," is what he goes with. Then he groans at himself. "I'm corny as fuck." He dips down under the water for a bit.

When he resurfaces, I say sternly, "You've found the only female under the age of fifty in the building to mess around with. That's what this is."

But it's too late. A flattered sizzle goes down my spine at the exact moment that he puts his hand low down on my back, only a wafer of wet fabric between us.

"Learn to take a compliment. Appreciate yourself. You're sublime." That's the last word I ever thought would be applied to me.

"That's kind of you to say."

"Oh, I'm not kind. I nearly reverted to my old ways the other night, at your place. You should know my secret. I have a major Heaven-Sent-Francine-Percival kink."

"Okay, well, she is gorgeous."

"I love neat-and-tidy types who have label makers and smell like a bubble bath. All the soup cans in the cupboard with the labels facing the same way. The bath filling up at the same time every night. God, you walk around in this haze of bubbles. I just want to eat all your cheese and snuggle up in your bed. I can admit it."

"I'm pretty aware of that." My throat is making my voice weird. That was too many lush words for me to process. Bubbles, kink, snuggle, bed.

"You feel it, right?" His mask slips for a second as he looks down at my floating legs. Maybe he's considering the possibility that he's alone in this. "I think we've got an interesting sizzle."

I look at the word *GIVE*, written on his skin forever. He's always so brave. I'm going to try to be more like him.

I put my hand under his chin to tip his face up for my inspection, and his mouth opens in surprise. I look at his lips and the porcelain sharpness of his teeth. His stubble feels like wet sand on my palm. Men: so animal, growing bristles and beards. It must be a lot of effort to disguise it.

I decide to give him what he craves so badly. It's not exactly my well-kept secret. "Teddy, you're so pretty it's crazy."

Instantly he replies, "You're so pretty I need to buy a pencil sharpener."

He looks at my mouth and his pupils dial out, ink black, and everything on the edges of this moment washes away. I think he's going to kiss me. I've only just come out of romance retirement and I'm very inexperienced, but even I know that this is it.

I swear, he's going to do it. Another inch closer.

I haven't been kissed in years, and those were largely tongue-less. I don't remember how to, but Teddy does. We are suspended in this buoyant moment, knees touching. Then it's like he remembers something, blinking out of the building haze. Now we're floating a respectable distance apart.

To cover up the weird mix of disappointment and relief I'm feeling, I say, "I know you just want to defend your couch and cheddar territory." I'm getting fatigued and am sinking down to my chin in the water.

"According to your own Week 1 worksheet, which I photocopied and is now in the back pocket of my jeans, your dream guy is nothing like me. You want someone who'll stick around. Mature, generous, principled."

His fist is solemnly offered to me; I don't check which hand it is. I just rub the knuckles like a comfort. "You didn't have to make an ass of yourself just now, but it made their day. You just made a difference to a lot of people." I watch him turn over my words. "You've been interested in what goes on inside my head, and that means more than I can say."

"What's going on here?" Renata bawls from the sideline. "What did I talk to you about, at length, Theodore Prescott?" She gets to her feet and walks to the edge. I stare at the wet tiles beneath her feet with my heart even further up my throat.

Teddy looks back into my eyes. "Don't seduce Ruthie if I don't plan on sticking around, because she's a tender treasure that must be protected at all costs."

Renata barks: "Correct. And what are you doing right now?"

Second First Impression

"I'm explaining to her that I'm not her type," he says easily as he strokes through the water, away from me.

"Damn right. Get out of the pool. Now." Renata says it in a voice that cannot be disobeyed, and just like that, Teddy's up the ladder, leaving me to eventually climb up myself. Out of that cold water, on dry land, I sweat and shiver for the rest of the afternoon.

CHAPTER SIXTEEN

"You did good," Melanie says with her head inside my closet. "Your first worksheet was excellent. You were really honest about your dream man."

(Was I, though?)

"Thanks, Mel. And yours looks good too." I am sitting on my bed, reading her version of the worksheet: the dream job edition. "I think what I'm seeing here is that you don't like any job where the days are the same."

"Yeah. It makes me start to feel like I'm decaying." She tosses a handful of clothes on the bed, still on their hangers. "But don't try to distract me. We're talking about you. Bring on the Sasaki Method, Week 2."

My swimsuit is on a hanger from the curtain rail. It's been dry for three days now, but I haven't put it away because it's a reminder that what happened between Teddy and me was real.

I changed when I jumped in that pool. I got younger.

I've soaked myself in something that has made my skin sensitive. I've been breathless ever since we swam in the same water and he told me words like *sublime, sizzle, magnetic.* I need to walk around naked for a few minutes to recalibrate myself, but the moment I even touch a button or zip, he's knocking on my front door, asking to borrow something.

A knife, fork, plate, and frying pan have all gone next door. After dinner, he appropriates a squirt of washing-up detergent. He leans in my doorway drying my things with my dishcloth, telling me about the ridiculous tasks he performed for Renata, and I can't stop staring at the toes of his boots on the threshold to my apartment. He's creating a boundary for us. The fact that he sees a need to? I get a delicious shiver in my stomach.

Without thought I tell Melanie, "Teddy's made me doubt this whole project."

"Did you just tell me to my face that Teddy Prescott is making you doubt me and my Method?" Melanie throws a tweed blazer onto the bed with violence. "You're going to take advice from a man-child like him?"

I am compelled to defend him. "That's harsh."

"It's accurate." She holds up a blouse and makes a face. "Remember, he's a test. You need to stay strong and resist the urge."

"There's no urge," I begin to lie, but she holds up a hand.

"My mother says in any relationship, there's an adorer and an adoree. One who loves, and the one who is loved. You'll need to know which one you are."

"Adorer. Adore-ee." I sound out the unfamiliar made-up

word. I think of my mom and dad. That's pretty clear-cut. He doesn't even buy her a birthday present; she bakes him a triple-layered cake. "Give and take."

"Exactly. Theodore Prescott is permanently on the hunt for an adorer. And he will take all the adoration until you have no more. Then, like a big old honeybee, off he'll go, buzz, buzz, buzz . . ."

Teddy'd probably agree, but I wish she'd stop. "Just warning you, if he's home, he can hear you through the wall. He says bless-you when I sneeze."

Melanie makes a dismissive sound like *pffft*. "If he were home, he'd be here right now, lying on your bed with his head on your knee, trying to get you to notice how good-looking he is." She considers what she just said. "He lives to make you laugh. That's a direct quote."

I'm desperate to talk through this situation with someone. Is this my segue? "I wonder if he means the things he says to me."

Like a karate instructor, Mel barks: "Who cares. He's not your type."

So I've been told, by the man himself. "Is he . . . your type?"

(I mean, come on. He's everyone's type. Except mine, apparently.)

She considers it briefly, and I feel like something important is hanging in the balance. If Melanie decides she wants him, I will have to . . . I don't know what, exactly. Step aside? But I'm not standing in her way. I'll have to go dig a hole with my bare hands under Renata's lemon tree and attempt to bury this dazzle, two feet deep.

And I would do it, despite how much it would hurt. But only for Mel.

She shakes her head. "I mean, he's gorgeous, but the moment I met him I knew there's only room in my world for one gorgeous high-maintenance princess. And that's me. I'm looking for an adorer." She runs her fingers through her ponytail. "We'd have too much resentment between us. Hey, what's that ugly old bike parked out in the courtyard? I can't imagine he'd be caught dead on that."

"Don't let him hear you talk like that. He calls it the Dream Girl." Jealous of a motorbike: an unexpected personal low. "He got it out of storage. It's a 1939 Indian he inherited from his grandpa. They restored it together before he died, but Teddy needs to fix a few things on it. I'm pretty sure if it starts raining he'll bring it into his living room." I check the weather app.

He's working on it because he said he needs to keep busy at night. To keep himself out of my cottage. Said to my face so honestly, with a gleam in his eye.

"You sure do seem to know everything about him," Melanie remarks as she continues to judge all my clothes. The evaluation can be summarized as: nope, yuck, granny, hmm, maybe, why.

"He tells me everything." I am thinking over what she said. "You really think he's high maintenance? In terms of his needs, they're pretty basic. Just laugh at his jokes, make a lot of eye contact when he's telling you stories, and let him eat that container of leftover pasta in your fridge."

"Spoken like a true adorer." Melanie smells the armpit of my winter coat, like that's a normal thing to do. She checks the care label and the coat is put on the bed. "Don't let him take too much from you. He's shameless."

"He borrowed a drop of olive oil last night. I have no idea how I'm getting that back." I'm beginning to think life would be easier if I left my front door unlocked. "But he gives me things, too, all the time."

Flat, she challenges: "Like what."

Melanie will be hard to impress with any of the ephemera that Teddy presents me with. He picks me dahlias from the bank of the lake. Sure, I planted them so they're sort of mine already, but he doesn't know that. He drew red lipstick hearts on my rehab tortoises. He swept the leaves from the courtyard. Gingersnap cookies, still warm from the Parlonis' oven.

My favorites have been the little artworks he's created for me on the backs of receipts and menus. In the blank space in between Hawaiian Supreme and Mega Meatlovers, he drew a girl in a bathtub. *I'm gonna design you the perfect tattoo, it's just taking a while.*

He's a beautiful black cat, dropping feathers and ivy leaves on my doormat. He's given me nothing but kindness, friendship, and the diamond sparkles in his tortoiseshell eyes. In my tiny universe, he's showered me in riches.

"Still waiting to hear one single thing he's given you. Something that cost money in a store." When I hesitate, Melanie throws her hands in the air. "Ruthie, this is why I worry about you. You're too charitable, and he's going to be gone sooner than we think."

My stomach dips unhappily. "Did he say something?"

"No, but we know by now he lands on his feet. Knowing him, he'll find the exact money to buy into the tattoo studio on the street in a paper bag." Melanie opens my underwear drawer. Then closes it with a rueful headshake. "I need you to not get your feelings hurt by him, Ruthie. Don't forget, his family's company might be coming for this place, and he won't do a thing to help."

Anxiety spikes in me. "We don't know that PDC is going to be trouble."

"I read that binder of boring media printouts about PDC you gave me ages ago. I also found an interview with Jerry on-line. He was talking about that *life is change* crap he gave us in the first meeting. I thought he was just giving us an old-white-boss pep talk, but he really believes it. They don't buy sites and keep them the same."

To keep calm, I pick up a silk blouse off the bed and fold it carefully on my lap. "Providence is special, though, and it's managed perfectly. They'll see."

"I've worked a lot of places and the writing is on the wall. This place is going to change. You might get evicted. Teddy will be gone, and so will I. I mean, I'll only be a phone call away, and we'll still hang out. But I need to make sure you're going to be okay. Because I am your adorer."

In my tiny universe, I have never been this lucky.

Before I realize it, I've put my head down and I'm praying. The old reflex comes usually at selfish times—*Please God, let me get a good parking space.* But now I'm moved out of gratitude. For the first time in years, I'm thanking God for bringing these two people to me. I don't care that one day I will be sad. I have so much.

The silk shirt on my lap has a few hot wet dots on it now.

"According to your worksheet, you want someone strong and mature. Someone to show up for you and to support you when things get hard." Mel takes the folded silk shirt away from me, patting the tears. "It's your turn to get taken care of now. You deserve it."

With an emotion-thick voice I manage to say, "Maybe you should study to become a therapist." I make a note on her worksheet.

"Add it to my list of possibilities." She hums around for a few minutes until she seems to have finished in my wardrobe. "Okay. So this is the keep category." Just as I melt with relief— the pile on the bed is huge—she points backward at the tiny capsule collection that remains hanging in my closet.

"Mel, are you telling me that I cannot keep all my stuff?" Each has a memory attached; a moment of triumph when I found each on the thrift store rack. "This is a pure silk shirt. It had its tags."

She doesn't remotely care. "It's all going back where you found it. Everything here is just . . . old. These browns and yellowy-creams are not your colors. No offense."

I do take offense at the way she lifts the waistband of a wool skirt on one finger like disgusting seaweed. "I don't get paid enough to replace an entire wardrobe in one day. I can say that everything on this bed was a good purchase."

"You don't even own jeans, do you? You can wear this tonight"—she unhooks a black funeral dress out of the wardrobe and holds it up—"for your second-week activity." With ceremony, she takes a sheet out of her folder. Then she with-holds it.

"Teddy tried to get an early look at the full Sasaki Method. I caught him trying to log into my computer. He played the son-of-the-boss card. It was so undignified." She pulls a face at the memory. "He was all sweaty, trying to work out what we're going to do next."

"That reminds me. I know he got a copy of my first work-sheet from you."

"I truly don't know how that happened. He asked to read it, I told him to get lost. Then there was a giant Snickers in front of me. Then he was gone. I'm slightly sure he's a wizard or a vampire." She shakes herself out of the memory fog with some difficulty. Poor kid.

"I'm sure he came and saw you midafternoon, too, right when you're weakest. He's hard to resist."

"But you do." She considers that. "It's why he can't stop hounding you. He's never had a challenge before. From now on, let's get secretive so he doesn't sabotage everything."

I scan through the new Week 2 worksheet, which is largely blank, with lines added for writing. I look up at her. I'm not sure I completely understand the point of this. "All I have to do is go sit somewhere by myself for an hour and fill this out?"

"A place where people your age hang out. That's it. And while you're there, you're going to write about who Ruthie Midona is. I want you on a page. On dates, you need to be able to describe yourself quickly and positively. Like a job interview."

"You haven't organized some sort of surprise, have you? Is a male stripper going to come up to me?"

She laughs until she has to wipe her eyes. "I'll save that for Week 3."

"Sit by myself and fill out a worksheet." I ponder this. I don't know where I'll go. "Am I actually this sad?"

"You're not sad. You've got anxiety issues about leaving Providence and you're a door locker. Yes, I've noticed, and no, it's nothing to be embarrassed about. You like checklists and lists, so I thought this way would distract you. But being alone and off-site will be enough of a push outside your comfort zone. I've thought about this a lot, and I know you can do it."

She's really firm about this, holding my gaze, and I get that same rush of relief when I received my first worksheet. She's tailored it to my abilities with such care. "I'm really grateful you're taking the time—" I try to begin to describe my feelings, but she just waves her hands like my words are smoke.

"Don't forget, you're helping me back. What should I do?" She takes out a second copy of the worksheet and hands it to me.

I take a pen and amend the paragraph of instructions slightly. "I'd like to read about what you want your life to look like in ten years. I think maybe if we know where you want to end up, we can start to work backward."

"Ten years," she marvels. "I'll be thirty-two. Ancient." She hasn't looked around Providence lately if she thinks that.

"Put thought into where you want to live, what kind of house you have, whether you work full-time, part-time. Pretend that you're in an interview session in ten years, and they ask you about yourself."

She nods and puts the sheet away carefully. As she gathers up her things to leave, she says, "I'm going to give you a spoiler for next week. We're going clothes shopping at the thrift store, so put that in your diary for next Friday night. We are picking out some things that are more age-appropriate. Start to bag these up, okay? No cheating."

She turns and takes a photo of what remains. She counts the hangers. Nothing gets past her.

"No cheating. I promise." I am completely indoctrinated into her Sasaki Method cult.

"I'll have a draft of your new dating profile ready by Monday, so buckle up, buttercup. We are going to push the button on that, and we'll be off to the races." Over her shoulder she says, "And for the love of God, buy some new underwear."

Off she goes and I'm struck by how she has a bounce in her step. I think Melanie innately knows what Teddy told me: *Walk around like you're the shit.* Feel beautiful. Be sure of it. I can only dream of being as young as Melanie Sasaki.

But with her on my side, maybe I can get back to twenty-five again. She has put so much effort into helping me, more than anyone ever has. I owe it to her to apply myself to this process of self-discovery. There's no way she wouldn't be warning me so strongly off Teddy if it wasn't a total disaster on my horizon.

I go back inside, pick up her completed career worksheet, and begin to research careers to make a short list for her, so I have some hope of repaying her kindness.

CHAPTER SEVENTEEN

This building has a chalkboard sign by the door that has a hand-drawn picture of a plate. Stacked on top is a mess of chalk lines, some curved macaroni bits, and a protruding and phallic hot dog. Above it, in bold letters is: COME AND TRY OUR FRANKENFRIES.

It took me just over an hour to make it to Memory Lanes Bowling Alley. That sounds bad when you learn that the bowling alley is a sedate seven-minute drive from Providence, but my hatchback was surprised to see me and slow to start.

Then I had to dash back up to check my cottage door. Then I sat in my running car and approved some new forum members. I listened to a five-minute meditation. I left and drove back (twice). But I'm here now, and I consider this evening to be a victory.

I get a text from Teddy: Where r u? I'm lonely. I suspect he is hungry. Before I can reply, he begins compulsively texting, and the following are received in the space of a minute:

- My 1939 Dream Girl won't talk to me
- I am forming a search party with hounds
- Your little Turtle Mobile is gone
- Are you on a date????
- Drowning myself immediately in my bathtub
- Update—drowning in YOUR bathtub, I like it better

I'm laughing in my car like a dweeb. What was his original question? Where am I? I'm lonely for him, too. Before he can do anything rash, I reply: I'm out doing my homework. I send him a photo of the chalkboard.

A bunch of kids run past me inside the bowling alley, squealing with laughter. This was a good, safe choice. I'm not good at selfies, but I manage to get myself and the bowling alley sign into the same angled shot, which will serve as proof of attendance for Melanie. I'm even wearing the designated black dress and the cool evening air feels unfamiliar on my bare arms.

"ID," the bartender calls out in a forbidding voice when I reach the top of the stairs.

"Wow, okay," I reply and hand it to him. "I'm twenty-five."

He checks it, rechecks it, then chuffs a laugh. "You look about twelve."

I'll take being mistaken for twelve over a Golden Girls cosplayer any day. As I tuck my ID back into my purse I briefly consider getting wasted. Maybe I'll drink straight from that bottle of green stuff back there. I'll leave my car here all night and order my first ever Uber home. I'll crawl up the path to my cottage behind the tortoises. Maybe they'll eat my corpse.

"Can I get the Frankenfries and a regular Coke, please." Witness me, cutting loose.

The bartender is doubtful as he looks around me. "You by yourself? The Frankenfries are designed for a group of people. It's a very big portion. Doesn't make great leftovers."

I absolutely bet Teddy will eat the leftovers when I bring them home. He's like a vulture, picking at the carrion left behind by the Parlonis. I put my money on the counter and the transaction is completed.

With my glass of strong black aspirin in hand, I decide on a booth. Should I go beside that group of men, or that group of women? I choose the women, probably defeating the purpose of the Sasaki Method. The bartender shouldn't have felt so sorry for me. I have two great friends, they're just not here.

Oh, shit. I haven't messaged my forum friends in . . . (I scrabble around to find the group chat) . . . nine days. I have known them for a decade. I start to type out a few sentences to them but nothing seems right. How do I apologize for forgetting they exist? They'll be the ones I'll be trading *Heaven Sent* memes with when Melanie and Teddy move on. I'll work out how to explain my absence when I get home.

But: They didn't message me either.

Worksheet out. Pencil case unzipped. Earphones in. I may as well be sitting alone in the school library. Melanie's worksheet has a cute curling ribbon graphic as its border, and I take out a pink pencil to procrastinate. Carefully, perfectly, I color it as I think about the exercise at hand.

Who am I, exactly? I'm changing, so it's a fair question.

I liked myself a lot when I was neck-deep in chlorine water. I set aside all my inexperienced floundering and just put my hand on a beautiful man's chin. It was like a fantasy, but I lived it. I didn't get the kiss, but knowing he wanted to is enough for me.

I feel the booth cushion compress, I look up and Teddy is leaning his forearms on the table. He's brought his sketch-book. He is a sight for sore, sad eyes. When I pull out my earphones, he says to me with feeling, "I have never seen anything so beautiful in my entire fucking life." As I register the ripples those words make inside me, I see he's looking over my shoulder.

"And an order of Frankenfries," the bartender sets them down. "Teddy. What's up, man." (Of course Teddy knows everybody.) "When are you moving to Fairchild? I've got a friend I wanna send to you. He needs a touch-up on an old piece."

Teddy rubs his hands together and says to the plate, "I should be taking bookings by Christmas. Maybe leave it to the New Year so I can get settled."

"I'll let him know. Bet you can't tell, because he's such a mess," the bartender says to me with a grin, "but this guy is the best at what he does." He rolls up his sleeve to show me a beautifully rendered old-style naval anchor.

"I know he is. And he's not a mess." Teddy's eyes crinkle at my indignant defense. When the bartender leaves, I say, "You always turn up at the exact moment there's food."

Teddy rests his ankles against mine. "It's uncanny how lucky I am. Look at you, doing your homework on a Friday night. Why did you look so sad?"

"I just found out I'm not as beautiful as a plate of Franken-fries." I rub down from bare shoulder to my elbow and he watches the movement. "And I remembered you're moving away."

He steps over that and focuses on what he can give me: one hell of a compliment.

"You're sublime," he promises me and I get that pool-floating sensation. "You've got skin that keeps tattoo artists awake at night." Through the steam rising off the food, he's appraising me with a gleam in his eye.

"I guess a totally blank canvas must be appealing." I feel myself get bolder. "If I ever decided to do something crazy and you finally design me the perfect thing—"

"I couldn't do it to you. It'd be like tattooing a peach." Not paying attention to what he's doing, he scoops up fries heaped with what is clearly boiling hot macaroni into his mouth. It's a bad idea. Now he's struggling, cupping his hands over his mouth, his eyes sparkling green and brown. He's brought him-self to tears.

I find him a tissue in my bag. "But you've tattooed other girls. You think it wouldn't suit me?" He shakes his head, adamant. "I'd have to get it somewhere secret, so my parents wouldn't find out."

He swallows hard. "Somewhere secret." He literally exhales a plume of steam.

"I haven't even told you what I want." I wait until his eyebrow moves. "I want the *Heaven Sent* logo." Now he's laughing and reaching back to the plate. "Teddy, if you could just control yourself . . ." I use my fork to pull a single french fry out of the stack and I blow on it.

He leans over and bites it off my fork, because of course he does.

"I forgot, we share everything." I'm being sarcastic, but he just smiles, all satisfied.

"Now you're starting to understand." He has a nice big drink from my glass. Apparently, we even share straws.

"If I was out on a date, should I expect to get my own drink?"

He realizes what he's done. "Sorry, I've just started inhaling everything like always. I think I have some cash . . ." He begins fishing around in his pockets.

I shake my head. "Keep saving that cash. You're doing really well." I try to pull out another fry but it's overloaded and splats onto the table, narrowly missing my worksheet. "Meanwhile, this isn't going well at all."

"I had a dream last night that I paid Alistair for my share a week before the deadline. Do you think it's a sign?"

I've heard enough about his dreams to know that things go weird pretty fast in them. "Then what happened?"

"I knew it was a dream because he gave me my key to the front door and it was the size of a surfboard. I woke myself up trying to fit it in my pocket and I'd gotten my boxers down around my knees."

I laugh, even as thoughts of keys and locks distracts me. The relief of having some company has given way to nerves. I felt better about leaving Providence knowing that Teddy was staying behind. I know I don't have to be there 24/7. I'm just more comfortable when I am.

"I'm not sure if my homework counts now. It specifically says I have to sit alone."

He's eaten probably a quarter of the plate with his fingers. "She'll never know." He's got the blank sheet in front of him and he's written my name at the top in elegant stylized script. "I'll help. Tell me everything about you and I'll write it down. Start from the beginning. Ruthie Maree Midona was born at . . . midnight. Or noon. Am I close?"

I begin to gather up my pens.

He sighs. "If you're serious, I'll go. I just missed you so much. I got home and your windows were dark. I followed your patrol route. I went up to your little lookout spot by the dumpsters, where you like to look at the city lights."

I'm mildly disturbed. "Have you been stalking me?"

"Then I got your text. I remembered there's this group of four sketchy dudes who hang out here drinking all afternoon, and I got into this panic that they'd found you sitting alone and were putting roofies in your Coke. That's why I was so fast." He picks up my glass and drinks from it.

"Lucky they didn't roofie it, or we'd both be unconscious."

"I worry about you, out in the world, all soft and kind. It's horrible out here." He goes silent and we hear bowling balls hitting pins and a child's scream of joy. Down near the lanes there's a lit-up cake and people are singing happy birthday.

"The outside world is not horrible." I have to smile at myself. How could it be, when there's weird food and happy kids, and Teddy's legs wrapping mine up in a hug under the table? "I think you've been spending too much time at Providence to think that."

He opens his sketchbook to a new page and begins helping himself to my pencil case. "I'm so glad you're not on a date," he declares quite cheerfully.

I can be selfless and encourage him every step of the way as he saves for his share in the studio, but for me and my goals he won't do the same. "At some point soon, I'm going to be having a romantic candlelit dinner. At the same time, you're going to be sitting in your very own tattoo studio writing *Live Laugh Love* down a girl's back in Comic Sans."

"That's the most disgusting thing you could possibly say to me," he splutters.

I try another french fry; finally, this food volcano is safe enough to eat properly. I raise my fork. His protests die and he leans forward like he is anticipating something.

This mix should be wrong. But every forkful is a prism of salt and flavor, the textures alternating between crispy and velvet. Luxe, melty macaroni blends into the gravy. Childhood flashbacks from smoky hot dog chunks.

I don't know how long I'm in this haze. All I know is, nothing in life feels that bad when I'm eating carbs and fat. Everything will work out, because of cheese. Every time I glance up, he's smiling at me, his cheek resting plumply on his fist. The smattering of freckles across his nose are cinnamon-sweet. I'm in a pleasurable dream. He has a white haze of light around his head.

I am possibly having a food-related stroke. I scrape up more. "What is happening to me?" I feel a wet line on my face; it's a tear.

"My angel, that's heaven on a plate. I told you." He hasn't taken a single fry or sketched a single line during my endless gorge. "When you enjoy yourself, you really do."

I really should do some work. I dig through my supplies. "Actually, I might need that pencil back. It's my only one. I need to be able to erase off the worksheet."

He starts sketching with it, declining the request. "I think you need to write in ink. You know who you are. Thanks in advance for the Live Laugh Love nightmare tonight, by the way. You're going to hear me crying through the wall." He regards me with curiosity then bursts out laughing. "You know you're funny as hell, right? Everything you say is so on point."

I'm surprised and want to change the subject. "Oh thanks. So did you design all your own tattoos?"

"You think someone else designed me? You don't recognize talent when you see it?" He's grinning. "I drew them, Alistair did them for me. Sometimes when he was pissed off with me he'd press extra hard. So all of it was agony." There's truth in the joke.

"Do they all mean something?" He just smiles at that. "How many do you have?" It slips out before I can censor myself. How many girls have asked that same question? I get my answer.

"I don't know. You can count them for me if you want." (Insert here the predictable eyebrows, sparkling eyes, sinful smile, my heart fluttering, etc.) He unhinges his jaw to eat more

fries. Chewing, he says, "Tidy girls like to be nice and organized, huh?" He reaches over for my hand and begins padding
my finger up his arm. "One, two . . ."

I want to keep going and have to cover it up. "All seductive with your mouthful of mush. Hold me back." It's intensely
gratifying to make him snort-laugh like that.

"Want help with the worksheet? I'll write in all your facts.
We'll circle back to your time of birth. What was your college
degree?" He's poised and ready.

My smile fades. "My parents couldn't afford to send me to
college. I did a business administration course."

"Must have been some wild parties."

"It was one long orgy." I'm lucky he wasn't drinking because
he would have sprayed me. "I was the youngest by twenty
years, easily."

"Kinky."

I notice a woman at the bar watching us. Well, she's watching Teddy. I guess I'll have to get used to that, but I can't say
I'll ever like it. "Most people were retraining for new careers. I
could finally relax." I've said too much there, and the memory
twinges too close to a nerve. I push the plate at Teddy. "Here,
eat more."

He won't be distracted. "Why could you relax?"

"I'm just more comfortable with older people." I twist my
fingers together as he just sits and stares at me, wanting more.
"I got bullied a lot at school, obviously. But being in a class
with adults I felt safe again."

"Is that why you ended up at Providence? Elderly people can't hurt you?" He thinks on that. "That's not true. Renata isn't strong enough to use a pepper grinder, but she's also more lethal than a cage fighter. I've been studying her for scientific purposes."

"My parents knew my boss, Sylvia, through the church. You know how women in the eighteen hundreds just got sent to be a governess? It was like that. I didn't apply; they basically sent me here. I really need to work out how to repackage that for when I'm telling some guy about it on a date."

I look over at the bar again. That girl is still watching us. I think she knows Teddy.

Teddy's a little indignant. "You described it just fine. Why do you need to repackage anything?"

"That's the whole point of this exercise. It's interview prep."

"I guess you could say that you used your connections to get the job," he suggests. "Sounds like Sylvia is a hard-ass. She wouldn't have taken you if you were useless."

"I guess," I admit. "I'm really good at my job. Please mention it when you're talking to your dad."

"I'm good at my job, too. My real job, not the one where I order Gucci sweat suits online in extra-extra-extra small. Can you tell Alistair? I need to think of some way to impress the shit out of him next time I see him. I haven't exactly been involved in the business side of the studio here. Got any good ideas, Administration Angel?"

"Sounds like you're going to have to hire and be a boss. Are you ready for that?"

He's self-conscious. "I mean, I'm not interested in being a 'boss,' but I want to put together a good team."

"Do you guys have customer accounts?" I watch as he thinks. I've got no real idea of what's involved in his kind of business but I try. "If someone needed to come back multiple times to get more color done, how would you record how much they had left to pay or the quote they'd been given for the total price?"

"We just write it down in the book."

"What about scheduling the appointment?"

"The book."

"Payroll? Client information?"

"I think you know the answer."

"Administration Angel recommends you impress the hell out of Alistair by getting a quote on a software package. Something that texts clients about their next appointment, things like that. Maybe the two locations can be linked together so you can see each other's weekly takings. Something that can handle payroll and tax. He might say that the book is cheaper, but at least you made a suggestion."

"Angel . . ." He sighs, and before he can finish that thought, the woman who has been watching from her stool at the bar walks up to our table. She has something to say. As she gets closer, both Teddy and I notice something at the exact same time, judging from his intake of breath.

She's really, really pregnant.

CHAPTER EIGHTEEN

Teddy? Teddy Prescott," the woman says, passing her hand over her full stomach. "I've been looking for you for the longest time."

His expression dials through denial, anger, bargaining, depression, and acceptance. He's sighing, nodding, and mentally picking out a car seat when she erupts into cackles.

"Oh, come on. We were together six years ago. Sorry to scare you."

He lays his head down on his arms and dies. To me, she mouths, *Not sorry*.

I feel like I've had six years shaved off my life-span. "Geez, Teddy. Learn how calendars work."

Teddy sits up and tries to recover. "Anna. How are you? What are you doing here?" He's staring then blinking away, fascinated and horrified by the huge drum under her skintight clothes. "Do you need us to drive you to the hospital? How many babies are in there?" He scans the floor for broken waters. His boots make scrabbling sounds on the floor.

She ticks her answers off on her fingers. "Not in labor just yet, but my husband will drive me when I am. One baby. And I'm Brianna, not Anna."

Teddy replies, "Sorry. You know how I am with names."

"I know how you are." Brianna is a little sad now. As an aside to me she adds, "I never thought he'd forget my name, though. I guess some people never change."

I begin to slide out of the booth, desperate to get away. "Would you like to sit down?"

"Thank you, but no. I just wanted to say hi." She glances at the childish mess on our table, momentarily distracted. I know she's estimating my age; it's all people ever seem to do to me.

I take a stab at lightening the tense vibe. "I'm teaching Teddy how to read, the poor thing never learned." They both let out identical quacks of amused surprise. "He's starting a business and has sought my services."

"You're a nice girl, volunteering your time like that. He's not a quick learner," Brianna says with a grin, but it fades off. "You're not *with* him, are you?"

Imagine being able to say yes. "No, of course I'm not."

"Oh good. He'll randomly disappear forever and forget your name. At least, that was my experience."

On her inner forearm is a bluebird tattoo that I recognize as Teddy's work. What is this stab through the meatiest part of my rib cage? What's the point of jealousy right now? There are girls walking around everywhere with his art on their body. But I'm not one of them.

"He's fun to be with, but when he's gone, he's really gone.

And it's not worth it to have to miss him. Nice to meet you. Goodbye, Teddy." She leaves, and when she reaches the top of the stairs, her husband dashes up to hold her arm as she slowly clomps down.

The action is so doting and sweet my throat squeezes with emotion.

Imagine having someone who was so afraid that I'd fall. I'd really, really love to have something like that. Teddy's going to try to put on a casual front, but he's clearly affected. He won't lift his eyes. His pencil is scratching in one spot on the pad, nearly tearing the page.

"Are you okay?"

"It went better than it usually does," Teddy says with a cheer he doesn't feel. "She didn't pour a drink over my head or slap me."

"Was what she just said unfair?" I watch him consider it. Then he shakes his head. "How many girls have you done that to?" I mean *disappoint* and *hurt* and *leave*. He understands exactly. Before he even opens his mouth, I know what the answer will be, because his eyes confess.

"All of them. It's like my mom says. Nothing lasts forever."

"Tell me about her. Your mom."

"She's very pretty, with nicer hair than me. Impossible, right?" He tries to joke but I don't smile. "Her name's Ruby. Ruby . . ." He pauses to think. "Hardiman. Grant. No, she's Ruby Murphy now. Weird to not know your own mom's name."

"How many times has she been married?"

"Sometimes, I barely have enough time to pick up my suit from the dry cleaner for the next wedding. Six times. And as you've just found out tonight, I am a lot like her."

His eyes search mine. "You know I'm going to leave, right? And you're not going to try to stop me?"

"Of course not. Because you're going to be the manager of your own studio. And one day, I'm going to drive all the way up to visit you to get my tattoo. Everyone's got one except me. Brianna had a bluebird by you."

He seems surprised. "How do you know it was mine?"

"I know talent when I see it." I smile when he does. "I'd know you anywhere, Theodore Prescott."

"If the studio doesn't work out for me, I don't know what I'm going to do," he confesses in a hush. "I'm thousands away from what I need. Alistair is talking about checking out shopfronts, and I can tell he thinks I'm not going to come through."

My phone interrupts and the caller ID makes us look at each other in panic. "It's the Parlonis. Hello? What's happened?"

It's Renata. She bawls over a loud din, "Ruthie, what is this godawful noise?" In the background, I hear a faint siren. "We're all deaf and half dead, but this is still managing to keep us all awake. Half of them are out on the pavement wondering if it's the fire brigade."

The sound sinks into me. "The office alarm's going off."

Renata says, "Well, go fix it. I don't know how you can't hear it. I cannot get ahold of Theodore. I have no one here to fix

207

this noise. It's not much to ask, is it? Peace and quiet? Do you know how much we pay to live here?" She lets out a screech of frustration.

"I'm sorry. I'll be five minutes. Please don't tell Sylvia. I know I locked the door. I know I did."

"It's just tripped. There's nothing to steal in the office." Teddy thinks he is helping but those words are congealing the food in my stomach. I'm sweating. I'm feeling like an animal, nothing but base reactions. He tries to catch my hand and I shy backward. "We'll go together," he says, but he's too slow. He's a person who's never in a rush. He's no use to me. "Ruthie, wait for me."

I'm already running down the stairs, my hand skimming the handrail. If I fall, I'll catch myself. I don't think of him as I run to my car. I actually don't have any thoughts at all.

I drive home like I've got Brianna in labor on my back seat. I run up the path toward my squalling baby office. I trip on a paver when I try to dodge a tortoise. For a moment I see myself from above and this windmill-limbed frantic sprint is sad to witness. This moment now begins to intercut with my memories of being sixteen and careless, distracted by a boy.

The alarm's going off, but I can't hear anything except my heartbeat.

My hand is jarring on the doorknob and it's not until I register pain in my wrist that I realize that the door is locked. I drop my keys twice, unlock the door, fall inside, disarm the alarm, and sit on Melanie's desk. I proceed to have a wheezing, squeaking panic attack.

"What happened?" Teddy says from the open doorway. Turns out he can hurry when he wants to. "Was it locked?" He asks this like he really knows me. "Breathe, breathe." He moves me into Mel's chair and makes me put my head between my knees. My airways have turned into a one-way street.

I don't know what he says to me next, but through the fuzzy blackness, he somehow coaches me to exhale once.

When I can, I reply, "Yes, it was locked. Nothing happened. The alarm was tripped." I ease up. Why did he have to follow? The last guy who witnessed this meltdown was Adam. Every time he looked at me, he had the memory of it in his eyes. I know this is very unattractive.

When Teddy kneels down between my feet and opens his arms, I crumple down into him. The smell of his body through his T-shirt is familiar to me now. That's how long he's been lingering in my doorway, following me around, noticing and questioning everything I do. Part of his delicious scent has adhered to my couch cushion. My scarf smells like him, my pillow, my entire bathroom . . .

Wait a second. "Have you been using my shampoo? That's theft. No wonder you've been extra lustrous lately."

He pulls back and won't be distracted. "Can you tell me what happened?" He doesn't mean right now. He means the years-ago thing. "Most people don't check every door the way you do."

"How on earth did you steal shampoo without me noticing?" I'm pushing away until the wheels of the chair begin to roll. "I wish I'd spoken to Brianna a little more, to find out if you've always been like this. If you want something from me, just ask."

"What I want to know is this story that's been eating you up." His hands pull the chair back. "An alarm going off and ruining your night out is annoying, but it isn't the end of the world. But it felt like it was to you. You can tell me."

I blow out a breath. It's been years since I've spoken out loud about this. "When I was sixteen I learned the importance of security. That's all."

He shakes his head. "That's all? I don't think so."

I've never had anyone ask me about this, so I don't know where to start. The beginning, I suppose?

"When I was sixteen, our church had a huge fund-raising event to raise money for . . . something. A hurricane, or an earthquake. The event was a really big deal. The local radio station was broadcasting from it. There were games, a pageant, a pie-eating contest, the works. It was really wholesome. It was like an episode of *Heaven Sent*."

"I can picture it. Just FYI, I imagine your dad as Pastor Pierce."

I smile reluctantly. "I wish. Anyway, my boyfriend, Adam, came along. I thought I was in love. He went to a different school, so spending the day together was a treat. Chaperoned by his parents and mine, of course." When I think back to that day, all I can remember is the color of Adam's polo top and the stench of bloody smoke coming off the grilling steaks. "Our parents approved of the relationship. Everything was perfect."

Teddy's starting to grimace. "I hate the part of the story

where something goes wrong for you. But it's coming." He shuffles closer on his knees. "This is the part that hurts, isn't it?"

I take a deep breath. "There was a charity auction that boosted the total. At the end of the day, we counted ten thousand dollars. It was a huge amount, more than we'd ever imagined, and it was cash. People had been really generous. Ten thousand dollars. My dad told me to go and put it in his office."

"Oh." Teddy's got a doomed note in his voice. "Oh shit."

Talking about this only feels possible because Teddy is such a good listener. It's what I've always liked best about him. His expression is always changing as I speak. His face softens with sympathy or pinches with concern, his eyes flaring with surprise or loyal outrage hardening his brow. The way he listens to me makes it feel possible to talk about the moment where I lost my confidence and my faith.

"I took the money up to his office. I was talking to Adam as I put it in the bottom drawer of Dad's desk. The money got stolen early that evening, probably when we were all eating leftovers from the barbecue."

Teddy's looking grim. "What did the police say?"

"My parents didn't call them. It was too humiliating for them to admit it to everyone that the huge fund raiser had been for nothing because their daughter didn't lock the door. There was no forced entry."

"Ruthie," Teddy says with such sympathy.

"My dad was so angry. He said I was too caught up in myself and a boy to do the one thing he'd asked me to. Ten thousand dollars. Gone."

"The only person who's at fault is the person who stole that money."

"So the last bad thing to happen was that my parents used what little there was in my college fund to cover the amount that was stolen. They talked for a long time and considered covering it up completely. But it wasn't enough of a lesson. Dad made me stand up in front of everyone on Sunday and explain my carelessness. And I was giving up my dream of becoming a vet to make it right."

"That's complete bullshit." Teddy is lit with anger. He looks like a devil, kneeling at my feet.

I'm taken aback by how infuriated he is. "Why are you mad? I deserved it."

"They should have stood up for you. If you said you locked the door, you did it."

"But I didn't. I just can't remember. It's the black spot in my memory. And I swore to myself that I'd never feel that way again. From that point on, I've used checklists and routine to manage myself. I was hoping you and Melanie hadn't noticed."

"And what about Adam? Did he stand up for you?" Teddy's eyes narrow when I look away. "Your mom? Surely she believed you?" He falls silent. "You could have been a vet, but instead all your college money was spent on a hurricane. I can't believe how much of yourself you've had to give over the years."

"I wasn't delusional; I didn't think I'd actually be a vet one day, but maybe a vet nurse? Once the savings account went to zero, we all knew it wasn't going to happen for me. What the actual worst part was, my dad could find forgiveness for anyone in that congregation, but not for me. He lost faith in me, and I lost my faith in God."

Teddy leans back from me to see my face better.

"I think I have to go punch a hole in a fence or something. Ruthie, I'm going to tell you something, and you need to believe me, okay? Are you ready?" I nod. "What happened to you was shitty and I'm sorry. And I want you to know that it's time to let it go." He considers my face and decides to take a risk. "I've got a therapist I see sometimes. I could give you her details."

I have a cleaned-out cathartic feeling in my chest. I wipe my eyes. "Is that why you're such a good listener?"

"Am I?" He's similarly flustered. "I didn't think I was."

"You are the best listener I've ever known." I drag my fingertips through another section of his hair, admiring the glassy shine my shampoo has bestowed. "I've thought sometimes I should see someone about my mental health. What do you see a therapist for?"

"How to cope with having hair this good." He gets to his feet and helps me up. "Reset the alarm. I'll lock the door." We do that, and it's only when we're walking up the hill that I realize that we're holding hands, and he completely sidestepped my serious question with a silly reply.

"Can we talk about what you go to a therapist for?"

Teddy sidesteps a tortoise this time. "I want you to know that I'll always take your side. Even when I'm in Fairchild, you just call me, okay?" He's making his voice cheerful and it's making me feel worse. He's just taken me apart completely and learned the worst moment of my life. And he won't give me anything back. But I can't make him.

"I wish you trusted me like I trust you."

"I'm not a guy you should trust. I thought Brianna just explained that."

I trail him into our courtyard. In the dark, the Dream Girl sits, where he's taken her apart, too. "Could I go for a ride on her before you leave? How are you taking two bikes with you, anyway?"

"I'll definitely take you for a ride. I promise." He uses my keys and unlocks my door, puts me on the couch, and switches on lamps. Now he's in the kitchen like it's his, taking my favorite mug out of the cabinet. "Hmm. Sleepy Time Tea or hot chocolate?" He looks over at me. "What are you waiting for? It's time for *Heaven Sent*."

As he adjusts the crooked pillow behind my back, then hands me a steaming mug, I think that this is surely what it must feel like to be adored.

"I'm sorry I stole your shampoo," he says as he presses play on the episode. "I don't suppose I could have a spare key? I really want to have a bath in your tub with all the candles lit. It's something I want to do before I go."

After all I've shared tonight, this request seems like a tiny thing. "Sure thing."

CHAPTER NINETEEN

A ll we need is a stunning photo and we're ready to go live on your dating profile," Melanie tells me. "Here, put this on. And this, this, this." She tosses random cosmetics at my head from across the office. "This, this, this."

I lower my arms when it's safe. "You're forgetting. We don't do this in work hours." I get up from my chair to collect the makeup, but I'm so stiff I have to stay bent over. "Oh, my back." My computer glasses swing on their chain and whack me in the face.

"You old granny," Mel says with affection. "If you're not careful I'll load a pic of your bum, bent over just like that. You'd get plenty of messages from weirdos."

"I will kill"—I get down to ground level and pick up a lipstick—"you"—a blush—"Melanie Sasaki." Highlighter. Eyelash curler. She even threw a makeup brush. I straighten up with difficulty. "I swear, I feel it in my joints when a storm is coming through."

"You are aging rapidly by the day. By week six I'll be dyeing your white hair back to brown. I've got to get you out of here before I go." She takes a long swig of the massive bottle of pale green juice on her desk. I already know from her earlier swigs that it tastes like celery had diarrhea. It's Wednesday and day three of Mel's cleanse. I'm desperate for her resolve to break. But even as she complains and overshares, I've been laughing.

I once thought I wouldn't last in the same room with her until lunchtime without screaming, but now time's passing too quickly. "Your end date is a month away now. So soon."

"The temp agency is already sending me through new roles to look at. They think I'll say yes to anything. I usually do, but I'm tired. I hope we think of my dream job before then."

I ask the following, even though I know what the answer will be. "Would you consider working for the Parlonis?"

She gives me a Look. "Wow, you really despise me, huh. Do you know what they made Teddy do yesterday at lunchtime? They got McDonald's and he had to plate it up like a five-star restaurant." She searches in her phone. "Look at this nonsense."

He's cut the Big Macs into tiny wedges. They're laid down sideways beside a Jenga-style stack of fries, a nugget, and an artistic squiggle of Sweet and Sour Sauce. I can't exactly tell Mel that I have already seen this photo, while Teddy was lying on my couch with his head on a cushion. A cushion that was on my lap.

Since my false-alarm meltdown last Friday, Teddy has stopped trying to keep himself out of my cottage. There's been no threshold-lingering; instead, he's been soaking up my hospitality and I mean that literally. He's been soaking in my bathtub, singing "Wonderwall" through the unlocked door. Melanie would have a nosebleed if she knew. I really don't know how it's happened, so I wouldn't be able to explain it.

He hasn't made me feel like shit for my meltdown, and he's come with me on each nightly security round. He washes the dishes and he knows every single subplot and backstory of *Heaven Sent*. It feels like Teddy's been sent to me. I know that thinking like that won't help.

I steer us back to work.

"As one of your last projects, I was hoping for your help planning the Christmas party. I was thinking of doing a vintage prom theme this year. Imagine all the ladies in pretty dresses."

"Yes, yes, yes," Melanie enthuses. "Parties are kind of my thing. I love organizing. I love inviting people, I love seeing them have a good time. I live for that." Out comes her notebook and she begins scribbling. "Food. Decorations. Playlist. Invites. Food. What I'm going to wear. Oh my God, I can do my hair in a beehive. Eyeliner. Food."

She pretends to chew her next mouthful of juice before swallowing.

In my Midona Project dedicated notebook, on the page titled POSSIBLE CAREERS FOR MEL I write *Event Planner*. "Let's start with invitations. I usually give four weeks' notice of the date, so they need to go out this week. Do you have any design skills?"

"I have been temping for ten thousand years. I have every skill." The thought dims her light. Melanie looks around. "I can't believe I'm going to say this, and it may be the juice talking, but I'll be sad to move on from here. I'm tired of new people, new desks. It'd be nice to rest awhile."

"You're not scared of old people anymore?"

She blows out a breath. "I was at first. I found your photo album and the funeral programs in your drawer. I'm scared of that aspect of being here. But if we just keep everyone happy and busy, I think everything will be okay. And besides, you're here."

Melanie takes a phone call from a resident. When she hangs up, I agree with her. "It's our job to make their lives as lovely as we can." I check my in-box. There's one from Dorothea at PDC marked "Request." Before I can even read to the bottom of the email, Melanie says, "I sent it to her."

"Thank you."

PDC sent a surveyor here yesterday. I walked around the site with him, trying to work out the purpose of his visit. I tried my best to demonstrate the virtues of our lake and hillside. He finally told me: *Unless you're a qualified surveyor, too, I think you've helped me enough.*

Red with embarrassment, I slunk back to find a message from Rose Prescott on my desk. She made me dig out an asbestos assessment report from 1994 because she obviously hates me. Melanie picked the cobwebs out of my hair after I emerged from the file storage abyss.

It was worth it to hear the grudging approval in Rose's voice when I called her back.

I will give Melanie some good feedback now. "You've been

doing a really great job. I couldn't have gotten through these last few weeks without you." This gives her a rosy glow. "Using your design skills, could you mock up something that looks like a 1950s-era prom invitation?"

"Cute. I can do that. Might team up with the old Tedster on this one, seeing as though he's 'so inspired lately.'" (She uses quotation fingers.) Now she narrows her eyes. "What's inspiring him so much, do you think?"

It's me and the safe white page that is my cottage. It's because Teddy finally knows exactly what he's doing every night, and it's cleared the disorganized restlessness out of him. *I have never been this peaceful, Ruthie.* But I can't tell her that.

I shrug in answer to her question. "Great idea about the invitations, let's get him involved. I really hope you'll come, even though your contract will be over. We'll give one to Teddy," I add on lightly. "He won't be able to make it, but he'll know he's always welcome."

She rolls her eyes. "He's finally sorted out his tax situation. Get this: He got a refund. He thought he was going to jail but gets a check instead. Was he kissed by a leprechaun at birth? His account is filling up nicely." She looks up from her party planning checklist. "Nobody ever made saving for a life dream look so effortless. I hate him."

Teddy tells me everything, but he didn't tell me that.

"Me too." We're both liars who are going to miss him badly. "He's absolutely unbelievable."

"So here's what we're going with for your dating profile,"

Melanie begins, consulting her screen. We are distracted by a black-clad figure at the door. "Oh, go away please, we're doing some serious stuff."

"I will not go away," Teddy says indignantly, sitting in the visitor chair at my desk. "I'm staying until the food comes. Who's unbelievable?"

"Food." Melanie is distracted again. Mel says her juice cleanse is to release toxins from her organs; which organs, she will not say. My observation is that the juice is releasing dizzy spells and bouts of random paranoia. With eyes like a wolf, she asks Teddy, "What did they order?"

"Big salads."

"Salads," she echoes in grief.

To make conversation I say to him, "I heard you had a tax windfall."

"Yes. I didn't expect my next Good Samaritan to be the tax-ation department. I was going to tell you." Except he didn't, because news of his progress makes a very hidden part of me very sad, and he knows it.

Once upon a time, I sank gratefully into my silent candlelit bathroom like a temple. I thought that my routine was sacred and untouchable, but I know that things have changed for me now. Having him sitting on my couch in the evenings, and Melanie across from me during the day, has spoiled me. I'm beginning to worry for myself.

"So what's going on here?" Teddy asks Melanie in a tired voice.

"I was just about to read out Ruthie's dating profile and take her photo. Except of course I wasn't going to do that during office hours," she adds, in response to whatever my expression is. "I was going to do that at 5:01 P.M., after Ruthie and I cross-reference the water charges on Providence's account to the payments we've made."

"Guys, I do not care about what you do in here." Teddy drapes himself back in his chair and pulls the elastic tie out of his hair. He shakes out the beautiful mess with his hands. "Rose is going to turn it into an alpaca ranch just to mess with me. Just enjoy it while it lasts."

Stroke, slide, his hands sort through his hair until my fingertips burn on the armrests of my chair. It's not just me affected by it.

"Quit tormenting me," Melanie says to Teddy with temper. She gets up, runs to the bathroom, and slams the door behind her. The juice has cleansed her at least four times since 9:00 A.M.

He blinks at me like his feelings are hurt. "What'd I do?"

"You've been making her feel like her hair is inferior. She wears her ponytail extension every day now. It's hard on the scalp." I'm unsettled as I go over his comment. "Alpaca ranch, huh? Have you heard something?"

Teddy continues sorting through his hair with his head tipped back. Up to the ceiling, he replies, "No, but even if I did, I couldn't tell you. Board members and shares and whatever. Don't wanna get sued by my own dad, that'd be awkward." He yawns. There's those back molars I've been missing. "Rose would be first up in the witness box."

"A surveyor was here."

He winces. "That's never a good sign. Stop looking at me with those huge brown eyes. I know what you want from me, and I can't do it."

Melanie comes out with her ponytail redone. "Teddy, what conditioner do you use?"

"I rinse it in rainwater with a capful of vodka."

"Really," Mel marvels, leaning on her desk with eyes like cartoon spirals. "Does it have to be cold water?"

"Very cold. Like ice." He drops his hands out of his hair. "You got a Tangle Teezer in your bag, Mel? 'Course you do, you're a girl. Come brush me."

"Can I practice a basket braid on you?" (He nods.) She approaches him unsteadily and puts both her hands into his hair, making his eyes droop into slits. My eyes probably are, too. She's up to her wrists in that gleaming black stuff. I love her, but I want to scream at her.

And he's watching for my reaction and I've got to hold it together.

"It's got to be a wig. It's too perfect." Melanie tugs around on his hairline until he whimpers. "Okay, that does it. Ruthie's bones told me that it's going to rain. I'm going to put a bucket under the garage's downpipe."

I save her some effort. "He's kidding about that. Please eat this before you faint." I pass her a banana. It makes her relinquish his hair and I hiss out the suffocating green steam building in my lungs. His nostrils flare and I swear he scents it. His

222

mouth quirks. I want to stick his head in a bucket of dirty mop water.

"My cleanse," Melanie says, a lamb bleat. "My toxins." We watch her violently skin the fruit and chomp it in half. Through her disgusting mouthful, she says something to him like, "Before you ask, no, I won't tell you what Ruthie's dating profile will say."

"I'll swipe through all the girls in the world until I find her."

"You would," she says darkly after a hard swallow.

"Sounds like he already has." Wow, I really said that. I turn back to my computer and open an email from the maintenance contractor while Teddy just stares at me. "So it looks like they're sending an electrician next Thursday." I reply to the email, diarize it, all under his bright-hot hazel eyes.

Mel contributes the following insight: "Banana good."

"Why are you on the juice?" Teddy asks her.

"I met a guy for a date down at the Thunderdome. He said I was bigger than he expected." This isn't what she told me about the juice cleanse. But it's okay. Teddy has a way about him that draws the truth out.

I'm instantly angry. "Excuse me, he said what?"

"My profile says I'm half Japanese, and he made an assumption." She smooths her hands down her front. "I should be smaller."

Teddy's equally affronted. "You're planning on changing yourself based on some dude's imagination? You're smarter than that, Mel."

"I just haven't been having much luck lately," she says defensively. "I'm sorry, Ruthie, but it's a jungle out there."

"He saved you a lot of time, revealing himself as a jerk up front. Don't change anything about yourself. You can have my yogurt." The spoon I hold out is snatched by a desperate hand.

Melanie throws the banana skin at the bin and it sticks to the wall above. "Thanks, Mom and Dad, you're the best." She goes to the fridge. Silence fills the office, apart from rhythmic scraping, swallowing sounds, and *mmm*. When she's back at her desk, she makes a decision. "I'll read out Ruthie's profile, but only because I want a decent guy's perspective."

That's troubling for him. "Find someone else then."

"Twenty-five-year-old cute-as-a-button brunette—"

I hold up my hand. "Objection."

"Overruled," Presiding Judge Theodore Prescott says. "So far very accurate."

Bananas mixed with yogurt are a hell of a drug. Melanie is getting some color back in her cheeks. "Just let me say the whole thing. No interrupting. Twenty-five-year-old cute-as-a-button brunette seeks old-fashioned soul mate to set her world on fire. No casual hookups, weirdos, little dicks, broke dudes, or fugs."

I am aghast. "Melanie. Take that last bit off."

"I loaned her some of my dating profile," she says to Teddy with a grin. "It's too good."

"Well, it rules me out." He hauls himself to his feet when he hears a scooter. "I'm sure you'll debate that in my absence."

"Broke dude," we both say in unison to his departing back.

"He's also a weirdo," Melanie adds. I cut her off with a head-shake before she can ponder the rest.

"I am feeling so much better, but I need some air," Melanie says when Teddy walks in holding the delivered takeout. "Why don't I walk these up to the girls. I want to talk to Aggie about careers. Did you know she was a fancy lawyer?" She detangles the bags out of his hand and walks off up the hill.

The light leaves the room. This is traditionally the time that makes me feel like life is over, but it's just beginning, because he is here. The zesty lemon flecks in his eyes are the only bright things.

This is it. Another moment I'll look back on one day with either a headshake or a mental high five. I had a gorgeous, single next-door neighbor, a risky one for sure, but I am a champion at guarding my feelings. I have been training for this big, tattooed mistake all my life. If I ask him to just give me the last few weeks he has left, what would he say?

Before I can take this chance, he lifts his phone and says, "Here, I'll take your dating profile photo. Oh, man," he says in despair to the screen.

"Show me."

He holds the screen up. For a dating profile photo, it's not the best. I'm at a desk with glasses around my neck and yes, brown and cream is not my best palette, but I look like someone who has integrity, clear skin with a flush, a light in her eyes, and a fond softness to her mouth.

"I look like a pretty little dweeb. At least it's truthful advertising." My joke doesn't make him smile. He sinks down lower, staring at the screen, polishing a smudge off the glass with his thumb. His chest rises and falls on a deep breath.

I'm going to take a page out of his book. If I say it light and joking, he won't know that it's serious. "I'm worried I won't remember how to kiss. I haven't kissed anyone since Adam. My prom night feels like a long time ago now."

He's momentarily dumbstruck as he considers the length of my drought. He leans forward, elbows on knees. "Don't worry for a second. You should see your mouth when you talk. When you smile," he adds when I do now. "I think you're a good kisser."

I wonder if I could possibly convince him to test the theory?

I look across at the time. "Would you like to come over for dinner on Friday night, after I go clothes shopping with Mel?" The mere mention of food has him nodding. He rubs his palms up and down his thighs. I wonder if this is a little underhanded, having a kiss-related motive. I should be up front. "I think I should tell you that I will probably try for a good-night kiss. For purely scientific reasons."

He's gaping at my boldness, and laughing, and concerned. "That's not a good idea. My self-control around you has been pretty impressive. We don't want me falling back into old patterns."

I stay brave. "I wouldn't mind. So knowing this motive, are you still coming to dinner? I can't exactly invite myself over to your nuclear bunker. It's really a shame your dad couldn't fix you up with a cozier abode."

"He said I could have an empty town house." He shrugs carelessly. "The Parlonis told me on my second day I could have their spare room. I've got some very comfy options. But I'll stay right where I am."

"Why?"

"Because you're my neighbor."

I am utterly charmed and I'm sure he sees it. I stretch my arms over my head.

"Thanks for the profile photo. When Mel gets back, she's going to push the button. Let the dicks rain down upon me." I put my face in my hands. "Let me rephrase."

"Don't remind me about all those jerks with dicks," he says in a withering tone. He attaches my photo to a text and a second later his phone chimes in his pocket. "About Friday. I'm gonna be a good boy, so don't get your hopes up." I don't know if it's the lengthening shadows playing tricks on my eyes, but he seems kind of nervous. Why would he be? It's just me.

"One of these days I'm going to be a bad girl. Maybe you'll be around to witness it." I can't believe the things I'm brave enough to say to him these days. It kind of suits me. Then I utterly ruin my sexy bad girl aura, but I don't think he minds. "Now, let's talk about software packages. What have you found that might suit your studio?"

CHAPTER TWENTY

I had to invite them," Melanie says when we pull up in front of the thrift store, parking her tiny car behind a rather conspicuous Rolls-Royce Phantom. "They were both asking me when and where we're doing the makeover, and I said here, and this time, and it all just worked out this way. What's the big deal?" She is breathless.

"It's not a big deal. Why are you so nervous?" I mean, now I am, too, if Teddy is inside.

"I've got a lot riding on this third week," is all she'll reply.

When we go inside, we find Renata talking to Kurt, the regular sales assistant behind the counter. She's saying to him, "Well, how much will you give me for a vintage Hermès riding jacket? I don't like the buttons on it. I could use the closet space."

"We don't buy clothes," he says in a slow patient voice, like they've been through this already. "Haven't you ever given clothes to Goodwill?"

Renata picks through a tray of rings on the counter, tossing each aside like a parrot rejecting seeds. "If I donated it, how much would you sell it for?"

Teddy says from the back in the men's section, "It says right there, all jackets are three dollars."

"Three dollars?" Renata roars. "Has the world gone mad?"

"Donating is not mandatory, but we do appreciate it," Kurt tells her, gathering up the jewelry. He brightens when he sees me. "Oh, hi, Ruthie. How's it going?"

Kurt is in his midtwenties and hallelujah, he finally did something about that hair. It used to be a longish bowl cut, tangling in his eyelashes when he talked, but now he's got a haircut and a forehead. I'd always kind of assumed there'd be some zits lurking under there, but he's revealed to be clear-complexioned and mildly attractive.

If I'd never felt Teddy Prescott's vibrations before, I might even think Kurt is cute.

"I'm good thanks, Kurt. Hi, Renata and Teddy, thanks for coming. No Aggie today?" I look to the back racks.

"She's too weary," Renata says, eyes down and her lips pressed thin.

I look at the rack behind the counter. Like I knew he would, Kurt turns around and retrieves a small selection of garments. "What have we got?"

"I know you said you don't wear red," he begins, "but this is sort of your style. Or is it too short again?"

From the back, an incensed Teddy straightens to his full height with a face like a bull. He's preparing to charge, but Melanie comes forward instead.

She shakes Kurt's hand. "Melanie Sasaki, founder of the Method." (That makes absolutely no sense and he's weirded out.) "Let's take a look. Oof, too short. And this one is a big no," she scolds, weeding out a brown dress. "That's what the old Ruthie would have gone for. No more brown librarian clothes. But the others are okay. We're going to have a montage shortly."

"Don't be messing with her tidy vibe," Teddy bellows from the back.

Renata pats the stack of clothes on the counter. "Add them to her dressing room," she tells Kurt like we're in a boutique. "Now, explain the meaning of this." She snaps her fingers at Teddy and he comes forward at me like a mob henchman, pulling out an envelope from his jeans back pocket. It's the invitation to the Christmas party.

I steel myself for the impending argument. "What part of the invitation do you need me to explain?"

"The theme. 'Vintage prom.'" Renata's stare is like lasers as she takes the card from Teddy's hand and flaps it at me. "Did you do this to taunt me?"

I'm taken aback. "Excuse me?" I look at Teddy but he shrugs. "I work all year for this party. And I'd never taunt you with anything."

"You somehow knew I didn't go to my prom. My biggest life regret, and you knew. How?" She looks back down at the pastel invitation. "You googled it, didn't you? I saw a program on TV that said everyone's secrets are on the internet now."

"I don't think that applies if you were born before 1930,"

Teddy quips and earns himself a punch in the stomach from his tiny employer. It wouldn't have made much of a dent but he doubles over, anyway, holding his midsection. "Call . . . security—" He gasps overdramatically at Kurt, who dithers helplessly.

"Renata, I'm not a mind reader." I try to remain patient despite somehow always being in the wrong. This is something that is clearly very painful for her. "Now's your chance to come to our special Providence Prom."

"And I'll have to attend as an old person," Renata says through gritted teeth. "I was supposed to go as myself, when I was young. I wanted to walk in with my true love, in front of absolutely everybody. But Aggie said we couldn't."

"Why?" I ask, but Melanie has been bristling at Renata's tone and cuts in.

"Most people are excited. I'm arranging for a clothing hire company to come up the week before, for anyone who wants to hire a dress. My invitations turned out so beautifully. Even you have to admit that."

Renata is caught on a detail. "Hire a dress? Hire. A. Dress? This just gets worse and worse."

Melanie shrugs. "Do what you want. You are not forced to attend."

I cut in: "But we hope you do. You could walk in wearing something totally spectacular." The prospect of this tempts her. "We're doing prom king and queen. All the music will be the same as . . . back then."

Teddy says to me, "My dad got an invite. Melanie said you

even sent one to Rose. But where's mine?" He seems genuinely hurt now. His hand is still cradling his stomach. "Didn't I tell you when we first met that I love costume parties?"

"It's here." I take it out of my purse. "I was going to give it to you tonight."

"Tonight," Melanie says slowly. Suspiciously. "What's happening tonight?"

"I want to organize my true-love tattoo." Renata unfolds the Christmas invitation again. She is fascinated by this thing. She gives me that look again, sharp and assessing. "I've got a few things I want to do. Teddy here has a contact."

He translates. "Renata wants a consult from Alistair."

"I've told him a prison tat will do fine, but he flatly refuses, obstinate boy," Renata tells me. "Imagine me with a lonely teardrop." She indicates the deep creases on her cheek. "Well, I want you to design it, Teddy, even if you insist that your friend does the inking. If it turns out terribly—"

"It'll turn out amazing. Thanks for the invite," he adds, tucking it in his pocket. We all hear the note of regret in his voice.

Renata says, "Ruthie, name a single boy who came back to visit once he left."

"To be fair, you destroyed each and every one," I say with a faint smile. I want Teddy to push back against her claim but the silence stretches on until maybe he's accepting that it's likely true. "You never tell me how close you're getting to your goal."

He turns away to riffle listlessly through a nearby rack of women's pajamas and won't reply.

Renata says, "I told Aggie to pay him below minimum wage, but she wouldn't listen. And because he's too well paid, I'm going to have to get a new boy. It's impossible hiring around Christmastime." She hides her sadness with selfishness. I'll try to do the same.

"Maybe I'll get some peace and quiet in the evenings." Teddy doesn't smile and I feel terrible. I say to Renata, "So I take it you RSVP no to my kind invitation?"

"Don't go that far," she says grudgingly. "Let me talk to Aggie about it. Might be time to right that wrong." I wonder if this true love of hers could possibly still be alive?

I realize that Melanie isn't contributing anymore and am not surprised to see she's in a trance, swiping her finger left and right on her phone. She says to the room in general, "And we've got another ding."

She means my dating profile has had a match and a message has come through. I think that's how it works? She hasn't actually let me take charge of it. Holding the phone protectively to her chest, she adds, "Let me check it first." She peeks and exhales. "Okay, it's clean." Teddy pulls a face anyway.

Renata takes the phone forcibly from Melanie's hand and squints at the screen. "No. Not for Ruthie."

I hold out a hand. "I'll decide."

"What's happening?" Kurt asks me. He's effectively pinned behind the counter by a bunch of crazy people.

"I've got another solitary match on MatchUp. Also known as a miracle." I extend my hand and look at the message. Like the

233

ones I've seen so far, it's a simple *how r u*. A standard-looking guy, sitting on the hood of a car. "Not overly inspiring. Oh, hey, there's my wool skirt."

I had donated back all the clothes rejected by Melanie's assessment. I visit with the skirt like it's my friend, but I can see now that it's a heavy material in a joyless fawn brown. I can do better. I start browsing.

"I'm on MatchUp," Kurt tells me, leaning on the counter.

"What has become of us," I reply to him, pulling a rueful face.

Teddy steps behind me in the narrow aisle between skirts and trousers and presses himself up against my back. The coat hanger I'm holding on to makes a long squeak across the rail.

"Still on for dinner tonight?" The innocent question feels anything but. "I thought about what you suggested we have for dessert." His forearm slides across my collarbones and I'm squeezed gently. I am engulfed in the warmth of him, the padded muscles, the lines drawn all over him. And what's with how nicely we fit together?

"Oy!" Melanie bellows before I can answer. "Get off her. We talked about this." She bustles through, grabs Teddy by his clothes, and drags him to the back of the store. They begin having a hissy conversation that I'm very interested in, but I can't eavesdrop because Renata is tugging on my sleeve.

She hands me a dress. "Here. Hold this up against you. Hmmm, add it to her change room," she tells Kurt. To me, she adds grudgingly, "This place is interesting. It feels like dumpster diving. Who knows what I might find." She disappears face first into a rack of sweaters.

Sorry, I mouth at Kurt, but he just smiles at me. I go to the counter. "She thinks we're in a boutique."

"I got that impression." He glances to where Melanie is scolding a downcast, cowering Teddy. "You haven't brought friends with you before."

"I didn't have friends before." I realize with a jolt that it's been days, maybe even a week, since I last messaged my forum friends in our group chat, and it was about an admin matter. We've had ten years of chitchat, deep confessions, and quality memes. "Well, I mean I had no real-life friends under the age of seventy."

"What about me?" Kurt's playful and wounded. "I've been saving you all the good stuff for the past year."

"Of course. You're a very good thrift store friend. Well, I'd better get started." I go into the change room and consult the very random stack of clothing. It seems like everyone has a different idea of who I should be. After a false start, where I can't pull a leather skirt up my thighs, I drop the next dress down over my head. It fits, and in thrift store shopping, that's three-quarters of the battle won.

"Melanie, could you zip me, please?" Do I think I'm in a boutique now? I open the door a fraction and she slips in.

"Boy oh boy," she drawls loudly as she drags up the zip. "What a pair of knockers you got there. This dress does them justice."

"Well, I'm not coming out now." I press my hands to the hot-pink dots forming on my cheeks. "But you make a good point."

Melanie checks the tag. "Four dollars. Sold. First date dress located," she adds in a shout to the rest of our entourage.

"I can't wear this."

"Teddy, give us a guy's opinion." She turns the handle. He falls onto us; he was pressed against the door. She's annoyed, they exchange a look. Their earlier argument still wafts in the air. "Ruthie turns up for a first date in this. The reaction from her date is . . . ?"

Teddy looks at me in the dress. He opens his mouth, sticks his fist into it, and bites.

"Okay, good," Melanie says briskly, pushes him backward, and closes the door on him again. "Look at yourself, Ruthie. Really look. You can actually see your"—she struggles to find a word that isn't knockers—"your outline."

It's true. I really can. And it's not bad.

"I'm a guy," Kurt says to us. "I held that dress for her instead of putting it out on the floor. Don't I get a look?"

"You're pushing my buttons, buddy," Teddy snaps at him.

"I'm the official judge on this," Renata says. "Let me in." She is admitted by our bodyguard Teddy. The space is getting claustrophobic. I can't believe I'm pressed in by people who care. "Yes, I think this could work. I wonder if they could tailor it higher on the calf. She's on the petite side."

Melanie sighs. "There is no on-site tailor, Mrs. Parloni."

"Can I come in, too?" Teddy says through the door hinge.

"In your dreams," Renata tells him.

"I'm going to need someone to leave, or I can't get this off." I watch as Melanie and Renata stare at each other. Who will assert their supremacy? To my surprise, Renata relents. "Actually, Mel," I say, "you go out too. I'm your boss, you can't see me in my underwear."

Now that I'm alone, I can look at myself in this dress. I bite my own fist. Hot damn. I look exactly my age.

And after this amazing find, nothing quite compares, but between Melanie and Renata, a capsule wardrobe is building. The entire process is underscored by heated debate. "I'll buy her new ones," Renata argues from the denim rack when I poke my face out to see what's going on. "No, I draw the line at used jeans. Look at this pair. There's a hole in the crotch."

"Stop thrusting your bony old fingers through it," Melanie cries. "I'm having a nightmare tonight."

"I've never heard the word *crotch* said with such violence," I tell Teddy to make him laugh, but he's gone all serious. I square myself back at the mirror to look at the pink dress I'm wearing now. Compared to the miracle dress, this one is a little lackluster. "Thanks for coming along to help me today."

He's dry. "I'm so selfless, coming along to watch you try on dresses. What a saint."

"No, I really mean it. Everyone's moral support has really made me . . . well, made me feel like I can do this. I can finally look at myself, and see something different, and I can put myself out there." I smooth out some creases in the dress. He doesn't reply and I feel a twinge of self-consciousness. "Was that too deep and meaningful?"

Melanie approaches, eyes critical on my dress. "Too short. I mean, it looks great, but you'll never wear it."

I confess to Melanie, "It's stupid. I've always wanted to try on a jumpsuit, but I never had the courage."

"Kurt. Jumpsuits." Melanie actually clicks her fingers. He

237

actually leaps to action. Renata toddles along behind them as they disappear, shouting about how Emilio Pucci does a nice silk one.

"Okay, these are the keepers," I say to myself as I look at the garments hooked on the wall. "I've had my one miracle today." I'm grabbing at my back for the zip, when Teddy slides through the inch of open door, walks me backward, and closes the door behind us.

"I can't stand this." He cups my chin with his warm palm, eyes on my mouth. "I can't be out there while you're in here. The worst part of this whole thing is, you don't know the truth about you."

I'm surprised by how wretched he sounds. "I don't know what?"

"It hurts that you don't know you're lovely, exactly how you are. You don't need to change. You don't need to put on a dress, like it's going to fix something. You don't have anything that needs fixing."

"I know," I manage to say with no air. "But changing just a few things will make me feel like I'm turning over a new leaf, and I'll be able to convince someone else too."

"You're the thousand-dollar dress on the rack in this thrift store and I can't believe no one's picked you up yet." He's frustrated with me. "What the fuck does it take for you to believe me, or lose this composure?"

I guess all it takes is the invitation to lose it.

I pull him down with two handfuls of clothes, and I get the

kiss I've been thinking about since the moment I first saw him. He knows I need help in this moment, and his hands hold me steady. We're making a firm, warm, confident press together. I can handle this, it's completely fine. In fact, the feel of his finger underneath my ear is giving me more of a shiver than our mouths. It's a privilege to smell his skin this close.

What was I worried about? I'm doing it and it's fine. As the thought crystallizes and I relax, he moves our lips and his hand slides the zip down my back, and I feel it everywhere. That's the part I've forgotten about. Movement. He's easing my mouth open in a confident way. I know it's practice he's gotten with a lot of other girls but I can hardly care when I'm in the hands of someone so capable.

My stomach is in free fall, and this kiss gives me an adrenaline boost I could not have anticipated. It's obscene, this beautiful mouth on mine. I pull him closer, closer, closer. *Show me what you know. Teach me what I don't.* I don't care that he's leaving when I could have him for this moment in time.

There are hundreds of minutes that could be filled with kissing before he disappears.

And as suddenly as it began, I am now back in that lonely place: life when I am not being kissed by Teddy Prescott. I didn't even get my hands into his hair.

He's resisting my hands as I try to pull him down again, but any rejection I might feel is stroked away by his palm on my bare back. In a blink, I realize he needs a moment to compose himself. I know this is someone who's kissed a lot of girls, so to see him so shocked makes me dizzy. "Whoa, you're good," he breathes like it's a confession. "You're so, so good at kissing."

"Can I help with anything, Ruthie?" Kurt says through the door. Even he thinks he works at a boutique now. What is he going to do? Go grab me a different size?

Teddy pulls his hand out of my dress, and just as I think we're done, he reaches down and spreads his hand on my butt. We stare into each other's eyes. His are sharp with jealousy. "No, I'm fine," I say in a very strange voice.

"Hey, I'm going to send you a friend request, if you want to message later," Kurt says in a confiding tone through the door. Teddy's hand on my butt is squeezing tighter and I don't have a brain cell left to answer. "Well, yeah," Kurt says after a long silence. Poor guy, how awkward. "Think on it."

"Yeah, think on it," Teddy whispers against my earlobe. "You want him in here with you, not me?" His perfect teeth bite. I want to nail the door shut. "Maybe next time I'll give you a real kiss."

"A real one?" My skeleton slithers out the soles of my feet.

He laughs and rubs a thumb across my burning cheek. When I take a sidelong glance at the mirror, I see our differences full length; he's so big, so dangerous-looking, but the hand on my chin is artful and light. All this time, I thought we were mismatched, but under the clothes, down to the skin, I think we're more nicely matched than I thought. I am a fantastic color after a few touches of his mouth. He's supernatural.

"You like looking at us in the mirror. I'll remember that. Do you know what I'm saying?" His mouth lifts in a sexy smile. "No, don't be embarrassed. It's more fun for us both if you tell me the truth about what you like."

"I don't know what I like." That's pure honesty. "But I'm pretty open-minded."

"Ohh boy. I'd better get out of here before I get carried away." He smirks in the direction of Kurt. "I'm glad I'm around to fend off your admirers."

"Ruthie," Melanie says through the door. "We couldn't find any jumpsuits, but I found you the cutest playsuit." I open the door half an inch and she hands it in. "I don't know where Teddy is, but I've got to reel him in," she says through the door hinge. "He's being ridiculous."

"He usually is," I reply just to make him pull that affronted face.

"So Kurt's into you, and he's pretty much what you wrote on your clipboard."

"Yeah, I guess," my voice squeaks when the big hand on my butt squeezes again.

"Teddy's deliberately sabotaging you. He can't be a part of the Sasaki Method if he deliberately derails things, just to keep himself on your couch. I'll go see if he's outside . . ." Her grumbling voice disappears.

I look up at him. "Is she wrong?"

"Not really. I'll be damned if I give up my place as Ruthie's Favorite Man." That's all he thinks about. Himself, my cheese, my couch, my adoration. He doesn't think about what happens to me after he leaves. After Mel leaves.

When Sylvia returns, and winter comes to Providence, I will be alone and it will be harder than ever before.

"Out," I tell him, and he obeys. He's clearly got a lot of experience sneaking out on stunned girls, because there's no screech from Melanie or Renata. Kurt doesn't say something like, *Get out of this store, you pervert.* Nothing happens. Where Teddy's concerned, it's always a perfect crime.

I spend a total of $67. In thrift world, that's enough clothes to fill a tractor's front bucket. Every single piece has been jointly signed off by Melanie and Renata, so I'm confident, and as Kurt stuffs everything into bags I'm noticing a color palette has emerged: pinks, yellows, and grays. I'm still in a daze from what Teddy did to me, and formulating the speech I'm going to give him about how real friends show support, when Kurt pushes a pad and a pen over the counter.

"Give me your number if you want, I'll text you." He has a lot of tension in his eyes. It's a big risk he's taking, and I know how scary it must be to do this. Melanie is watching from the door. She gives me thumbs-up.

And yes, I've thought about it.

- Kurt's nice.
- He's in my league.
- He's a permanent resident.

- I am fairly sure he won't murder me.
- He's been thinking about me and the clothes I'd like, for a year.

I write out my number. I've got to be realistic about what I can expect from the Sasaki Method. I can't fully focus on whether Kurt could be a good match for me when Teddy is filling up the air I breathe with his crackling energy.

"Let's grab dinner," Kurt says, right as a familiar hand slides up my back, clasping the nape of my neck. Kurt takes the notepad back with his eyes averted. Teddy's the big bear, and he's staking his claim on the girl with the cheese.

"Thanks for your help today," I say to Kurt, trying to shake free of the warm palm. No one can say I'm not professional when I have a goal in mind. "Dinner sounds great. Talk to you soon. And thanks for the clothes, as always."

Because Renata is still inside paying for some obscure designer piece she dug up, I'm free to have a word with Teddy. I push through the door and when we're on the pavement I turn on him. "Explain to me how you're being a good friend when you do things like that."

"You don't like kissing me in change rooms?" He smirks. "You grabbed me, remember. I felt your heart pounding. That boring guy could never do it for you."

"You pretend to be helping me, but it's only ever to serve yourself. I have been trying really hard to support your goal, even though it means you're moving away. I do that because

I know what it means to you. I swallow down how much it's going to hurt."

"I really don't want to hurt you."

"Is that why you won't talk to me about how close you are to leaving? How much money have you saved?"

"I called Alistair yesterday to tell him I can transfer half now."

"That's amazing. See," I add with my arms spread out wide and a hole in my chest. "That's how to be pleased for your friend and the progress they're making. And what did Alistair say? I bet he was happy."

"He told me it was payment in full or nothing. He doesn't trust me to actually make it. At this point in time, you're the only person on earth who thinks I can. And that's why I don't want to give you up. You can't seem to see any reason why I can't have my keys by Christmas."

I'm perplexed. "You're absolutely going to do it. You're Teddy Prescott."

"Yeah. I'm me. I've never finished anything important."

"Those look pretty finished to me." I point at his tattoos. They're only lines, black ink and no color, but each is perfectly done. He twists away like he's irritated by my belief in him.

"Alistair told me I wouldn't have the patience to sit there and get them filled in. He's probably right."

"Seems like a lot of people have been telling you what you're like. It's time to decide if you believe them." Just as he's about to reply, we're interrupted.

"Can you guys give Ruthie a lift home?" Melanie yells from halfway down the block. She's got her car door open. "Thanks, love you, bye. Oh wait," she shouts, lifting her arm. "Ruthie got another ding. We'll go through them all on Monday."

"What's the problem here?" Renata says as she emerges from the store.

"Just me, taking too much, as usual," Teddy replies to his employer, holding up his TAKE hand.

"You ain't wrong, Theodore Prescott," Renata says as he opens the car door for her. "You were a very selfish boy today. She's not your plaything, or a way to pass time. She's a real person."

He is silent for the rest of the drive home.

CHAPTER TWENTY-ONE

It's dark by the time we escape the Parlonis, and Teddy comes with me as I conduct my security rounds.

I go through my checklist, twisting doorknobs, and jolting firmly on the dumpster's roller door. I pretend he's not even there, to get in the practice for when he's gone. We stand against the chain-link fence side by side and as I stare at the lights below, his face is just turned to me.

I finally speak. "You're messing up all my plans." My anger has burned out, leaving me cold and sad.

"You're messing up mine."

"How?"

"You believe that I can achieve my goal. You are so completely sure that I'm going to leave here on schedule and that I'll have my own key to the studio." He says it like I'm wrong.

"Should I be sorry for that?"

"No. It's just no one ever has before. I can't quite process this kind of total confidence. It's because I haven't disappointed you yet." He turns his face away into shadow. "And I keep finding myself wondering what would happen if I just gave up. This isn't so bad at all."

"Take it from someone who had a dream once and never pursued it. You've got to keep going. Keep pushing." It's starting to require more and more energy to keep up this façade of platonic-friend cheerleader. "I pick a light down there and I visit it every night. If you have a day where Renata's humiliated you, or you're sick of living in poverty, just come up here and visit your light."

"Which one's yours?" He stares at the town. "And what are you wishing for?"

"You know what I wish for. That's why I got so mad at you today. I don't have that many chances in my life, so every single one counts."

I walk back down the hill, my big shadow right behind.

"What if I don't want to succeed," he says to my back when I'm unlocking my cottage door. "What if I just want to spend it all on a vacation? Or maybe I'll just mooch around Providence indefinitely."

I feel a few things. My heart soars with hope, of course. My head quickly shuts it down. "You can't be too sure that Providence is going to exist indefinitely. I'm getting less confident about it by the day."

"I'll just retire here, now."

"No you won't." I open my door and walk inside to drop my thrift store purchases on the couch. For once, he doesn't follow me inside. "Sometimes it's really hard being the selfless one," I grouch to myself.

Outside in the courtyard, the full moon is giving his hair a silver cast. He looks like an erotic nightmare, a black shape that should make me want to run. He's sitting on a courtyard chair, long legs kicked out in angles. A lap has taken shape, but it would be a challenge to sit on. The thought rattles me and I'm glad of the dark. I go to close my front door when he speaks.

"You think you're done with me?"

How the hell am I meant to respond? "Ahh . . ."

"Because I'm not done with you."

You know that special, husky manipulative voice he's so good at putting on whenever he needs something from me? It's in its purest form right now. I lose balance; one of my knees has unlocked. It's that kind of voice.

"It's late."

"I really don't think we reached our full potential." His hand slides down his thigh and pats it. "Come here. Get your real kiss."

Surely he's a test, sent my way, because how is it possible to resist an offer like that?

He keeps talking. "I want you to do what you did to me in the change room. Just longer and hotter. And kinda . . . wrap my hair around your hand." His legs move in a restless way. "I'm gonna put my hand into the pocket of your cardigan real slow."

"What has come over you?" My feet take me closer.

He glints a smile back at me. "I got a taste of you. And I'm being the brave one. I know you're just gonna go inside and sweat over me all night."

"What's it like being this arrogant?" I make him blink with that. "I have never met anyone in my entire life who was so sure that he was irresistible."

"Irresistible to you."

I ignore that. "Was it how you were raised? You've got four sisters, right? Were you the spoiled baby, indulged in every way, and when you're not getting a thousand percent of someone's attention you feel weird?"

The silence that falls over the courtyard now is absolutely piercing.

"I didn't meet my sisters until I was eight years old. So, no, I don't think I've got something psychological going on. But I'll check with my therapist to be sure." His eyes are sharpening now until I feel the dangerous press of his gaze through my clothes. "I'm just a regular guy who likes kissing you. And I was selflessly offering myself up as someone you could let yourself be reckless and selfish with."

I try not to be distracted. "I thought you had three full sisters, and Rose was the half sister."

"They're all my half sisters," he explains patiently like I'm a real dummy. "Didn't find that little nugget of info when you stalked my dad online? They're all from his first marriage. The one I kind of ruined."

"I didn't stalk . . . Okay, I did. Sorry. I didn't know."

"I'm getting a real good picture of who you think I am.

Spoiled rich Prescott son, lying around waiting to inherit, completely addicted to attention."

"You won't let me get close enough to actually understand who you are. You are real good at sidestepping."

He continues like I didn't say anything, "I wish you could get a second first impression of me, but I can't work out how to do it."

"You thought I was elderly, and I'm scared your first impression was right. That's why I'm trying so hard to be twenty-five years old. Tell me why you go to see a therapist. Is it because of your family?"

"Yes, of course it is. Nobody wanted me completely as a kid and now I have this fucked-up reflex to make everybody love me. I've done it to you, as well," he adds, unaware of how the words *love me* drop through me like a stone into water. "I know what I do, and I want to be different with you."

"The reason you want your tattoo studio so bad is because . . ." I leave the sentence hanging in the night air. Again, that hand pats his leg. "No, answer me. I know it's more than just a thing to write on your résumé. You want it by Christmas so you can . . ."

He can't tolerate the silence I've left. "I want to see the look on Rose's face when I tell her."

"Ah." Most guys work their whole lives to prove something to their father. But Teddy is trying desperately to impress his sister. "Is Rose the one person you could never charm?"

"Pretty much. The other three, Poppy, Lil, and Daisy, they all think I'm a hopeless dope, but they love me. Rose thinks I'm a talentless homeless person. She despises me for what I did to their family."

"What did you do?"

"I was born and it all went downhill from there." Like he's put an invisible rope around me, I'm reeled in closer without any conscious effort. I'm standing between his boots now. I think he's got powers. "That kiss in the thrift store? That wasn't an ordinary kiss. I have had hundreds of kisses, and that one took the cake. Please don't ask me to talk about the family stuff." His voice gets gentle and inexplicably my eyes prick with tears. "Just put your mouth on me again."

I tip his head back with my knuckles under his jaw and the spark in his eyes and the lick of his tongue against his lip is almost too much. I need to ask him to do something important for me. "When you eventually leave, please do it really gently, okay?"

He nods. I now have everything I want in this little courtyard: a willing partner in this exploration I want to make; someone who cares for me, will keep me safe, and will make sure I don't hurt too much when I'm left behind. This is a greater guarantee than any man on a dating app could give me.

Our kiss feels like relief, like leaning on your closed bedroom door after the worst day. Everything is simple now. We're letting our bodies do what they need to do. This kiss is a sink-down-deep groan. I move a leg to step over his thigh; my skirt is too tight and I'm hobbled by my own demureness. I pull it up midthigh, and I climb onto his lap, using the square buckle of his belt and his collarbone to steady myself. He wasn't ready for either touch.

I finally put my hands into his hair. Now my entire world is cool, dark velvet. The groan I make is frankly embarrassing, and he laughs into my mouth.

"You're so horny for my hair, I knew it," he tells me on an inward breath, and I kiss that smiling mouth until I eventually take his outward exhalation into me.

He's not wrong. I slide my fingertips through the dense, silky blackness. I scratch his scalp. I make a fist and tug, which affects him most strongly. He can't catch his breath, tortured by that soft tugging sting. It turns out that I really like getting Teddy Prescott this far gone, and I have to lean back to check the progress I'm making. His eyes are bright with flecks of green and amber.

"I love your tortoiseshell eyes," I tell him honestly, and the way he blinks makes my stomach flip. Did I just give Teddy a strong emotion?

I've found someone I can trust myself with, and I decide to toss aside that careful shield I have to maintain around him and his dangerous charm. I can be sure I held out longer than anyone ever did. I look at his perfect bottom lip and think about the way it's always lifting up on a wicked smile. Now I kiss it. I lick it.

Speaking of teeth, his are white and lovely. I press my tongue on his canine just to feel the pain. He permits me the kind of access I'd never imagined I'd want, putting my tongue against his, everything wet, sharp, soft.

Hair, mouth, and teeth . . . I'm now adding skin into my luscious free fall into Teddy's orbit. Men's skin is vastly different from women's, I know that now as I cup my hands on his jaw, tingling my fingertips on his stubble before sliding down his throat. It's a thicker, warmer hide than my own; it can withstand a nail scratch and the soft drag of my teeth.

His hands spread wider, squeezing, like it's hurting him to not put his hands all over my body. "If you touch me, I'll get really carried away," I say into the side of his neck as I find a pulse point. "How flattering," I remark as I open my mouth over it. The sound he makes is pure sex. I understand vampires now. Above, the sky is black and flecked with gunpowder stars.

"Ruthie." I hear a note of warning and his hands flex on me.

In my voice there's just a plea. "Just a little longer. I'm enjoying myself so much." I go to fit our lips together again, when he puts a hand on my jaw.

"My turn," he says.

He's moving his hand. I feel a soft, stretchy tug on my shoulder. He's put a fist into my cardigan pocket. I laugh into his mouth.

I'm not allowed to be amused for long; he's got things for me to do.

He wants me to take whatever he gives me with grateful attention. I must tell him he's gorgeous with every twist of my mouth. I shudder and melt with every change of tempo and every unexpected deepening. He's sketching on me, that's how it feels; lightness, the suggestion of shapes, darker lines then digging into the page. Back to shading at the edges. I'm not remotely scared of this bigger picture we're creating now; my hands are trying to find the edges of his clothes.

"Settle, settle," he soothes me as he huffs warm air against the side of my neck. It feels like he can't bear to remove his mouth from me. I'm right—I feel a lick, sliding into a mouth twist and the scrape of teeth. If he wants to do that randomly all over my body, that would be great.

"Ruthie, what the hell," he says through a mouthful of my shoulder. "Yum." He's losing focus, a husky slur to his voice. The shoulder of my cardigan interrupts his progress and he bites the entire thing in his mouth. A big quack of laughter comes out of me, echoing louder off the stone walls of the courtyard.

"Don't eat this cardigan, please. I need it."

"I don't," he replies, and his hand slides down the sides of my body.

I feel his fists grip the hemline of my skirt and I go completely rigid. What underwear am I wearing? Plain white cotton. Teddy stands, I'm steadied on my feet and he retreats behind the courtyard table to put a physical barrier between us.

"Sorry," Teddy blurts. "You see?" He's got beautiful color in his face, eyes glittering, the ink on his arms contrasting with the dusky flush, veins cording and fists flexing. "I always get carried away."

"You didn't. It's okay, I was just remembering that my underwear isn't sexy." I have to prove that I'm not crazy-in-love with him, but what I say next is so brutally honest I wince partway through saying it. "That was the best kiss I ever had."

"Then why do you look so guilty?"

"I probably was too intense." As I start to rewind what I just did to him, the sounds I made, I begin to curl up into myself inside.

"Hey. You've got nothing to be ashamed about. You're amazing." He says it in a really kind way. It's also the start of a sentence that girls like me hear all the time. *You're amazing, but I want to just stay friends.*

"Did I come on too strong?"

Teddy laughs and takes out his keys. "I'm a big boy. I can handle you. But we'd better stop here. Close your door on me before I follow you in."

CHAPTER TWENTY-TWO

Week 4 of the Sasaki Method is here and I don't care about it anymore, but it is imperative that Melanie and Teddy don't notice because I do have some pride left. It's Friday evening and we are all lying by the lake. In the middle of us is an empty pizza box. TJ is allowed to graze near the picnic blanket edge, always under the watchful eye of his father.

Melanie's telling me now, "I've been chatting on your MatchUp account with three nice guys for the entire week. No dicks, no foreign princes, no requests for Western Union money transfers, no requests for nudes. I think we've got some real contenders."

"That bar is so low TJ couldn't fit under it," Teddy remarks acidly, reaching out a hand to turn his tortoise 90 degrees. Then we make eye contact and Teddy blushes sunset pink.

I always assumed it would be me dorking out after our kiss, but the opposite has happened. I've kept my cool. Meanwhile, Teddy's gotten so flustered he's been:

- Dropping bags of takeout
- Walking into hedges/flailing in spiderwebs/slipping on duck droppings
- Losing his train of thought so badly that Renata has accused him of stealing medication

This is what keeps my heart beating too fast in my chest all day long: he's acting so weird because he can't recover from how I kissed him. And I'm the only one who knows.

Melanie snaps at him, "Go away if you're going to be difficult. Anyhow, here we are, Ruthie. Week 4, you take over your MatchUp app. Here's your username and password." This is presented to me with ceremony, typed at the top of the Week 4 worksheet, which outlines the activity for this week.

I summarize the requirement out loud for Teddy's benefit. "Goal: One date at the Thunderdome. Method: Flirty messaging and chatting online with two guys, bonus points for flirty conversation with two guys in real life."

"I can't stop thinking about you. One in the bag, beautiful." Teddy holds up a hand for me to high-five. I can't slap it; Melanie is too scary for me to risk it. Lowering it back down, he says, "What, aren't I a guy?"

He looks into my eyes and now we're traveling back in time; I'm straddling him, I'm kissing him until his breath catches in his chest and his hands tighten on my body—

"You're absolutely not a guy." Melanie is sick of this. "Your constant attempts to derail this to keep the attention on yourself are really annoying." Stacked beside her on the blanket are an assortment of what are presumably her reference books, their titles including:

- *True Love and Astrology*
- *His Aura, Her Aura, Their Aura*
- *Crystals for Luck, Love, and Sexual Energy*
- *Best Baby Names*

The last one is a worry, and it's full of purple sticky tabs. "I have warned you about getting carried away." I pull it out of the stack.

"What the hell," Teddy echoes faintly when he reads the spine.

She shakes her head. "No, no. I'm looking up the names of the guys I'm messaging for you."

I open to a tab and scan down the page, searching for a clue. A faint pencil mark is beside a name and I read it out. "Paul. 'Small, humble, restrained.'"

She shrugs. "I decided he's no good for you."

I lower the book. "Just so I'm clear. You're choosing guys for me based on the meaning of their name?"

She nods like that's not very, very strange. "My top pick for you on MatchUp is Brendan. That means sword, which is kinda hot."

Teddy flops down onto his back, wriggles, and puts his head on my lap. Side note—I'm wearing new tight jeans. To the office. On a Friday. And they made Teddy go shy for a bit. With his heavy head on my legs, he looks up at the baby book in my hands.

I would bet a billion dollars that I know what he'll say next. What else would someone so in love with themselves say next? I'm already leafing through to the letter T. From my lap, Teddy says, "Tell me what Ruthie means."

A billion dollars down the drain. I gape down at him.

Teddy reaches out sideways to turn TJ again. I privately think that TJ wants to keep walking and would be perfectly fine if he did. But Teddy is truly devoted to his little friend. He's amended the lyrics of his bellowed shower song to "Wondershell." He's asked me, is it possible to keep TJ? *Fairchild is crazy close to the Reptile Zoo. Twenty-five minutes. I could put him in day care. Did you know that, Ruthie, how close it is to where I'll be?*

Melanie says, "I know it sounds insane, but I think that people are a lot like their name meaning. Like, Melanie means black. And look." She holds her black ponytail up like proof. "I've ruled out a few contenders that couldn't go through to the next round. One guy's name meant *dairy man*. Can you even imagine?"

I think of all the possibilities she's probably deleted. "I am lucky anyone wants to message me at all, but you're ruling out Paul because his name means *small*? He could be seven feet tall." Out of the corner of my eye, Teddy's legs stretch. "He could be my soul mate, and you just decided based on an ancient name meaning?"

Melanie shakes her head. "I asked him. He was five two."

Teddy takes the book from me and my hands drop into my lap/his hair. Melanie doesn't seem to notice, so I'll just untangle this one messy section. It's like knitting. Something repetitive and soothing to occupy myself with in the evenings, on the couch as *Heaven Sent* fills me with that scrummy kind of comfy nostalgia.

Threading my fingers through Teddy's hair is an addictive action that I can do for hours.

He flips through the book. "R. Let's see. Rhiannon, Rhonda, Rose—" On that last one, he stumbles. "Rowena, Rukmini, Ruth." He reads the definition and lowers the book. "Uncanny. You know what, Mel? You could write a sequel to the Sasaki Method. Whittle down your romantic options according to name meanings. I believe it now."

She's smug. "I've already got the title. *The Sasaki Meaning.*"

Teddy and I say in perfect, disbelieving unison: "Holy shit."

"So what's Ruth mean?" She's preparing to be cheeky, that much is clear. Once upon a time, seeing this impending joke at my expense would have had me battening down the hatches. Now, I'm smiling. I'm having another one of those *where-am-I* moments. Friends, picnic, lake, sunset.

She delivers her zinger. "Let me guess. Ruth means *administrator.*"

I throw a pizza crust at her head. "It means *employer.*"

Teddy reads out of the baby book: "Ruth." He aims a big smile up at me and I feel it in my heart. "Kind. Compassionate friend or companion."

"Sexy, huh," I say.

From this angle I can see he's finished reading the description, but he keeps going.

"Brown-eyed sublime being. She of soft, deep cardigan pockets. Bubble-bath taker. Pool jumper. Cheese provider. Sunset glower. Heaven sent."

It's the loveliest description of me I have ever heard. I pass my hand through his beautiful hair. "That's more interesting than the original meaning. Being both a Ruth and a Virgo has been my cross to bear."

Melanie says, "You're a Leo, Teddy. It's so obvious. Look at the lion, lying there being groomed by the virgin."

I have to laugh. "Oof, way too close to the truth." I see the question Mel is too afraid to ask. "I lost my virginity at prom. And . . . that was the last time. Teddy knows this already."

"After a drought that long, I will give you a pass to have a one-night stand during the Sasaki Method program." She looks at my hands in his hair, his endless legs carelessly kicked out. She compresses her lips. "A one-night stand with a stranger, not this one here. So what's the name Theodore mean, anyway?"

"Guess." If he was hoping for flattery, he is sorely disappointed.

Me: "Vagabond."

Melanie: "Infant bear."

Me: "Lord of legs."

Melanie: "Train wreck."

Me: "Hot mess."

Melanie: "Lazy rich boy."

He laughs and hates us. "Shut up, both of you. You're so wrong. I was named perfectly." He reaches out a hand and turns TJ back toward us again.

I leaf through T and read out loud: "Theodore. You've got to be kidding me." I close my eyes. "God's gift."

Melanie's howls echo off the hillside.

"You think I'm God's gift?" He snuggles himself up a little on my thighs. He makes me feel like I've got the best lap there is. "Thank you, Ruthie. You always make me feel good about myself."

"Back to the matter at hand, making Ruthie feel good about herself," Melanie tells him in a warning tone. "Open the app, Ms. Midona. Now open the messages. The top three or so are our potential Mr. Ruthies."

"How many guys have you been messaging as me?" I scroll down a few hundred yards. "Mel, this is crazy. How much time have you spent doing this?"

"I've been trawling the ocean for you," she defends herself. "You should be thanking me. That sexy glasses guy named Christopher has asked if you want to get coffee." There's a bear growl from my lap.

"How did I get this many matches? Did you photoshop my head onto a hot bikini?" No, she didn't. It's just the picture Teddy took of me at my desk. Flattery is an unexpected cozy fire I've stumbled upon, and I'm feeling a glow. "Weird."

Teddy is sour. "Random guys make you feel more flattered than I ever could."

I press his frown line away with my fingertips. "That's because they're not after my Wi-Fi password."

Mel remembers something. "Where's your janky old motorbike? It's gone from the courtyard."

"I assume it's in his bed. Handlebars on the pillows." Every time I get him to grin, it feels like I've won something.

She takes my phone from me and begins typing. "If you have no objections, we'll go with Brendan. No objections from Ruthie," she clarifies as Teddy opens his mouth to speak. She stares at the screen, then smiles. "Instant reply. He's keen. Next Thursday. I've got a date too. We can both be in the Thunderdome and I'll take care of you from afar."

"Sounds good." Also sounds scary.

Mel checks the time. "Whoops, sun's going down. I've gotta go. Read over Week 4. Chat to guys on MatchUp. Go flirt with two real guys, I don't care if they're nerds at the library. Just get some real practice in on someone who isn't Teddy. Then we'll set up a date for this coming Thursday."

"She can practice on me any old day," Teddy says, stretching and snuggling again.

She smiles down at him with all her teeth. "Enjoy that lap while it lasts, bucko."

"I sure will," he replies in the exact same faux-sweet tone.

Melanie gathers up all her belongings, which takes quite a lot of time, and off she goes. "Bye," she calls into the powder-pink sunset. "Teddy, you gotta get ready to let her go."

"Watch where you walk," Teddy shouts after her, up on one elbow. He's got a hand caged over TJ. "Ugh, she's not watching," he mutters to himself before rolling back down onto my lap with a groan.

Every time he looks up and seeks eye contact with me, I know that complete dazzlification has occurred. I've got a date with someone called Brendan next week. Or was it Brandon? The sword guy. How could I think of anyone else when I have this person comfortably weighing me down?

Teddy says, "I was wondering if you'd like to come on a field trip with me and the Parlonis on Sunday."

I watch his brow crease and his nervous lip lick. "Where are we going?"

"Alistair will be up at the new studio to check the progress of the fit-out. He mentioned it like he doesn't think I'd want to go. I can kill two birds with one stone. Renata can get a quote from him on how much her true-love piece will be and whether he agrees to do it. She'll finally stop hassling me about it. Anyway, come with us. They're both going to fall asleep in the back seat. We can listen to this *Heaven Sent* podcast I found."

He knows how to make things tempting. "With what happened last time, the alarm . . . I don't think I can." I see the disappointment in his eyes when he nods and blinks away across the lake without a word. I argue back anyway. "How could I just leave?"

"I'll tuck in every resident. I'll put a protective force field over Providence." He turns his face back up to mine and my heart misses several beats. I start to die when he murmurs, "I'll check that every single door is locked. I'll carry you over my shoulder and put you in the passenger seat. It'll be easy."

"I still don't know why you require me."

"I'm nervous about seeing Alistair and I want to show off to you about which room at the studio is going to be mine. Why do I require you? What a weird question. I always require

264

you." He's got that little line between his eyebrows again. "What exactly do you think is going on here?" He gestures vaguely around us and my heart squiggles with nerves. When I turn to look at the beautiful backdrop to this moment, I see something.

A golden bonnet tortoise is making its way over to us. I see some red on it, then relax when it's not blood. It's Sharpie. "Hey. Look. It's Number One. Teddy, it's my first tortoise."

He's smiling up at me from my lap. "You never forget a face? This girl is so cute," he adds to himself.

I lean sideways and pick up the tortoise. He's a healthy boy now, big as a paperback, kicking and protesting his midair situation with vigor. I look down at Teddy and try to suppress my smile at his rapt expression. "I'm just going to have a moment here with this tortoise, which might be weird, but who knows when I'll see him again."

"Have your moment."

I say to the gimlet-eyed creature, "Number One, when I first picked you up, I didn't know a thing. But you made me realize that I can still help without being a vet. You gave me hope. You were the one who changed everything for me and I hope we meet again someday. Let me just . . ." I put the tortoise back down on the blanket, take a few photos of him, and then rummage through my bag. Using my headphone cord, I measure across the shell and mark it with a hair clip. "I can record his size in his chart."

When I let it go, Number One stomps off, fuming. "Letting them go is the hardest part. I was so careless. I should have known the marker would stain." I apply hand sanitizer and wonder if this might be a good segue into convincing Teddy to release TJ. "Now that rare, precious creature is marked forever because of me."

The combination of words I've chosen sound like a magic spell verse under this pink glitter swirl-sky. With the weight of this man's head on my legs, I feel a swell of melancholy I could never have anticipated. And like always, because we share everything, Teddy feels it.

"You are not careless." He says it with such quiet confidence that it salves that little crack in my heart.

"We're lying right in the middle of all your hard work and kindness. Your mark is all over everything." He looks at his tattooed forearm, then sighs up at the sky. "I wish I could be even a fraction of the person you are. Sometimes, I lose all composure when you look at me. You've got this look that just . . . levels me flat."

"I'm not that great," I say dolefully, and it makes him laugh. "Teddy, you're a good person. I personally guarantee it. You're very vain, but why wouldn't you be." I sift my fingertips through his black silk. "And you've done something no one else has."

"What?" His eyes are full of starlight now. I cannot believe I have him here, holding me down, this rare, precious creature. He is going to break my heart when he walks off into the night.

"You stayed longer than any other boy." I bend and press a kiss on his forehead. "For however long you stay, I'm glad I had you here. There's no one else in the world who could compare to you." These are words he loves to hear and I hope it's because it's me saying them. Now I've got to say something that might hurt him. "Do you think it's time to let TJ go now?"

Second First Impressions

Teddy looks sideways at his tortoise, always at arm's length. "I don't think he's ready."

"I think he's got to hit the road, just like Number One. And just like you will soon."

"You always talk like you're saying goodbye to me. Other girls have talked to me like I'm going to be a permanent fixture and it made me want to get up and walk out of rooms. But this is worse." His eyes search mine.

"Worse, how?" I'm combing my fingers through his hair, and when I find no knots, I realize I've just been sitting here stroking him. "It's okay. I've always known that you're leaving."

"You expecting me to leave makes me . . . itch." He taps a finger on his chest, and without thought I begin to scratch him through his T-shirt. He's laughing, he's sad. "Stop always trying to give things to me. I don't deserve your lovely scratching."

He rolls off me and the loss of his weight on me is as dreadful as I anticipated. He picks up TJ and says to him, "Ruthie thinks you're ready." Then to me, "Are you sure I can't take him with me? I'd take perfect care of him."

I kneel up too. "I know you would. But he's got to find a wife. Or a husband. I don't actually know if that's a male tortoise. This is where he belongs. I don't think living his life in a tank in your new place will compare to this."

We look up at the celestial dome forming above us as the sun sinks lower. The sky is a thousand shades of violet. A breeze skates over us. I can smell pollen and Renata's perfume that Teddy is gassed to death in. (He calls it *Spiteful Number Five*.) There's the sludgy mud of the lake bank and the wool of the blanket, too. Providence is safe, held in this cupped dome of silver pinprick stars, and maybe for tonight I can let myself rest.

"I'm really tired of looking after everything," I confess without context, but he just nods and puts TJ down. We watch him walk toward the general direction of the lake. "I'm really proud of you. My first one walked off like that and it kinda hurt my feelings."

"Yeah. Well, maybe we should go home. Did you see the fancy ice creams I put in the freezer? I've been living for them." The way he talks is like we live together, forever, nestled up together under a blanket.

I know that's not how things are, but gosh it would be nice to have a big, bold, passionate memory to return to when I'm alone again. We're facing each other now, kneeling, close enough to touch.

I've got to grab this moment while my big rare creature remains with me on this picnic blanket. I need to do something big, or else I'll be left with nothing but what-ifs. "I'm fairly inexperienced at these things, but this feels like a really romantic setting."

"It is." He's looking at me with a spark of interest in his eyes. "You're finally noticing that?"

I'm being drawn into his black pupils like he's hypnotizing me. "Could I ask you to kiss me, please?"

"Your wish is my command," he says, leaning down. Just a fraction before he touches my lips with his, he says, "But only if you come to the tattoo studio."

"Yes," I say, and I get my wish. It is everything I hoped it would be.

CHAPTER TWENTY-THREE

A re we there?" Renata asks from the back seat, yawning like a kid. "That was quick."

It wasn't quick. It was a very long drive, and Teddy and I listened to almost eleven episodes of the *Heaven Sent* podcast. My hamstrings are tight from sitting, and my stomach hurts from laughing at everything Teddy says. Is it legal to have such a gorgeous side profile?

"Aggie. Aggie." Renata is nudging her sister. "We're here at the tattoo parlor. Aggie." I twist in my seat. Aggie is resting against the door, eyes closed, mouth open. My heart jumps in fright and Renata begins to shake her. "Wake. Up."

Aggie makes a deep, dry gurgle and sits upright. Everyone breathes out.

"I thought you were dead," Renata accuses her.

"Not quite," Aggie replies. She allows Renata to fuss over her, and she does for a few long moments, straightening Aggie's collar, patting her hand. When I look in the rearview mirror,

I see Renata's eyes are glossed in tears. "It's all right, it's all right," Aggie repeats.

"You really scared me," Renata retorts, her voice breaking on a sob. "And look how close I am to my tattoo. I would have been too late."

"Well, you're not," Aggie replies. They lean together, foreheads touching. It's a moment that Teddy and I are now intruding on and we get out of the car. I'm missing something, but I can't work it out.

"Phew, that felt like a close one," Teddy says. "Does that kind of moment happen a lot for you?"

"Yes, it does. I've found plenty of people who have passed away."

"Really." Teddy is surprised. "How do you deal with it?"

"I've got a checklist that guides me through it." I look over at him and see that answer isn't remotely enough. "Then, after the funeral company has left and their family members have gone home, I cry in the bath." I don't want to remember the last time that happened, just over four months ago. Tiny, frail Mrs. Higgins didn't answer her door when I checked in on her. I found her in bed, ice cold. And I let these three coax me off the property again, leaving everyone behind.

"Please tell me about your studio," I say with a lump in my throat. "Please help me think of something else."

Teddy puts an arm around my shoulder. "This is my place. Well, it will be. What do you think? The sign got done yesterday" On the front window is an old-fashioned sailor tattoo, an anchor with a scroll over the top. I read the name of the studio out loud. "Always and Forever. That's quite a romantic name for a tattoo studio."

"That's what I've always thought, too. You go on in, I'll get the gals out."

Walking into a place like this should be a miniexercise under the Sasaki Method, because it takes guts. I'm in an almost-finished waiting area. There's a black couch still wrapped in plastic, an unplugged computer, and an empty cabinet stacked with boxes of jewelry. Loose on the counter are printed photos of tattoos. The sore-looking skin with new ink that makes me wince, but I begin to find Teddy's work.

"There, there, there," I touch my fingers across the photos.

"Can I help you?" A man walks out, then looks past me and sees Teddy outside. "He actually showed up."

I don't like that tone. I indicate the photos. "I was just picking which ones were designed by Teddy."

"Pretty easy to spot that kind of talent. We'll hang them up on that wall there. I'm Alistair." He's a bearded guy, older than I'd imagined and dressed in crumpled flannel. He looks more like a construction worker, more so because he's got paint on his forearm and a layer of dust.

I hold out a hand. "I'm Ruthie Midona. I'm Teddy's neighbor."

"You're Ruthie," he repeats, like I'm famous. We shake hands. "Well, I didn't see that coming."

"How do you mean?"

"You're not what I expected," Alistair says, which is intriguing, and it's frustrating when he gets distracted by the sight of the Parlonis holding on to Teddy's arms. "Wow. I didn't think he'd last a week doing that."

"Me neither. But he works twelve-hour days for them. He never complains, and believe me, they give him a lot to complain about."

"I'm giving her the tour," Teddy yells from outside, weighed down by his elderly employers. "Wait for me."

"I hope you're going to stop giving him a hard time," I say to Alistair quietly. "He's working his ass off to make this happen and he wants this so badly. Make him feel like you actually want him here, okay?"

Alistair blinks, hesitates, turns an embarrassed color, and goes to open the front door. "You're just in time. I need your thoughts on the paint the contractor's suggested."

Teddy smiles brightly, then reflexively looks at me, and I'm in love.

I always thought that love would feel like something gentle, but this isn't. I feel a clawing, desperate need to hold his heart in my hand and to fend off anything that might damage it. The world outside Providence is a chaotic, restless thing, full of disappointments and pain. I am the only one careful enough to hold on to something so precious.

"Fetch the needle, I'm not getting any younger," Renata says to Alistair.

"We agreed that this is a consult, to get started on the design," Teddy tells Renata when she opens her mouth to argue. "I'm not designing it for you and that's final. Alistair is the best."

Judging from what I've seen in the waiting room, Teddy is the best. I wish he would realize it. I'm surprised by how quickly I've adjusted to this I'm-in-love revelation. It's like picking up a coat in a thrift store and shrugging it on; it fits. I don't need to look in a mirror to know it. Now I just carry on wearing it. My back aches from that huge drive. I don't know how many more times I could do that.

Alistair takes Renata and Aggie into a small room off the hallway and seats them. "So what are we doing here?"

"I've got some ideas," Renata says, digging in her Birkin for her notepad. "It's a tribute to the love of my life."

Has he passed away? How long ago was their affair? I know she's never married. In that YouTube footage of Renata abusing Karl Lagerfeld, it's Aggie seated beside her, looking young and lovely. There was some kind of tension between them that went as far back as their prom night. Maybe they were both in love with the same man. I'm rather pleased with my juicy theory and decide to discuss it with Teddy later.

"You are going to make her lifelong wish come true," Aggie observes to Alistair. "She couldn't sleep last night, just tossed and turned."

"I'm honored," Alistair says, smiling at them both. "I think I'll need to look at your skin to see if it's suitable for the piece."

"Why?" Renata goes very still, like a snake before striking. Alistair doesn't know her, and he blunders on.

"You're older than my average client. I've never worked on anyone as old . . ." He trails off and realizes he's just pulled the pin on a grenade. Teddy and I are already halfway down the hall when she detonates.

We go into a room at the end of the corridor. It's got a bench for the client, a counter, and a stool. "This will be my room," Teddy tells me and I watch him smooth his hands down on the countertops. "I like this one because I can see all the way down to the front desk. I can't wait until I have my own photos on the wall here. So what do you think?"

It's the second time he's asked that and he's nervous for my answer. "It's great, Teddy. But every boss has an office. Where's yours?"

The question surprises him. "I didn't think about that. I'm going to be living upstairs, so I guess I could work out of the spare room? I'm going to talk to Alistair about the things I want to do here."

Now I notice he's got a bulging file under one arm. He says, "I got a quote for the software. And I downloaded a free trial and mocked up how it'll look. It was your idea. It's things like that that'll make him take me seriously."

"You take yourself seriously. That's the most important thing. I'm proud of you."

"Thank you," he says with such sincerity that I know it's one of the first goodbyes we will have. I abruptly don't want to hear it, but he continues, "You've helped me get my confidence for this. I don't know how to run a business. Between you and Alistair, I know I'll have someone to ask when I don't know something."

So I'll be back at Providence, at my desk, receiving a call when he doesn't know how to add a new client to the database. In the background, I'll hear pretty girls leaning on the glass counter-top, picking out their piercing jewelry, waiting for him to get off the phone to flirt with him. I've always known what's been happening here, but it still makes me feel small. I've helped plenty of handsome boys with their homework or the Parlonis over the years. "Would it be okay if I go wait in the car?"

He's crushed. "But I've waited a long time to be in this room, and I want to be in it with you. Come sit down." He pats the bench seat that I guess clients lie on. I edge my butt up. He asks, "What's happening with you?"

"Let's pretend I'm a new client." I put my arm out in the hopes that he'll touch me.

He laughs and wheels over his stool. "Okay, New Client, what do you want?"

"I want to be entered correctly into your new database with a reminder of my next appointment. And I want a bluebird tattoo."

He's startled. "What's the significance of that?"

"I saw the one you did on Brianna. It was beautiful, and I was jealous of it. So one imaginary bluebird, please." He wheels away, grabs a pen, and wheels back. Uncapping it, he looks at my skin with indecision. I say, "Go ahead."

He hesitates on my inner arm. "You literally have no hair or freckles. Is this skin even real?" He rubs a thumb over it, then his palm. Creating a warm friction bloom between us, he polishes across my skin with admiration in his eyes. "How could I even put a dot on this?"

"I want you to surprise me." I look up at the ceiling and feel the cold touch of the pen. "High-school Ruthie is gagging right now. She's telling me to not trust you, and that you're going to write something mean on me."

"I won't." The icy tickle of the pen begins moving on me. "So how's the Providence review coming along?"

I close my eyes, tired just thinking about it.

"Rose seems really unhappy with everything I've provided. No matter what I give her, she asks me, 'Where's the rest?' I don't think she realizes that it's a really small office and things are probably a lot more simple than she's used to. I'm doing my best without Sylvia."

"If Dad's life philosophy is *Life is change*, Rose's is *Where's the rest?*" Teddy repeats softly. The pen on me pauses, and I swear I feel it skip and wobble. "But Melanie told me that you've been really holding it together. I'm real proud of you."

There's more of that goodbye feeling. I look up at the ceiling. "When Rose finds out that you're part owner here, she'll be really impressed."

"She'll ask me how long until I get bored and move on. I'd better get out of Providence before she does something really spiteful." He moves the pen, ticking in some detail. I like the sensation of his big hand holding my elbow and the brush of his knuckles. "This place is nothing that will impress her."

I hear how sad that makes him. "Why is she so mean to you?"

He smiles at the dark murder in my voice. "She's paranoid that I'm going to come to my senses one day and try to get into Dad's seat. She hates that I'm the only son." The pen pauses.

"She's the only one who makes a big deal out of that. Maybe some of the board members have said something to her."

I tip my face over to watch his face, but I avoid looking down at my arm. It's probably my only chance to wear his art on my body, and I want the full impact of a final grand reveal. "Anyone who knows you knows you're not interested in stealing her job."

"Yeah, and she doesn't know me. She's always been like a guard dog, growling every time I come too close." He blinks up at my face and notices my attention. "No peeking."

"Of course I wouldn't. Aren't I trustworthy?" I smile when he does.

"You're very trustworthy," he says like a realization, eyes intensifying on his work. "I bet you keep secrets for the rest of your life."

"I haven't been given too many to keep." I hug my free arm across myself. "Is that the issue Rose has with you? She thinks you're going to one day turn up in a suit and demand all that you're rightfully entitled to as the male Prescott?"

"That's the thing," he says, pausing the pen strokes. He sits back. "I'm not entitled."

"I know that. You never come across like that."

"I mean it kind of literally. I'm from Dad's second marriage. I was a love child." He puts quotations around that phrase. "I told you I didn't meet my sisters until I was eight. That's because I had no idea they existed. And they really didn't know about me."

"Oh, gosh. Was Jerry—your dad—involved with your life?"

He looks sideways, remembering. "My only early memories

were that he traveled a lot. Mom said he was always away on a big business trip, and when he came back, he'd give me art supplies, which I loved. But what was actually happening was, he was going home to his wife, Dianne Prescott, and her four daughters. And in between his visits, we ran out of money. Mom is not a budgeter. I'm told that I'm spooky-similar to her."

I have a feeling it's Rose who's told him that. "So how did they find out about you?"

"It was a big fiasco, caused by my mom, of course. She's dramatic," he adds wryly. "And she can drink too much, although she's gotten a handle on it lately. She turned up at Jerry and Dianne's vow renewal ceremony, drunk as a skunk, and you know that part in the ceremony where they ask—"

"If anyone knows any reason why these two should not be married—" I supply, filled with a mix of fascination and horror. "She didn't."

"She did. She blew up their entire marriage. Dianne packed her bags, emptied an account, filed for divorce. The official line is she went to stay at a health spa in Switzerland, but I think she had a breakdown."

"How awful."

"So imagine all that wreckage. Left behind were four flowery girls. Daisy, Lily, Poppy, and Rose. They were confused by where their mommy was and why their parents were no longer married. Dad walks me into the living room, told the girls I was their new brother, then got a work call and left the room."

He leans forward, recaptures my wrist in a warm grip, and

278

begins drawing again like he needs the distraction. "Awkward is not a word that can properly convey that moment."

"Were they mean to you?"

"Daisy, Poppy, and Lily were younger than me. I told them they could dress me up any way they wanted. That made them happy, and when I grew my hair they practiced hairstyles on me. They all loved me straightaway. My name until I was almost thirteen was . . ." He stops himself and laughs. "Why do I tell you everything?"

I have a lump in my throat. I need him to tell me everything, forever. "Please tell me that nickname. I can keep a secret, remember."

He stands, grasps the bottom of his T-shirt, and stretches it up. He's searching on himself like he's scratching through the kitchen junk drawer for a pair of scissors. "Fine. Here." He turns to the side, and as I try to focus on the art and not the body (difficult), I spot what he's showing me. Another flower tattoo hidden in the mix.

"Your nickname was Sunflower? That suits you." Now that I've dutifully admired his art, I can now give myself a second to look at his body as he pulls the T-shirt back down. How ribs and muscles can coexist together so closely, I have no idea.

He drops back heavily onto the stool. "But Rose was my age. Actually, we're less than six months apart. How Dad managed to juggle two newborns at once . . . well, scratch that. He didn't juggle much. Mom says he only dropped in twice a week, disguised as a gym visit."

"But he and your mom were in love," I venture. "They got married in the end, right?" I know there won't be a happy ending.

"That's what's so bad about it. They were married for eighteen months. Turns out, Mom liked having a rich-guy secret boyfriend who dropped in twice a week with some cash. She's due to trade in her current husband any day now. I worry all the time that I'm like that. I have been like that," he clarifies in the quietest voice.

"I think you can be any way you want to be."

He's doing tiny touches of the pen now on my arm, and I sense that it's almost over.

"Rose is furious, twenty years later, that I ever walked into that living room. You were completely right when you said Rose is the only girl I've never been able to charm. And I'm telling you this because I am not going to be able to save Providence from her. Me being there is making it more dangerous by the day."

"Does she know you have a tattoo for her? I've seen it on the back of your arm. It's so beautiful."

"They all have one," he says lightly, like it means nothing to walk around with tributes to each. "But that rose hurt worse than all of them put together."

"Let her know that she's important to you, and you'd like a chance to make a fresh impression. I think the next time you walk into a room that she's in, it'll be different."

"There's no point in trying," he explains patiently. "I just accept things like this. It hurts too much otherwise. Thanks for being such a good listener, Ruthie Midona. I hope you like your temporary tattoo."

He gets up to go check in with Renata, and I am left sitting behind, stunned at the creation on my arm. It's an angel, around five inches tall. She's got flowing robes—or is it a cardigan?—wrapping a neat, curvy frame, tiny pointed bare toes and wings out, she's reaching up to the heavens. And in her hands, smaller than half a fingernail in size, is the unmistakable outline of a tortoise.

I don't like it. I love it.

I can see what we could be, in another reality where his dream wasn't too far away and I hadn't made a lifelong commitment to Providence. I'm probably going to have to take his advice and just accept it. It hurts too much otherwise.

"Come on, I want to give you the rest of the tour," Teddy says from the hallway. "Want to see my new bedroom?"

CHAPTER TWENTY-FOUR

'm too quiet on the drive home. The Parlonis aren't; they're collapsed sideways onto each other, openmouthed snoring. "Are you tired?" Teddy asks me. "Are you hungry? I can stop somewhere."

"I'm fine." I hate how bland I sound. I need to do better. "It's all just feeling pretty real, seeing your studio and your apartment."

"It's nice, huh." Teddy's smiling and wrapped up in the glow of his new future. "My commute time will be even shorter than at Providence. I can fall down those stairs in about twenty seconds. What did you think of the bathroom?" This is the second time he's asked me. "I lay in the tub to check that it's comfortable."

Let the record reflect that I was really, really supportive as he took me upstairs to parade me around his new apartment. With his lovely warm give-take hands cupped on my shoulders, I was walked around and dutifully admired:

- The bathroom ("Wow, it's brand-new—I love those tiles!")

- The kitchen ("You could fit a turkey in this oven, Teddy!")
- The living room ("Please don't find a couch on the side of the road.")
- The view ("I bet that tree is pretty when the leaves change.")

The more I gave him, the happier and more excited he became. I couldn't say anything about the bedroom, because I'll never be in it. But it was lovely, too. I have a full-body shiver just thinking of how he walked me in and massaged my shoulders while detailing the apartment's heating system to me. It's superior, naturally.

"I think the spare room will be a good office space," he enthuses now, reaching over to squeeze my leg before he turns down the air-conditioning and angles the vent away from me. "If I put my desk under the window, I'll probably get distracted all the time. There's room enough for two desks."

"I guess there is. It's a nice big space." It will be filled with sunlight in the mornings. "Set yourself up two desks, one for your art."

"Which wall would you put your desk on?"

I'm all out of opinions. "I don't know. The back wall." We're almost back to Providence. I just need to maintain this pleased façade a little longer, and then I can sink into the bath and feel sorry for myself. I've always known this was coming. My residents don't move away and send me postcards. Now I have to begin to deal with the slow death of this special friendship.

283

He says, "I'll put my desk under the window. Nice and sunny for some herbs in pots there, too." Decision made, he's humming and happy as he drives us up to the upper parking lot so the Parlonis have less distance to walk. They're bleary-eyed and tired, and Aggie is so heavy in the brace of my arm I'm exhausted by the time we unlock their door.

The visit to Always and Forever (Fairchild location) was a success. Alistair was stunned that Teddy had turned up, let alone selected a new software to implement, but he hid it well. Their discussion became increasingly animated, from storage space to sanitation contractors. Alistair is now convinced of Teddy's new professional approach and Teddy is muddy-piglet happy.

I am truly happy for him.

"I never saw the tattoo design," I say to Renata as she settles into her armchair.

"I like a grand reveal. I'm having it done next Tuesday." She looks over to the kitchen, opens her mouth to bellow, then realizes that Teddy is already microwaving something for them. "Good," she grumbles. "What a shame I have to find a new boy when I'd just gotten this one the way I like him."

"It is a shame, but we knew it would happen." I put the TV remote within her reach and unbuckle her shoes for her. Aggie is already sound asleep. "I'm going to go now. Good night," I call out in the general direction of the kitchen.

"Wait," Teddy replies, just like I knew he would, but I can't wait anymore.

The cold night air outside brings every frustration I've been packing down to the surface. He's so oblivious. That's what always gets me about Teddy; he's so wrapped up in himself, always taking, not realizing how terrible it feels to be left behind. I pass by town house number 15 where I found Mrs. Higgins. She had framed photographs of her husband and children beside her bed. At this rate, I can't say I'll have the same when someone finds me someday.

I'm having a mix of emotions: premature sorrow for the loss for Teddy; a sinking sensation that my time at Providence will just be punctuated by people I care about leaving. I loved Teddy's new apartment. My cottage is dark and cold in comparison and I know I'll never have the courage to find a new place, box my belongings, and leave.

One day, Teddy's going to find a girl who's exactly his type, and she's going to use that nice new oven and heavenly deep bathtub. "Goddamn it," I yell up at the sky when I get to my front door. "Goddamn it."

I've got the key in the door when I hear his jogging footsteps. I've got it closed by the time he skids into the courtyard.

"Open up," he says. "What are you yelling about?"

"I'm tired. I'm having a bath. Good night." I look at the little tortoise-angel on my arm. It's going to fade as soon as I soak it. My frustration twists tighter. Can I have anything for myself, forever?

"I'll just come in," he says and uses the key I gave him. Now he's in the doorway, backlit by the courtyard light and circling moths. He's all I'm ever going to want. I have a date on Thursday, and it will be the first audition of my second choice. No one is ever going to measure up.

"What's got you all riled up, Tidy Girl?" He reaches for me, maybe to smooth the hair back from my face, but my grenade pin is caught on his pinky.

"Don't call me that."

"But that's what I call you," he protests, sinking down about a foot shorter. He looks like I've smacked him with a rolled-up newspaper. "What's happening? I'll fix it. Tell me, tell me," he says, crowding closer, sounding like he cares about me so much.

I push him with my hands on his chest. "Can't you tell when someone just wants to be left alone? This is my place. Give me that key."

"I want to understand what's going on. Is it something I said?"

"It's just really frustrating how you never think about how things feel for me." I hate the concern and care in his eyes. I need to make him get out. "I've done what you wanted. I came with you, I kept you awake on the long drive. I saw your studio and your new apartment. What more do you want?"

That's an easy answer, apparently. "I want you to be happy."

"Impossible."

"How did tonight make you feel?"

"Like I always do. Left behind." I can't stop the words. "You just rubbed your new life in my face, and look where I am again. I'm back at Providence, where I'm probably going to be forever because I'm terrified of change and making a bad decision."

"I wasn't rubbing it in your face. I wanted to impress you."

"Why? Why bother? Are you trying to have a redo of your

relationship with Rose or something?" The thought takes hold the moment I say it out loud. "You are. You're trying to charm me to convince yourself you still can. I'm nothing more than a challenge you're passing the time with. You won't be satisfied until I'm desperately in love with you." I put a lot of sarcasm into that.

His eyebrows go down. "I wanted to impress you because you're really important to me."

"I've helped enough handsome boys with their homework to know that the moment you get that studio key, the exam's over and I will no longer be required."

He's completely bewildered. "No longer required?"

"How could I be? You're leaving. Me." I make myself put the words together. "You're leaving me. You're leaving me to go start a new life, and I'll be back here with no one to care about me. No one to take care of me or to stand up for me. Sylvia will come back and put me in my place. I'll have to watch PDC change this place and every person up that hill will eventually die. And here's Ruthie. Forever. Stuck right here."

"It kills me that you can't leave." He ignores my flapping hands and gathers me into a heavenly hug. "I was trying to impress you tonight because I wanted to show you that there's a whole world out there for you, if you want it. You're like a rabbit in a trap. This place is bad for you."

I'm inclined to agree, but I shake my head automatically against his chest.

"I want to take you with me. That's why I wanted you to love that bathtub."

Have you ever been caught off guard by the sound of your own heartbeat? Maybe you've pressed your ear weirdly on your pillow, and now all you can hear is your own proof of life. You are confronted with your mortality in a base, clock-ticking kind of way: you have an engine room, and it has a finite time-line. What a miracle and a privilege.

I'm feeling like that now as his words sink into me.

"My entire life, I have prayed." He says that softly above my head, cuddling me closer. "In every chaotic fuck-up moment I've ever had, I've said this random prayer in my mind. I wished I could find some kind of peace. Every lost wallet moment. During the divorce, when my mom turned up and threw fits on Dad's front lawn. When neither of them could agree on who would take me. Always knowing I was in the wrong place. I prayed for peace, quiet, certainty. And it's you. I'm in love with you."

I take my ear off his chest and look up at him. "Wait, what?"

It's the only words I get out before he holds my jaw in his hands and kisses me. I don't have to ask him to repeat it now, because he's telling me again with a smile on his lips and a laugh in his throat. Furniture touches the back of my body: counter, couch, wall? I'm not sure. All I know for sure is, Teddy Prescott loves me, and he is not holding it in anymore. Best of all: I believe him.

How many times have I wondered what it would be like to be his sole focus? I know now. He's playful and affectionate with his mouth and hands, with a tremor in his body like he's one second away from laughing out loud up at the ceiling.

He gets his wish when I pull his T-shirt off: he puts my wallpaper all over himself. The contrast of his sticker book-ink against the flowers and vines is something to behold. I behold him for several long moments, while he shivers and puts his hand in his hair, his breath coming light and fast.

I realize what's putting that look in his eyes. He's out on the ledge.

I step out with him and take his hand. "I am in love with you, too."

His relief is my relief. It's always been like that, from the moment I rescued him at the gas station. He sags, exhales, and reaches for me. Now I'm flat on the fairy-tale flowers, being woken from my slumber by true love's kiss.

Tidy, messy. Give, take. Adorer, adoree. Together, we can be all these things. It's the most natural thing in the world to be walking backward across the threshold into the one room Teddy has never ventured into, until now. He breaks his mouth from mine and gets overexcited.

"I have had dreams about this." For a minute or two, I let him pick around on my dresser. I always thought it was because he had a reflex to take and acquire, but it's because he just desperately wants to know me. His fingertip slides along the back of my hairbrush and he picks up a jar of moisturizer to read the label. "Aw," he says fondly, "how cute. You don't have wrinkles. Your face," he says as he pulls me close again, "is all I dream about."

As I am pushed gently onto my bed, he says into my mouth, "Please tell me what your bear is called."

"Teddy."

So it turns out that getting naked with someone can be fun.

I follow the patterns and lines along his body, all those flowers and jewels. Wishbones, goldfish, a queen of hearts card. I kiss a rabbit, a diamond ring, a crown. There's a scary skull on his side, but I kiss it on the cheek. An entire section is just feathers and leaves. He's a masterpiece, every inch, and I tell him this. (He laughs and says thank you.) My hands unbuckle his belt for something to do.

My unexciting white shirt and denim skirt are the most exciting thing that has ever happened to Teddy. The way he looks at me is with such frank appreciation that surely I'm misunderstanding this? It knocks me out of the moment and I have to get his eyes back on mine.

"How am I sexy? I mean, I have a label maker, for heaven's sake." He collapses into my arms like his joints have lost all strength. He's got a hard shape in the front of his expensive jeans. I am very, very sexy.

I thought he'd be suave and dark-eyed-smooth, unhooking my bra with a fingertip, but he's not the Casanova I always assumed he'd be. Teddy's a hot mess in bed, but I mean it in the best possible way. For starters, he's easily distracted. He sees a freckle on my collarbone and loses composure. His mouth muffled against me, I think he says something like, *I saw this and I wanted to do this.* Disorganized to the bone, he's taken off one of my socks, undone the zip of my skirt, the bottom two buttons of my shirt (and a random middle one) and then forgot everything to pull the blankets over us.

"I'm dreaming," he says, twisting kisses on my neck. "I'm in my bed, having one of my Ruthie dreams." I feel him stretch; he's reaching out to touch the wall.

I am probably dreaming myself; held in the patterned cradle of this bicep, I am kissed tenderly by someone who thinks the sun shines out of me. It's not until I feel the warmth of his torso on mine and my sheets on my legs that I realize he's peeled off my clothes. I guess he does have significant skills.

He feels me go still. We float together breathlessly, like in the swimming pool.

"Want to keep going?" he asks, and his eyes roll closed when I nod and put my hand in his hair. We sink. We gasp for air. He shows me things from my feverish midnight fantasies: what it looks like to see his tattooed hand on my breast, the weightless black silk of his hair on my pillow. Everything is fracturing around me now, the tiny flowers on my wallpaper and the daisies on his forearm as he slides his hand down, even lower down, and he tells me I'm like a dream.

He gloats at how turned on he's gotten me. He demands ten different compliments and praises before he'll move his fingertips. I get to four or five when he laughs and relents. I give him probably twenty more compliments after that. I never came close to finding satisfaction with my first boyfriend, Adam; I was too concerned about his comfort and the experience he was having. I never thought about my body as anything other than an instrument for him to find pleasure. All Teddy wants to do is make me smile and shiver, and his own body doesn't seem to concern him. It's his typical unhurried style that brings about my first orgasm. It takes me by surprise, because he didn't seem to have a specific agenda, just a gently nudging thumb.

"Oh, nice," he says as I shudder and spasm with his give hand between my thighs. If I ever thought touching him in return would be awkward, I was wrong: we are friends above all else, and we can talk about these things: I can tell him how I want to try this, and this . . . He lets me. "Perfect," I tell him, when his penis is revealed. "But I thought there'd be a tattoo. Or a big metal piercing."

"Some things are sacred," Teddy explains with a half laugh. "I hope you're not too disappointed." He groans when I show him I'm not, and then links his fingers over mine. I give and take until he's dewy with sweat.

When I decide I would like to take, he obliges with good humor and a courtly kiss on my cheek. "In the drawer," I say, nodding sideways. "Melanie insisted I buy condoms. She said every pilgrim needed supplies for their journey, something like that."

Teddy bites off the cellophane from the pack and spits it on the floor. "Glad you did, but they're all mine now. Did you know," he says in my ear, "I'm ruining all your dating plans from this point onward?"

I'm distracted, because we haven't settled who's staying and who's going, but Teddy arranges my limbs, asks me twice if I'm okay, puts his mouth under my ear, and pulls my knee up onto his hip. We forget everything now.

"More," I say, and we shiver and stretch against each other, until I have him. The tenderness in his fingers as he pulls some hair away from my eyes has me wanting to hide my face in his shoulder, but he won't allow it; my face is tipped back and he watches my eyes as he moves. He's open for feedback, and when a perfect alignment is achieved, he laughs at the look on my face. "Oh, there we go. Come this way, if you can," he invites me. "But if you can't, no pressure. I've got a lot of tricks up my sleeve."

"It feels like I'm going to come, if you stay just like that—and I do this—"

I try to banish my thoughts. The bed squeaks and I'm so alive. I'm twenty-five and my blood is banging through my veins and his hazel eyes look at me with such amused affection, the way he always looks at me, and I tip over the edge and I'm coming, and he's praising me, holding my shaking torso in a hug.

It's pleasure, more than I've ever experienced, because it's shared with him.

"Nice?" he asks me and I wordlessly nod. "Okay, good. Can you keep going?" Now we're moving again. I still feel the after-shocks inside me, and now Teddy is taking his turn to move in the way that feels best for him; everything's silky smooth and easy, but there's a new angle and a new kind of friction.

"Let me just," he starts a sentence but never finishes it.

His breath is coming too short; there's physical effort that has his muscles straining and he's working so hard. I firm up my spine and give back to him when I feel him starting to flag. It's what causes him to groan, freeze, then dissolve into shuddering spasms.

I don't know what to do now, so I put my arms around his shoulders and hug him until the tension melts out entirely and we're dropped back into this room: two people who know each other fully now, and we kiss each other on the cheek. I always wondered what an afterglow would feel like: gratitude, and a smile, and I'm so glad. I tell him as much.

"I really didn't expect it to be so good, right out of the gate," I confess, which makes him laugh. "No, but really, so good. Once I found that angle . . ."

"It's all about the angles, in my experience," he says, then seems to wince at his words. "I mean—"

"It's okay. You knew what you were doing, and I was glad." We hug together for a long time. We confess every little moment that we wanted each other. He's out-of-his-mind horny when he sees me wearing my glasses. I tell him that the craftmanship on the butt of his jeans is art. The sound of the pipes filling my bathtub can make him hard. The shine in his hair gives me a candle-flicker in my uterus.

I tell him things that I cannot believe I have the courage to. "I want to be tattooed on you." He just nods in reply, and our kisses are just a continuation of this intoxicating conversation.

I notice the time on my clock. "I might need to go check the office."

"Nothing says afterglow of mind-blowing sex like checking an office," he agrees. "But I already rechecked it for you. It's okay, Tidy Girl. Everything's safe. You're safe." He kisses my temple and pulls a blanket up over me.

How accepting he's been of my compulsive tendencies is humbling. "This is probably a weird time to ask, but can I get the name of your therapist?"

He laughs a lot. "I traumatized you that badly tonight?" His smile fades. "Yes. Of course. I'll take you. I'll hold your hand in the waiting room. It's going to be okay."

The rest of the night is fabulous.

We have a bath together, and it's infinitely more satisfying than talking through the wall. Teddy smells like a pink unicorn when he towels me off and tosses me back on the bed. The second time he sinks himself into me, I'm readier for the sensation and we find a looser, fast tempo. We change things up, three times, four times, laughing and handing each other pillows to prop each other up, until we can't stop moving and there are no thoughts. I tighten, an impossible orgasm ripples outward like a stone dropped in a lake. Teddy follows soon after.

I make macaroni and cheese, wearing a towel as a dress. "This casual look works for you," Teddy tells me from the stool at the counter as we eat. "You spoil me a lot."

"I actually like spoiling people. I bring Melanie a spare yogurt every afternoon. She hasn't noticed yet. It's my love language." The word *love* clangs and I falter—did I imagine the whole thing? When I check his face, he's looking goofy-happy, eyes closed and smiling with his cheek on his folded fist. "Are you okay?"

"Just in love with my dream girl."

I grin. "Dream Girl is currently parked . . . where is that bike, anyway? You're taking me for a ride on it, remember." I take our bowls to the sink and begin to fill them with hot water. He doesn't say anything. "Right? You're letting me have a ride?"

"I'm really sorry. I got it running and listed it for sale. I thought I had time, but I got an offer within hours. I know you guys thought that one was a piece of junk, but Indians are really collectible."

"Oh." I have his heart now, but it's ridiculous how hurt I feel. "Did you get a good price?"

"A fortune." He doesn't sound that happy about it. "I never talk to you about this, because your eyes get really sad, but I've almost saved enough." Enough to make him leave, just as I've finally gotten him.

"Let's go to bed," I tell him, because that's an easy thing to reply. He follows me without question into my bedroom, where we lie skin to skin, and I force myself to feel every sensation, to catalog them with archival precision. I'm making memories I'm going to need one day.

All things considered, I'm still the luckiest girl alive.

CHAPTER TWENTY-FIVE

'm a mess. A zombie. It's now Monday morning and I'm at my desk staring at my computer, trying to work out what the hell I'm looking at. Why does the screen look different? The screen is bright blue, when usually it's a sage green. Has last night's intense, perfect sex with Teddy changed my eyesight?

"What's up, girl. Ugh, you look rough," Melanie says as she sails in, bright and early for once. "What's happened to you?"

I'm weak-legged, swollen-lipped, heavy-headed, and wrung out. Nobody deserves to experience so much pleasure in one single night. I woke up wrapped in Teddy. He tipped my face toward a ray of daylight on my pillow to describe the exact brown of my eyes, before hopping out of bed to make me tea.

Melanie's still staring at me, so I'll stick with the easy explanation. "There's something wrong with the computer." I type my password and nothing happens. I put on my computer glasses and squint at the tiny pop-up. "Admin Access Only. What does that mean? We don't even have an admin."

"It means that head office has locked the network. I've seen this happen in lots of offices. You need to call PDC." She yawns and goes into the bathroom with her makeup bag.

"I don't know if they'll even be there this early." I dial the number for Rose Prescott's assistant. It goes to voice mail. I leave one, asking her to call me. Mel reappears, this time with makeup on. "Now what do we do?"

She grins and swivels in her chair. "Want to strategize for your date?"

"Not during work hours." I'm going to have to work out a way of telling her thanks but no thanks, the Sasaki Method is now coming to an end. I've already canceled that date in the app on my walk down the hill. I'm hoping to have this conversation with her when I might have some answers to what she'll ask next: *Are you leaving here? Is he staying here?*

I blame extreme tiredness for how long it takes me to realize there's someone standing in the doorway. "Can I help you?"

A gray-haired man in a suit comes in, sets a small suitcase against the wall, and reaches in his jacket pocket. "I'm Duncan O'Neill. I'm a financial auditor, contracted by PDC. Rose Prescott is the head of the review. I'm reporting to her for this next part of the process."

"This is news to me."

"Financial auditor," Melanie repeats. "You guys think someone is stealing." Duncan looks at her sharply, but she says to me, "I've temped at places where this has happened before. It's why you can't log into the system. We're locked out and he's going to go through all your files and accounts. Is that right?"

"Yes, more or less," Duncan says, a little flustered. "Rose has identified some anomalies."

I'm already dialing her number. She answers on the second ring. "Duncan has arrived, I take it."

"You're on speakerphone with Melanie and Duncan. Could you please fill me in on this? I would have appreciated some advance notice."

"That's not how this kind of audit works. Ruthie, I'm going to be up front with you," Rose says. She sounds as tired as I am. "I have been turning myself inside out, trying to understand the set of books you've provided me. The income from the residents, minus wages and the costs of running the site, do not equal what is in the account."

"I don't understand. I run a report every Monday, and it's always exactly right."

Rose loses her patience. "Yeah, yeah, you do everything perfectly. You'd think you were single-handedly running the Hilton in Paris, not thirty-nine old town houses."

Is that a trick question? "There's forty, which you'd know if you even came to visit the place you want to change so much." I await my fate, the air caught in my lungs.

Duncan leans across to speak to the phone. "I need you to call me on my cell, Rose. Urgently."

"Yes. I think we've found our issue."

"Me?" I look at Duncan. "I can open my personal bank account here on the screen right now. I'm living paycheck to paycheck. Whatever you think I've done, it wasn't me." I've spoken these kind of words before, but this time, I'm willing to defend myself to the death.

Rose sighs. "You're not the one on a cruise. Just let Duncan do his work, give him anything he asks for, and do not call Sylvia. If she tries to contact you, I want you to hang up. Are we clear? I've been monitoring your outgoing emails and I know you've been keeping her abreast of everything that happens here."

Teddy poses in the doorway, pretending to do bicep curls with a large paper bag. "I came by to bring my beautiful girl a hot breakfast. Don't worry, I brought you some hash browns, Mel. Uh, hi," he now says to Duncan. "I didn't bring you anything. Sorry. You're in a meeting." He does a cute head duck and one of those *awkward!* grimaces. "Ignore me." He wades through to my desk. "I'll leave this here for you."

As his hand tucks some hair behind my ear, I manage: "Teddy, this is an auditor. We're being audited for missing funds. And your sister is on speakerphone."

"Half sister," Rose snaps automatically, and it's dreadful seeing the light drain from his eyes. Very calmly, she asks: "Are you sleeping with one of the office staff, Theodore? Which one of them is your beautiful girl? Who gets a hot breakfast?" She's sarcastic and I hate her.

Duncan wants to climb out the window. Melanie puffs herself up in outrage. Teddy begins to flounder, and it's up to me now.

"Teddy and I are seeing each other, yes."

Melanie screams "WHAT?!" so loud that for a moment I go deaf. When the ringing subsides, Rose is launching into a scolding tirade. "I told you one thing. To stay away from the staff there, Theodore. So Dad didn't have to worry about you, I said fine. Sure. He can stay in that moldy maintenance hut. But there was only one thing you had to do. Keep your dick to yourself."

"Too bad. I'm in love with Ruthie." He declares this as fact and Melanie puts her hand on her hip. She's got nothing but accusation on her face.

I say in a small voice to Mel, "I'm sorry. I didn't know how to tell you."

"You open your mouth and you tell me. It's that easy. How long's this been going on? You've both been lying to my face?" Melanie looks between us both. The phone is silent. "You know what? I don't care anymore. Throw your heart away on someone who's going to leave and break your heart. I put so much effort into my Method, and for what?"

"I'm so grateful, I really am." I grab my notebook. "I want to talk to you about your career, I've got some ideas."

She snatches the keys for the rec center from my desk. "I'm going to hang decorations for the Christmas party." She's crying when she walks out.

Duncan clears his throat. "I'm going to set up . . ." He beats a hasty retreat to a far corner of the room with his laptop bag. Now it's just me, Teddy, and the silent phone.

In a remarkably professional voice I say, "Are you still on the line, Rose?"

"Theodore, pack your stuff and get out. If Ruthie wanted to, she could sue for sexual harassment. Your surname is Prescott. Your dad is the boss. She's felt pressure over the review, and you've probably promised her that you'll save the day there—"

I cut her off. "I'm an adult woman and we've been getting to know each other outside of work hours. He's promised me nothing. I'm not suing anybody."

She ignores me. "I mean it. Teddy, if you're not out by tonight, Duncan is going to call me."

Duncan's clearly aggrieved. Auditing someone's love life was not what he signed up for.

Teddy challenges her. "What'll you do? What's the thing you'll do if I don't leave?"

"I'll give Ruthie her notice. She was warned by my father to not get involved with you and she did. Plus there's been mishandling of some form in the front office there; for all we know she's a part of it. Teddy, you're a selfish little shit, but I'm genuinely curious what you'll decide, because you've never sacrificed yourself for another living soul as far as I'm aware. What's your choice?"

Teddy looks at me. "Please hold." He presses the button and says to me, "Well? Are you coming with me to Fairchild?"

"You expect me to just walk away, with that kind of cloud hanging over my reputation? I've done that before and it didn't work out so well for me." I gesture at the flashing light on the phone. "Come on, help me. Stand up for me. She's suggesting I've siphoned funds out of this place."

"Of course I know you didn't do it." He says it with the absolute confidence that I would have loved to hear from my parents. "Rose knows it too. But who cares? Let's quit this place in a blaze of glory. You know there's a world outside Providence, don't you?"

A resident scoots past and waves to me. If I walk out, they'll all be marooned here. "Who will take care of them?"

"I don't know, their families?" He winces at how uncaring he sounded. "I mean, we'd set them up with groceries so they'd be okay for a good long while. Rose will get someone new in to manage."

"No one can take care of Providence like I can."

"You've given all you can to this place. Take something for yourself."

The red hold light is flashing. All I can think about is that unlocked door that changed my life once.

"If I leave right now, I'll look guilty. Besides, I'm not the type who can just pack everything into a backpack and leave. I can't take that kind of risk."

"You think I'm a risk?" He's affronted. "You're the only one who's believed in me. I'm doing it because you thought I could. You've seen my studio and my apartment. The Reptile Zoo is twenty minutes away, and they have a pathway program for interns that will earn credits toward a veterinary nursing quali-fication." Teddy takes a deep breath. "I'm asking you to choose me, please."

It hasn't occurred to him that he has the option to put his own dream on hold to stay in town for me. I say the thing I know will stop him in his tracks. "You haven't paid for your share yet, though, have you?"

303

The red light flashes on my phone and I can't take it anymore. "Rose, thanks for waiting."

"Well, what's the decision? Who's leaving?"

I look up, and he's already walking out. "Teddy. It's Teddy who's leaving. Like he always said he would."

CHAPTER TWENTY-SIX

Quite a bit of drama," Melanie says from the top of her stepladder. She's pinning up our CHRISTMAS PROM banner and I am supervising for work safety purposes. "What a week. More drama than this place has ever seen."

The Sasaki Method has been abandoned, but really, everything's abandoned now that he's left.

After I hung up from Rose, I followed Teddy up the hill, to our cottages, where I found him stuffing his meager belongings into his bag. We had a fight that covered the same ground, in different and painful ways.

He hates that I can't put my faith in him and leave. I hate that he won't stay with me and make sure that Providence survives. We both yelled at each other things like, *You don't love me* and *This was a huge mistake.*

Bad stuff. Stuff that keeps me awake.

"You know what, Ruthie?" he'd said as he shouldered his backpack. "I can't make you leave. I can't sling you over my shoulder and carry you out of here. When you do come, I want you to walk out of here on your own two feet. But I'm really scared that you aren't brave enough to." He touched a thumb under my chin, walked out, and I grasped the locked doorknob of his cottage like a lifeline.

"I'm still pissed off at you," Melanie says now, but I'm not surprised. She says it about twice an hour, but the venom has worn off. "I told you to not fall in love with the first boy you saw. I told you he was a Lamborghini, and look what you've done. You've driven yourself into a wall. You're heartbroken."

"Yes." I can't do anything but agree, because I've seen what I look like in the mirror. I'm back to ninety-five years old.

"I put so much work into creating a program to find you a good man. A safe man." She wobbles a little on the ladder and I reach up a hand to steady her. "You didn't even go have one terrible unsatisfying date at the Thunderdome. I wanted to sit at the bar and spy on you and we could have gotten drunk afterward and bitched about men."

"I know."

"Then what happened?"

"I saw his hair at the gas station. Then he turned around, and . . . well, you know what he looks like. Then he laughed. I never told you, did I? He mistook me for an elderly woman. It was a correct first impression, really."

"You're not old," she protests.

"He adored me. I have no proof of it, and maybe it's fading by the day, but he really did. You said I deserved that. So, even if I never see him again, I won't regret it. One thing Providence has taught me is, life's short."

"He's not answering his phone."

"I know." At least it's not just me going to his voice mail. "Mel, you've done a great job here."

Melanie has arranged catering and bought alcohol, created a cohesive decoration scheme, and taken care of every last detail. For the first time ever, I will be attending as a guest. Mel's contract expires tomorrow, but she assures me she'll still come. Maybe. If she's not too pissed off with me.

"You've put in a lot of effort in the years gone by," she says like she's sorry for me. She climbs down the ladder and decides to tell me something. "And this is the last Christmas party. I'm sorry, Ruthie, but this site has been mismanaged to the point that I don't think PDC would get a fast-enough return to continue on like this. It was always their plan," she adds gently. "The end date on the tenancy agreements, December thirty-first, next year? That's your exit date, too. Maybe you should decide if you want to move that forward and leave on your own terms."

She goes off to search in a cupboard for more tinsel.

My phone pings; it's my forum friends chat. I wouldn't be surprised if they were messaging to ask me to step down as forum admin. I open the message and see it's a link.

ACTOR WHO PLAYS DAD IN HEAVEN SENT
CHARGED WITH SEXUAL ASSAULTS DATING
BACK TO 1990s

I read through the article, and it seems that no one on set was safe from the actor who played Pastor Pierce Percival. I sit down in a chair by the window and stare at the green world outside.

My pleasures in life are modest. A bath, dinner at the same time, and the uncomplicated, wholesome television show that parented me through the hardest years of my life. I had a childhood of bullying, loneliness, and wavering faith, but no matter what, I knew what time this show was on. And I think of little Teddy, sitting at his own television.

Everything ends. I know that better than anybody. But I really need something to hold on to. I blink my tears into my cardigan sleeve, and on the pavement outside, I see it: a tiny, determined little lump, edging across the path. How do they keep moving themselves, despite the endless stretch of lawn ahead? They just do, inch by inch.

I've got to inch my way out of this, too. "Mel, the tortoises are endangered. Surely that counts for something."

"It should," she says, thinking. "But PDC will have some environmental assessor on their payroll to write a report that says it'll be fine. You're the only one who cares about those tortoises, I think."

"That's true. I've got records for the last six years, showing how the population has grown with just the tiniest bit of care and attention."

"Oh, Miss Ruthie is looking determined. She's decided she ain't going down without a fight." How I've missed Mel's open, unguarded grin.

"I wanted to thank you, Mel. You were the first person I ever met who took my side."

She's puzzled by my wording. "How do you mean?"

"You've always believed in me. I know the Sasaki Method was not about dating. Not really. It was you trying to get me to think about myself. To consider myself as a candidate for the human race. You made me be twenty-five. And I'm really, really grateful to you." I put my arms around her and hug.

"Whoa, whoa. You're not about to do something crazy, are you?" she says into my shoulder.

"Not something crazy. Something administrative. I'm going to make a call to my contact at the Reptile Zoo, and see what paperwork we need to lodge to get an injunction to protect the site. Let's make things difficult for PDC. I should have done this years ago."

Mel squeezes me and we end our hug. "Years ago, you were under Sylvia's thumb. What's happening with the audit?"

"From what I can gather, Sylvia altered each of my reports to show the site had thirty-nine town houses, before she submitted them to PDC. It's why she never let me have any kind of independence. She skimmed the entire revenue from the fortieth house, thinking it was unlikely that the owners would set foot on-site. I never even noticed the website listed thirty-nine town houses. Duncan's said she's kept a second set of books for years."

Mel says, "I know she's a family friend. Do you actually think she did it?"

Sylvia was there the day of the church theft. She was at our post-fund raiser leftovers-and-lemonade celebration. She was trusted implicitly by my parents and able to walk wherever she liked on church grounds. She could have accessed a key. She was there when I told the congregation that I was a careless, foolish girl.

Two months after that day, she took a vacation to Tahiti and sent my parents a postcard, and she's been gaslighting me ever since.

"Yes," I tell Melanie. "I do think Sylvia stole the money." Now I've got another call to make after I ring the Reptile Zoo. I'll leave another voice mail for Teddy, asking him to forgive me for not being brave enough. When he calls me back, I'm going to tell him that he's right. Providence has taken enough from me. It's time for me to resume my life.

Then after I make those calls, I'm going to call my father.

CHAPTER TWENTY-SEVEN

Knowing the Parlonis are without an assistant, I go up in the hour before the Christmas party. I find keeping busy is the key to sanity these days. If I let myself stand still for one second, Teddy's voice rings in my ear.

I called Always and Forever Tattoo Studio in Fairchild, and he'd answered the phone, sounding so unspeakably proud of himself that I had to hang up. He did it. I must love him a lot, because I'm so happy for him that I cry myself to sleep.

I find the front door of the Parloni town house unlocked, but it doesn't affect me like it once might have. The sisters are dressed and ready, practicing their dance moves in their living room. Achingly slowly, they step out a box on the carpet. It's the slowest waltz I've ever seen.

Each woman is dressed in a lovely prom gown. They are strappy affairs, and the vibrancy of the fabric is juxtaposed with their loose, wrinkled skin. Aggie looks unwell, barely moving her feet as Renata steps around her. I have a strange feeling I'm interrupting something I shouldn't. What is this piece of bad history between them, connected to their prom, all those years ago?

"Your chaperone has arrived," I call to them, breaking the moment.

"Good, you're here. Come get dressed." Renata points at a hanging garment bag with CHANEL printed across the front. "I went down to your thrift store again."

I gape at her. "You found this at the thrift store?"

"Of course not," Renata booms. "Boy, she's gullible. No wonder Sylvia fleeced this place right under her nose."

"Who told you that?"

"A little bird told me."

Dammit, Melanie. It's not right to gossip. I unzip the bag. Inside, it's ivory feathers and satin edging, and a price tag I'm too afraid to flip over. "I don't understand why you did this for me."

"It's a thank-you," Aggie says, just as Renata says, "It's a goodbye gift."

"How did you know?" I have my resignation letter typed, printed, and signed. After the Christmas party, I'm going to send it to Rose Prescott and help her find a replacement. I've got somewhere I need to be, and some risks I need to take. "I can't accept this dress."

"You will take what I give you," Renata snaps. "And you will say thank you every day until you die. Thank you, Renata Parloni, for changing my life. Honestly, she's the most difficult girl I've ever met."

Aggie pats Renata's cheek. "She doesn't understand. How could she? Just let her alone."

I don't know why she's so annoyed. "I'll borrow it. Thank you very much." I think that's the best compromise I can broker at this point.

"The salesgirl said you can't sit down in it. You'll bend the feathers if you do," Renata yells as I go into the spare bedroom to strip down and carefully pull the magical dress down over my head. I would have loved for Teddy to have seen me in this, but when I walk into Always and Forever, I will be wearing my cool-girl cardigan. The one with foxes and mushrooms on it.

"I'll zip you up," Aggie says from the doorway.

"Are you unwell?"

"Just an acute lack of youth." Even pulling the zip causes her to grunt. "There. You look how I feel on the inside." A faint smile touches her mouth. "You know that you've done something extraordinary tonight, don't you?"

"I wouldn't say that. Melanie did all the work."

"You'll be helping us set something right." Aggie pulls my ponytail out from the neck of the dress with care. "Thank you for taking the dress. It means a lot to Ren that you did. We never had children. But you, dear Ruthie Maree, are the closest we ever got. You and Theodore. We're going to leave the door unlocked tonight. In case he comes back."

I exhale and nod. I pull my hair tie out and my hair tumbles around my shoulders. "Shall we go?"

"We'll be along shortly. You go ahead."

It's eerie, walking through Providence in my miraculous swan princess dress. The air buzzes with the sound of electric mobility scooters. Weaving side to side, the residents dodge the tortoises. I open the rec center doors, switch on the sparkling lights and mirror ball, and the walls fracture into every color, spinning around us. My phone has a text from Mel: Running a bit late, just hit play on the playlist. I do, and the first song is an old one. I hear voices whoop in excitement.

My residents stream in, dressed to the nines. Some have dates. Some have brought their families. I get to hug each one hello, but also goodbye. When they find out I'm leaving, they'll say it's a shame. Once they find out I'm running away to try to recapture the heart of the tattooed boy who cleaned the gutters shirtless for the Parlonis, they'll give me full endorsement.

"I have never in my life seen anything so beautiful," Mrs. Whittaker tells me in the doorway. I can't tell if she means the glittering room, or my dress. "If only I had a date. I bet you can't tell looking at me, but once upon a time, I had plenty of options."

"Three boyfriends at the same time. Yes, you told me. And I'm in awe. I'm hopefully about to get just one boyfriend, but he's a special one." Electric, dazzling, beautiful Theodore Prescott. Please hold on for me. I'll be there soon.

It's only when the room is mostly crowded that I notice the Parlonis are nowhere to be seen. I'm just walking to the door when they step in, and they are hand in hand. Now that I am in love, I understand everything.

The Parlonis are not sisters.

How have I never noticed the way they look at each other? The hands folded together, the times I've walked in to find them leaning together on the couch? They walk in together, backs remarkably straight, heads held high.

Renata looks around at the room, eyes defiant. I know now what their old wound was: they couldn't go to the prom with each other, and it's been carried around on their relationship like a scar.

If they were expecting a scene, they don't get it. If they were expecting judgment or disgust, there is none. The Parlonis are glanced at and then forgotten in favor of the refreshments. I walk over to them as they halt underneath the mirror ball that has somehow transformed the entire world tonight.

"Why didn't you tell me?" Renata used the word *gullible* earlier to describe me and I feel it now. "Didn't you trust me?"

"She finally gets it." Renata smiles, and in this light she looks about twenty years old. "My beloved wins yet another bet." She lifts Aggie's hand to her mouth and kisses it. "I owe you twenty dollars."

"Why didn't you tell me?" I ask again.

Renata replies. "Your father is a reverend. At first we didn't say, because I didn't want to find out that you're a jerk. And it's just easier. People have assumed we're sisters our whole lives. But not anymore." Renata looks around the room. "This feels like what I thought it would. Even if I'm old."

I smooth down a feather on my dress. "But you know I'm not a jerk. I really did think you were sisters. Did Teddy know?"

Aggie says, "He knew the first day." Both smile. "We weren't trying to keep a secret deliberately. We've just lived this way for a long time. It hasn't been . . ." She can't think of the word. I think it hasn't been easy.

Renata gives me a look. "It's our business. But times have changed. And your prom was just in time."

"You should get married." I hope I haven't overstepped as they carefully exchange looks. Then they smile.

"You're starting to get it," Renata tells me. There's approval in her eyes. "You're starting to realize that life is too short. You've got to find that person you love."

"I think I lost him."

Aggie speaks. "Then find him."

"I'm so glad she's not a jerk," Renata says as they walk to the dance floor. Her shawl slips from her shoulder and I see her tattoo: AGATHA FOREVER. It's perfect.

Together, they step into an easy waltzing shuffle. Other couples join them, and soon the dance floor is a slow-motion, creaking sway. There are walking frames. Some dancers sit down periodically to rest. It's the tamest, sweetest little party. I take the box of corsages that Melanie handmade and begin to tie them to frail wrists. Tonight, everyone feels twenty-five.

Tonight is a miracle.

I lean against the wall, just watching, and a woman walks in. She's tall, powerful, and would be chosen first for a school sport.

"This is actually quite lovely," Rose Prescott says as she sets down her overnight bag against the wall next to me. "You've got a nice taste level. I was just coming up to let you know my father is arriving in the morning. I wanted to go through the audit findings here, seeing as though he's always going on about how important that is." Rose isn't one to say something like, *thanks for the invitation*.

"Melanie says that you'll recommend that the site be developed once the tenancies expire."

"It's what we do. Surely you've realized it. Don't be looking so accusing," she adds defensively. "And don't take your anger at my father's son out on me."

"Why don't you ever call him your brother?"

"Because I don't want a brother."

"He loves you so much he's got a rose tattooed on himself. But you've probably never spent enough time with him to notice it. He's been heartbroken since he was a kid that you don't want anything to do with him."

Emotion flares in her eyes. "It's complicated."

"Working here, I've realized that it doesn't have to be. And that life goes by quick. One day you and I will look like them." I nod at the crowd. "I think it's time we both make peace with a few things."

"Teddy said he'd be here, didn't he," Rose says like she's making one last pitch to change my mind. "He promised you, I bet."

No, he didn't. I'd hoped. "He did. But if he has somewhere more important to be, I understand." I see a tall man in the doorway and my heart leaps.

But then Rose says, "Oh, there's my dad."

Jerry Prescott walks up to us, pulling a carry-on suitcase. "I just got into town, thought I'd come and see what all the fuss is about. This is amazing."

He turns around us, smiling at the slow-dancing seniors on the dance floor. His gaze does catch on the Parlonis and their romantic clinch, but if he's surprised he recovers well. "I want to congratulate you on a fantastic year of hard work, Ruthie, despite everything that's happened."

"Don't congratulate me too soon," I reply glumly. "Rose has bad news."

"Oh, yes. She briefed me quickly on that." Jerry's face grows serious. "Did she tell you that we never believed you were involved? The matter is now with law enforcement. Sylvia is disembarking in Noumea tomorrow morning, and she's going to be met by police. It looks like she was embezzling from the previous owners of Providence, too. Since she's been working here for over fifteen years, we'd say a loss of $400,000 is conservative. If only I'd taken a tour with you, like you offered, the day I arrived here, we might have picked it up sooner. Forty little town houses."

Rose sighs like she's beaten. "I already know what you're going to say, so I'll just agree and say that from now on, I will personally walk every site we ever buy."

The mirror ball turns, my eyes are dazzled by a starburst, and when they readjust to the dark room, I see a new silhouette in the doorway. It's another man I don't recognize. He's tall and dressed in a suit that looks like it was made for him. He's got a sharp, edgy haircut, the sides shaved close to his head and some length on top, shining blue-black in the scattered disco ball lights.

It's Teddy. He's come back, and—

"He got a haircut." Both Jerry and Rose gasp in unison.

Teddy spots us now and begins to walk over. The Parlonis see him and begin to make their way over to us, too.

"My, my, don't you look sharp," Jerry exclaims, clapping his son hard on the shoulder. "You wouldn't be out of place in PDC corporate headquarters, would he, Rose?"

Teddy's eyes are only on me. "I came back. I'm not too late, am I?"

I gesture around us. "I'd say you've got perfect timing, like always. Where's your beautiful hair?" He's so handsome and grown up, I stare at his polished leather shoes. It seems that Fairchild has changed him in a way I didn't anticipate. Now, the half-full packing boxes in my living room are terrifying.

He steps to stand beside me, and the warmth of his palm on my shoulder is a relief. "I did what Dad said to do. I got a haircut. I'm here to tell you that you win. I'm ready to grow up and be what you want me to be. Add me to the payroll." He's not speaking to me. His eyes are only on Rose.

"Wait a minute," Rose interrupts, but Jerry holds up a hand. "What do you have in mind?"

"I'll do whatever business course you want me to do, then I'll start work for PDC at the bottom of the ladder. In exchange, I want you to leave Providence how it is."

"I've just completed an evaluation that shows this place isn't a great deal for us," Rose says. "Once we give Ruthie appropriate back pay, the position is even worse."

I interrupt. "What back pay?"

"Sylvia has been paying you under the minimum wage for six years." Rose explains it like I'm a tad simple. "Haven't you ever wondered why you make so little?"

"But that's because I have accommodation here."

Rose sighs like, *Oh Ruthie*. "As part of my review, I also looked at your duties. You're performing a role much higher than your duty statement. We'll work out what all this means, but I'm sorry that you were taken advantage of. We'll do what we can to make it right." Rose looks at her father, who nods.

Teddy turns to her. "I'm sorry I exist. I mean it," he says when she goes to argue. "Me and Mom ruined your life, and I'm really, really sorry. All I've ever wanted was to impress you. I don't know if this will do it, but I've got to try, because I've tried everything else."

Rose is turning red. I can't tell if she's angry or upset.

"This is quite a sacrifice, Teddy," Jerry says. "What about your studio?"

"I'll sell my share. If it's what it takes to let this place survive, then it'll be worth it. Look at them." He encourages his father and sister to look around the room. "How can I let these people be uprooted from the last home they ever planned to have? All Ruthie has ever asked me to do is care about this place. Well, here I am, doing it."

The Parlonis have completed their arduous trek across the room to us.

"What did we miss? Holy shit," Renata splutters when she looks up at Teddy. "*Vogue Italia*, eat your heart out. Was he always that good-looking?"

I laugh. "Yes."

Renata has her arm hooked into Aggie's. "I've never been into men, so I'll take your word for it. Where's your hair, Theodore?"

"I donated it to someone who needs a wig more than you do." He smiles at her patent disappointment. "I'm here to do the right thing for once. I'm making a deal."

"Is this in regard to the future of Providence?" Aggie asks Jerry.

"Yes, ma'am. Nothing has been finalized, however," he adds with a glance at Rose. "Please, just enjoy your lovely evening."

Aggie won't be treated like an old dear. "I hope you've conducted environmental impact assessments?"

Rose fields that. "Of course, that's part of my evaluation."

"And you know that this site is home to an endangered species of tortoise, and there's been a care and rehabilitation program happening on-site for the last six years?" Aggie speaks calmly and deliberately and I see a glimpse of her as an attorney.

"What, the turtles around the place?" Rose scrunches her face in distaste, even as her mind pivots to a new position. "We'll make sure that whatever work happens here, no animals will be impacted."

"We need to go through the impact that any works will have on the golden bonnet tortoises. They're listed as critically endangered and there's more here than anywhere else on the planet. If you'd visited the site earlier and taken my tour, you'd know that," I tell Rose quietly.

Rose is flustered. She looks at her brother like she's having a bad dream. "This place means this much to you? You look like a goddamn lawyer or something, Teddy."

"Not quite," he replies, gesturing to the tattoos on his hands. "And yes. This place means this much to me, and Ruthie means the most."

I put a hand on his sleeve. "I don't want you to give up your studio for us."

"If it's what it takes. Well? You can start me at the bottom, as long as I can work out of this office." He says this to Rose. "I've got a lot of experience with menial tasks and humiliating requests."

"It's true," Renata says. "He barely complained."

Rose's face shows her struggle with various emotions, but then, with a look of resolve, she makes a decision. "All right, I'll recommend that Providence remain as . . . is. On the other side of that hillside is a vacant field. Maybe it doesn't have an endangered species. I think we should build affordable retirement housing, linking both sites. It'll be the best of both worlds; something changing, something staying the same. It was my second recommendation in my report," she adds. "The first one was to redevelop. But now that I've come here, I can see that it wouldn't be right."

Teddy nods. "I think that's a good idea. This is a nice place to live, and it shouldn't be exclusively for the insanely wealthy. I think you should also make sure that there's a plan in place to get a bit of diversity. This place is a little . . ." He trails off, aware of the Parlonis' stare.

"You can say it. This is where rich old white people come to die." Renata cackles at her own joke, then sobers. "I think that's a very good, mature suggestion to move us forward into the . . . what century is it? I don't know. But I'm impressed with you. There is a brain in that handsome head."

"And a big heart." Aggie pats his chest.

"Great, so everything's settled," Teddy says, but his smile doesn't reach his eyes. He's lost his life's dream, to secure mine. I bet he feels how I did when my college fund was emptied. Like me, he's planning on making the best of it. "Thank you, Rose. I promise I won't let you down."

"Ah, shit, Theodore," Rose groans. "Why'd you have to do this?" When he doesn't know what she means, she says, "You had to make a grand gesture. I've always thought you were the most self-centered person."

"He absolutely is not," Aggie defends. "We have employed in excess of one hundred young men. None of them are a patch on Theodore. I can assure you, no one cares more than he does."

"I'm sorry," Rose says to him unexpectedly. "I was horrible to you when we were kids."

"And adults, by the sounds of it," Renata adds.

Rose ignores that and says to Teddy, "It wasn't your fault."

"It was my fault," Jerry says. "It was my fault, and I left you all to sort it out yourselves. I was just too busy."

"You tried so hard to make me love you," Rose says, and her composure breaks. Tears fill her eyes. "And I wanted to. You were the easy target for how miserable I was. How miserable I am," Rose amends. "I'm sorry, Teddy. Ruthie said you have a rose tattoo." Her voice breaks. "I don't deserve it."

"Of course you do. I couldn't leave you out of the garden of sisters." He's so open and kind and that's what completely breaks her. She steps into his arms. It's the kind of hug that's twenty years in the making. He makes eye contact with me over the top of her head, and I see the emotion in him.

323

"I've been the worst sister to you. It's been really hard to resist you."

"You held out so long I think you're superhuman," he agrees with a smile. "Hey. If you're my sister, what does that make me?"

"Brother," Rose says like it's a weird word. She tries again and her voice is stronger. "Let's be brother and sister from now on."

He swirls her on the spot to the music. "Well, we're going to be working together now, so we can even be friends."

She shakes her head, and Jerry does too. "We're not going to make you do that."

"What?" It's Teddy's turn to be flustered. "But we just made a deal."

"We saw the commitment and passion we've been hoping to see in you for years," Jerry says. "But I'm not going to hold you to it. You're a tattoo artist, not a property developer. I know it now." It's his turn to hug his son.

"Could I bother either of you to help me get a drink?" Renata says, her voice old and feeble. "Over at the refreshment table over there?"

"We'd appreciate it," Aggie adds, and there's no way Jerry and Rose can say no. The two old ladies smile at us over their shoulders as they are escorted away. And now Teddy and I are alone.

He touches his thumb under my chin. "I've never seen anyone this beautiful. This dress. You look like an angel."

"And you look like a devil. A really hot devil. Your hair."

I raise up my hand and run it through the short cut. "I can't believe you did this."

"I hope it wasn't what you loved best about me. What? You love me, don't you?"

"What's it like being this self-confident?" I lean into him and he wraps me carefully in a hug. "I've been trying to call you."

"I know. I just needed to get myself sorted. I thought you'd understand." Then he goes still. "But if I'm too late, and you continued on with the Sasaki Method—"

"Relax. The Sasaki Method is a success, because I fell in love." I tip my face up and I get the kiss I've ached for every minute of every day since he left. What a privilege, to be so young. I have my entire life to know him, to laugh at him, to let him care for me in his sweet, clumsy ways. I can teach him how to give, and he can urge me to take.

I can have this kiss for the rest of my life, if I'm really careful.

The music changes, he takes my hand in his and we walk to the dance floor. "Oh, look," Teddy says to me, pointing discreetly. Renata is holding a square ring box behind her back. When they slowly move around, we see that Aggie has a ring box, too.

"It's a race to propose." He smiles. "Who will win, do you think?"

"I think they'll call it a draw." I'm smiling, too, when he kisses me again. And again. We only break apart when we hear someone clearing their throat.

It's Mrs. Whittaker. She leans in and tells me with feeling,

"Well done. Oh, hello dearie," she says with her eyeline behind us. "What a fancy . . . costume."

"I am only thirty minutes late." It's a breathless Melanie, dressed in a traditional Japanese yukata, teamed with an elaborate fifties beehive. She looks back at her watch. "Okay, more like forty-five minutes late. What the hell is going on here?" She's noticed Rose and Jerry, mingling with the residents. She definitely notices Teddy's hand on my waist. "I really didn't think you'd show up."

"I came back to rescue Ruthie. But I think the tortoises are going to rescue her, and this place. Their little way of saying thank you."

"My Sasaki Method. What a waste of a brilliant concept." She points at our joined hands. "Ruthie Midona, you wrote a list that would not describe Teddy in a million years."

"Lists aren't always right." When I say that, they both make identical theatrical gasps.

"So you decided to charm her for good. All the cheese you can eat. I was all set to pick out a bridesmaid's dress, and you had to just come along and ruin everything." Melanie unknowingly says something very hurtful to him, but Teddy doesn't flinch. Maybe one hug with his sister has balmed that wound.

He tells her, "Nothing's ruined. Ruthie's world is going to remain exactly the same."

I have something to tell them. "I'm leaving Providence. You've both given me some really good advice. It's time for me to see the world outside this place."

"So you're not planning on staying here until you die any-more?" Teddy asks with hope.

"No, I think I need to find something new for myself." I think of my forum, my clothes, the tortoise-littered paths I've walked a thousand times. "It's going to be scary, but I want to do it."

We are all distracted by the scene unfolding on the dance floor: two elderly women, offering each other rings. The semi-circle around them breaks into applause.

"We'll help you," Melanie says without thought. That's the kind of friend she is. She walks toward the Parlonis and begins taking photos.

"And will you help me, too?" I ask Teddy. "I mean, I can probably do it by myself, but if you were there, I wouldn't be so nervous when I go to the Reptile Zoo with my internship application."

His smile is brilliant. "Yes, I am going to help. I will do everything for you. It's my turn to give. So let me." He cups my jaw in his warm, tattooed hands, and as his lips touch mine, the mirror ball glitters me blind. I'm dazzled, I know I am. And I don't ever want it to end. And for a long time, it doesn't.

In the lull of silence between songs, Melanie screams in horror: "Oh my God, Teddy got his hair cut."

EPILOGUE

I'd know that door knock anywhere, always in the same pattern and cadence. "Coming." I open my door and Teddy's there, holding grocery bags in each hand and my mail in his mouth. "I couldn't use my key," he says through his teeth.

"What have we got here?" I take the envelopes out of his mouth. Now he's freed up to give me a hello kiss, and he sure does.

"I brought a bunch of stuff you're running low on." He begins to unpack the bags into my fridge. "Did you finish your essay?"

"Yeah, I turned that in earlier. Now I'm sitting here thinking about something really hard." I stack my textbooks away and sit back down at my laptop. "Have you ever had something that you held on to for a really long time for sentimental reasons?" I'm looking at my home page for my forum, Heaven Sent You Here.

"Sure, of course. Sentimentality is my bread and butter."

I look at his tattoos and smile. "It's time I admitted a secret. I was the administrator of a really big online forum."

He's finished unpacking the groceries and brings a wooden board over to the table. He's made a tiny cheese platter. "What's this forum? No. Don't tell me. It's for *Heaven Sent*."

"Yeah. I've been running it with my friends since we were fifteen. But with the Pastor Pierce court trial, no one can feel the same way anymore. I think it might be time to close it down."

Teddy leans over and cuts into the piece of cheese and hands me a preloaded cracker. When he sees the screen, he remembers something and laughs. "I'm a member of this."

"What?"

"Back when we lived at Providence, I joined up so I could impress you. No wonder you were always watching the exact episode I needed to keep up. I just thought you were magical and perfect."

"I'm okay with you thinking that." I watch as he begins making another little cracker-and-cheese combo, knowing it's for me. And sure enough, he's putting it in my hand before I've eaten the first one. "Slow down."

"I can't slow down with you," he argues. "You make me want to speed up everything."

He's been asking me to move in when my lease here ends. I do love my little studio apartment up on the fourth floor, and with the back pay from PDC I can afford it. But Teddy's apartment is closer to college, and his bed is the comfiest place on earth.

His bed is like quicksand, though—if I get in, I can't get out.

I nibble my thumb. "Do you think I should close it down? The other admins have told me it's up to me. This was a lot of time. A lot of memories." I look at the home page, which has barely changed since I was fifteen.

"I don't think you need it anymore," Teddy says. "You've let go of a lot since you left Providence, and it's only been good for you." He's meaning how I've been seeing a therapist and I don't need to recheck door handles until my palm is sore. "But you can leave it up. It won't do any harm just sitting there."

"It's getting negative."

I hate the posts about the actor on trial. It reminds me, too, that I'm going to have to be a witness in PDC's case against Sylvia Drummond. It didn't look good for her when the photographs of her disembarking the ship in a fancy outfit hit the news cycle. Her face was contorted in fury, and when she eventually called me, I was prepared to defend myself. And I had Teddy beside me, holding my hand through that call, and Rose Prescott by my other shoulder.

My parents are now sure that Sylvia was the one who took the church money.

"I got a text from Mel," Teddy says with his mouth full of cheese. "She's asked us to come and help set up for the Christmas party this year."

"Of course we will."

Mel ended up finding her dream job. She runs a full activity program for the residents of Providence, but it doesn't stop there. She travels across six retirement sites, coordinating a variety of craft sessions, outings, and dance parties. Every workday for Mel is different. She loves old people. And most importantly, she visits both the wealthy residents of Providence, and the stripped-back struggling residences downtown, spreading her sparkle.

I say to Teddy, "It'll be sad to go back, though."

A quiet settles over us and when Teddy looks at me, he's got memories in his eyes. He says gently, "She died happy, and it was because of you."

Renata Parloni's funeral was outrageous, and she would have loved it. Dubbed a *HOT OR NOT* magazine publishing pioneer by newspaper obituaries, her ceremony was attended by fashion designers, magazine moguls, and leggy models who peeked furtively at Teddy in his suit. He was too busy holding Aggie's arm to notice, and besides, I was on his other arm.

When the priest said that Renata was survived by her wife, Aggie Parloni, a ripple of applause went through the room.

Renata was outrageous in life, and in death, she did something even more outrageous. That thing she'd always joked about. She'd written me into her will. When Aggie told me, it was like the hundred-dollar-bill incident from a lifetime ago. I tried very hard to not take it. I didn't deserve it. I tried to slip it back, but it was no use.

Renata had decided that I was one of her beneficiaries, and now here I am. In a lovely little apartment in Fairchild, exhausted from a full day of study and work. I'm an intern at the Reptile Zoo and while I have a long, long road ahead of me in my dream to one day become a veterinarian, I am tackling the journey just like a golden bonnet tortoise: one inch at a time.

"I think I need to let a few old things go," I say to Teddy, and I go to the admin screen of Heaven Sent You Here. There's a deactivate page button. "If I hit this button, there's no going back."

"Would you want to go back?"

I think over the question seriously. I wouldn't have a tattoo of a tortoise on my shoulder blade. I wouldn't get to look at that red number 50 that Teddy put on the back of his hand as a reminder of how we found each other at Providence. I wouldn't be in love, and I wouldn't have someone love me.

"No, I wouldn't go back," I say, and I press the button, and it's okay. *Heaven Sent* supported and nourished me during that time of my life that I was alone and old before my time, but I don't need it now.

"Aw," Teddy says, linking his fingers into mine. Give. He always, always gives. "I'm really proud of you."

"It's growing back so fast." I put my free hand into his hair, which is tied back into a messy knot at the nape of his neck. "Your crowning glory. But I hope you've realized by now that you are not your hair. You're a business owner."

"I'm a tattoo artist," he replies, but he's smiling. He's shocked us all by being very, very good at paperwork. Who knew that underneath this chaotic surface was a hidden administrator, dying to be given the opportunity? It's such a turn-on. He grins at me now. "Just thinking about my hair has made you horny."

"Teddy, surely you know by now you could be bald and I'd want you."

"Don't tell Daisy at Christmas, she might get out the clippers."

"That reminds me. This Christmas, can I take you home to meet my churchy parents?" I repeat the dating advertisement

I wrote for myself, all that time ago, when I was lonely and internet dating felt like a good idea for about two seconds, and then a further two months.

(I should also mention, Melanie is shopping the Sasaki Method manuscript around to literary agents.)

I continue, trying to remember my secret advertisement. "I'm looking for a patient, safe cuddle-bug soul mate."

"Well, you found him." Teddy gets up and presses a kiss against my temple. "Let me get some food into you. Oops," he says and pulls on my cardigan. "You're buttoned all crooked. There. All better."

He goes into the kitchen and as he dishes up my dinner, he says, "Of course you can take me home to meet your churchy parents. And they will love me. They'll think I'm God's gift. I'm everybody's type."

It's true. He is.

And he's mine.

ACKNOWLEDGMENTS

How many times can one author be talked down off the ledge? Ask my agent, Taylor Haggerty. There's a reason this book is dedicated to her. Thank you for always being on my side, for being a sounding board and a wonderful friend. I can never thank you enough for all you've done for me, but a purple book with tortoises is a good start. Thank you to all the lovely people at Root Literary, too. What a stable to belong to! It's an honor. My editor, Carrie Feron, has guided this book to publication through some rocky waters. She, along with her colleagues at HarperCollins, have had exceptionally trying working conditions in 2020. Thank you, Carrie (and team), for helping me write the best book I can. I find your passion for storytelling very inspiring.

Roland, Tina, Katie, Delia, Sue and David, Lyn, Anne and Bob, and anyone who's ever asked me "How's the book going?" even when knowing the answer would be a big sigh: Thank you, I appreciate you. The main character of this book is named for

Acknowledgments

my late grandmother Ruth Lowes, and I cackle imagining the hijinks she would have had at Providence.

The seed of this book is based on a daydream I used to share with Kate Warnock, when we worked together more than ten years ago. We used to tell each other stories about when we were very old and rich. We'd live together in a retirement villa, and we would hire a young male assistant to be at our beck and call. It was such a treat to finally write out this daydream in full.

About the author

2 Meet Sally Thorne

3 A Letter from Sally

About the book

5 Melanie's Query Letter for
The Sasaki Method

Insights,
Interviews
& More . . .

Meet Sally Thorne

Katie Saarikko

SALLY THORNE is the *USA Today*
bestselling author of *The Hating
Game* and *99 Percent Mine*. She spends
her days climbing into fictional worlds of
her own creation. She lives in Canberra,
Australia, with her husband in a house
filled with vintage toys, too many
cushions, a haunted dollhouse, and
the world's sweetest pug. ∾

A Letter from Sally

In my last author essay, at the tail end of writing the very hard Second Book, I wrote that a blank Microsoft Word document felt like an abyss. I feel a lot of compassion for that Sally, and it makes me realize how far I've come.

As an author, I'm asked a lot about my writing process, and I usually make a joke about how I'm a mess. In truth, what happens when my hands are on the keyboard is something that makes me feel rather uncomfortable. I'm not in control. I never know what I'm going to write until I've written it, and I'm finally understanding that is okay. Word by word, over and over, it takes shape.

I've come to a realization that becoming good at something creative or worthwhile is a process of applying layers, and being willing to be really uncomfortable when the Thing is halfway done. It will look *yicky*. You will not like it. You will be pretty sure that you're not succeeding. This is when another layer must be applied.

When the Covid 19 pandemic required the entire world to stay home, I turned my office chair around 180 degrees to look at what had been sitting behind me for nine years: my custom-built Victorian-Gothic dollhouse. It was shameful to own something so incredible and the mere sight of it made me despair, because the truth was, it did not inspire me. I hadn't even opened it for two years. I wished I could call a tiny real estate agent to list it. Was breathing life into something so dusty and dormant even possible?

The first few times I opened the dollhouse's front door, I was uncomfortable. It was just as I remembered. It had not reached its potential, I knew it, and I didn't like it. I moved the velvet armchairs and used a lint roller to clean the carpets, then dusted the inch-tall porcelain vases with a paintbrush. Next, I turned the lights on and saw how my 1:12 scale chandeliers sparkled. I felt a corresponding sparkle in my heart.

Very small parcels started arriving in my mailbox. I began to spend so much time lost in these tiny rooms that I'd forget meals and the scary world outside my window. I hated the drab ▶

little bathroom, so I focused all my energy on it until it was an eccentric jungle of potted plants surrounding the brass claw-foot tub. Layer by layer, I began to love this dollhouse again. I christened it Blackthorne Manor—magic objects really shine when they have a name or title. It wasn't too late to give it a name, not even after so many years had passed.

I hope that this might inspire you to look at the project or dream that is perhaps sitting behind you right now, that thing in your life that could be your own personal source of magic and heart sparkles if you could just bring yourself to apply one new layer to it. You might shake your head: It's been too long! It's covered in dust!

A book starts off as a blank page. A dollhouse starts out as wood. Nothing starts out looking like the finished product, and if you can accept that and work through the discomfort (particularly if you have perfectionist tendencies), then you can end up with a finished product that is a tiny work of art and something only you can produce. It doesn't even require you to make a life-changing leap; just add one new layer of effort, attention, and time. Add a new layer to that dream, and just like the tortoises at Providence, make the journey, one inch at a time. They always get where they're going, and so will you.

A blank page is a gift. Make your mark on it.

I now have the opportunity to provide a little bonus piece here at the end of the book, and when I thought about what to include, I realized that Melanie Sasaki had not had her full moment in the sun. Ruthie Midona found love too early, derailing Melanie's carefully planned-out Sasaki Method, and I knew what I wanted to write.

Included here, just for fun, is what I imagine Melanie's query letter to a literary agent would look like as she takes her first step toward publishing *The Sasaki Method*. This is *not* a book I am planning on writing, but it is intended as a thank-you to the girl who put her heart and soul into matchmaking in *Second First Impressions*. ∾

Melanie's Query Letter for *The Sasaki Method*

melanie@thesasakimethod.com

Connor Randall Literary Agency
22 W 24th St, #900A, New York, NY
Attn: Harriet Schwartz

Dear Harriet,

We met in February at the Nonfiction Writers' Festival, and we talked briefly during the lunch buffet about the dating self-help book I have written. You laughed a lot at my pitch, complimented my hair, and gave me your business card. In my opinion, we hit it off, big-time. I really enjoyed the recent release by your client, Greer Johnson's *It's Not All About You*, which further convinced me I'd be a good fit for your agency.

I am now seeking representation for my debut nonfiction self-help book, *The Sasaki Method*.

This is the survival guide tucked in your backpack when hacking through the Tinder jungle. It's the book to give to a friend who's been off the market for a while, stuck in their shell, Too Busy for This Nonsense, or in any way feeling like they've missed the boat. Written with the tone of "annoyingly upbeat, nosy little sister" (source: my older sister, Genevieve), *The Sasaki Method* asks the reader to commit to an eight-week program of introspective goal setting ▸

5

Melanie's Query Letter for *The Sasaki Method* *(continued)*

and practical exercises. Self-love is the primary goal, then opening up the individual to romantic love. Hetero relationships are not referred to as the "norm," and the language and case studies are inclusive.

If any challenge is made to my credentials, I will only have to reference the number of successful true-love pairings I have orchestrated. I am a modern-day Emma Woodhouse. This is my gift and I want to share it.

In combination with the book will be an IOS app (currently in beta testing), and I have also recorded four podcast episodes. I believe this gives us options for establishing a stable marketing platform. I also have full synopsis prepared for two further books in this series: *The Sasaki Meaning* (identifying signals the Universe is sending you) and *The Sasaki Redemption* (how to redeem yourself in today's cancel culture). I have identified an imprint at Bexley and Gamin that I believe would be an ideal home for my books. I'd love to talk more about this with you.

Please find attached a sample of *The Sasaki Method*, and I remain on standby to submit a full manuscript if you should request it.

Yours,
Melanie Sasaki

* * *

FOREWORD

We all have a superpower, and mine is helping others find true love.

I've been this way as long as I can remember. Each of my Barbies was in a deeply committed relationship with a Ken doll—or another Barbie (I've always been an ally). I wasn't dressing up as a bride; I was throwing petals on my friend. I didn't have my own love affairs in high school, but instead was the one engineering promposals and connecting unrequited crushes.

Perhaps my belief in love comes from my father. He's Japanese, and he has always told me folk stories about the red string of fate—the idea that you and another are tied together, finding your way back to each other. Sometimes the string ties two individuals together who have something to learn from each other. Other times, it's true love. By day, I run activities programs for seniors, and they are less poetic about it: "There's someone for everyone, ain't there, dearie." It's true.

My sourpuss sister, Genevieve, had no hope of finding love until she finally engaged my services— and now she's engaged to the equally sourpuss Mark. In time, they'll birth some sour little kittens. I encouraged* (*borderline forced) my hairdresser Lin-Lin to ask out her deeply shy dog groomer, Margaret. I was their bridesmaid. At that same wedding, I found two sets of shy wallflowers, put them together on the dance floor, and now there are two new engagement rings on fingers.

I don't mean to brag, but my skills are uncanny.

Despite all my undeniable successes, I never thought to write a book until the red string of fate led me to Ruthie Midona, the person whom I needed to teach me something: my approach needed some flexibility. She shuffled around like an elderly woman until I overhauled her entire way of seeing herself. She was a chronic list maker, and for her it made sense to be led through my program with a series of checklists and journaling prompts, which form the basis of the book you are holding. Love happens at unexpected moments, and we'd agreed Ruthie would not fall in love with the first man she saw.

Now Ruthie's being smothered with kisses by a man who seemed completely wrong for her, and he's the first man she laid eyes on. That red string never gets it wrong, and unlikely puzzle pieces always fit together. It gave me a new perspective that has contributed to this book in a fundamental way. Plan, but also *go with it*. I have to dedicate this book to Ruthie, because without her, I doubt I would have had the inspiration to organize all my various techniques, solutions, and worldviews into a formal document. She loves a procedure manual. Thank you, Ruthie, for being the first participant of the Sasaki Method. I await my call that you are engaged to that rascal Theodore, and I remind you that a lilac bridesmaid's dress is what we agreed.

I'm sure you're not yet convinced about why I am qualified to help you break out of your shell and find that special someone, ▶

Melanie's Query Letter for *The Sasaki Method* *(continued)*

and truthfully, I have no formal qualifications. I'm not a psychologist. I have had every job from A(utomotive Parts Cataloger) to Z(umba Studio Administrator). But trust me, this is my gift. All I ask is that you go with it wholeheartedly. Eight weeks with me will change your life. You will find the book organized into eight parts, as follows:

- TURN-ONS AND DEALBREAKERS
- ME, MYSELF, AND I
- MELANIE'S MAKEOVER MONTAGE
- FIRST DATE MIDPOINT
- COMFORTING YOUR REJECTED INNER CHILD
- WHAT'S COOKING GOOD-LOOKING
- I'M ALL I NEED—BUT YOU CAN JOIN ME IF YOU'RE RESPECTFUL AND SEXY
- GRADUATION DAY

I have the Midas touch, and I want to touch you.

(Okay, maybe I'll revisit that phrasing in the editing process.) ◇

Don't miss Sally Thorne's addictive and globally bestselling debut, the perfect enemies to lovers romcom . . .

'I have a theory. Hating someone feels disturbingly similar to being in love with them.'

Now a major motion picture!

Available now from

PIATKUS

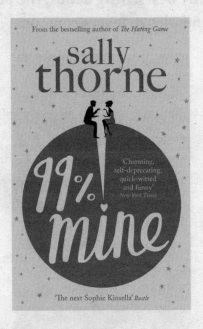